Appointment
with
Yesterday

by
christopher stratakis

A Novel in Four Parts
with a Prologue
and an Epilogue

978-0-9908871-7-1 Paperback

978-0-9977212-1-8 Hardback

978-0-9908871-8-8 eBook

IndieReader Publishing Services

Bloomfield, NJ

U.S.A.

Original cover images by Henry George Stratakis Allen, grandson of the author.

⚜

A poignant and compelling first novel, *Appointment with Yesterday* tells the story of Yanni, a cheeky and delightful Greek boy growing up in a small town on an island in the eastern Aegean.

Left in the care of his loving grandparents, Yanni endures the deprivation and terror of the German occupation during World War II, and finally leaves his beloved homeland and family to rejoin the parents who had left him behind to make a better life for themselves in America.

Filled with heartbreaking and heartwarming stories of love, devotion, disenchantment and dashed dreams, *Appointment with Yesterday* is, ultimately, the story of hardships overcome and a determined boy's journey toward finding his destiny.

⚜

For those who loved and nourished me.

Table of Contents

Prologue

The sea's sound floods my veins,
Above me the sun
Grinds like a millstone
The wind beats its full wings;
The world's axle throbs heavily.
I cannot hear my deepest breath.
And the sea grows calm to the sand's edge
And spreads deep inside me.

—From "Return" by Angelos Sikelianos

The old man leaned back on his chaise, gazing at the great expanse across the sea to the Turkish coast, misty in the haze of the warm afternoon sun. He was in a reflective mood, sitting on the comfortable veranda of his country home on the island of Erytha. A passing sailboat slid by, silent and graceful, as the sun-dappled

1

Aegean waters glistened and a few puffy clouds lazily blew through his line of vision.

"I cannot live without the sea," Yanni said, not realizing he'd spoken the words aloud.

My home is in New York, with my family, he thought. *But Erytha will always have my heart.*

He closed his eyes as images of his childhood, growing up on this quaint island, floated into his mind. The sound of the ships' horns as they pulled out of the harbor en route to bigger islands and the ports of the mainland. Ships laden with sweet, fragrant oranges from the graceful trees of orchards surrounding medieval mansions. The taste of the almond cookies his grandmother baked especially for him, the sugar leaving a fake moustache around his lips and sticky crumbs spilling out of his pockets. The sound of his uncle's thundering voice when Yanni misbehaved. The touch of the scratchy wool blanket he wrapped around himself in his rickety wooden bed with the uneven legs. The strange smell of the blood of a chicken, freshly slaughtered for the family's Sunday dinner. The sight of his grandfather's loving face as he tried, in vain, to scold Yanni for running home, late as usual. Endless games of soldiers, played with his friends in the fields, left him with skinned knees and dirt-grimed hands.

And always, the wondrously azure Aegean, his faithful companion, filling his eyes and his senses as he ran off to school every morning.

Suddenly, he heard his name being called. "Yanni!

Where are you? Hurry up!"

"I'm coming," he shouted. "Wait for me!"

The old man opened his eyes, expecting to see his school friends gathered on the narrow street beneath his bedroom window, begging him to come down and play one more game. Instead, he saw only the green grass of the lawn sloping down to the edge of the water. He stretched out his hand, as if to touch it, and sat up with a start.

Where am I? How did my hands become so wrinkled? he asked himself. *How can I be old, when I was so young just a few seconds ago? Ah, I must have been dreaming.*

"But I am old," Yanni said aloud, shaking his reverie away. "Older than I ever thought I'd be."

He picked up his diary, which he kept at hand, often jotting down memories as they came to him, then put it back down. He rarely reread these writings, for fear of seeing his own rambling thoughts scribbled on the pages in his fine, even hand. Thoughts betraying his innermost fears and misgivings, doubts and agonies.

Thoughts too painful to revisit.

Thoughts about the deprivation of his early years.

Thoughts of emptiness, and the struggle to survive during the war, when the Germans left the islanders to starve.

Thoughts of broken dreams and painful disillusionments, and even more pain when trying his utmost to cope with the upheavals in his life.

Thoughts of worry and fears that after a hard winter,

spring would never arrive.

Thoughts of his accomplishments, of the ambition still pulsating after a lifetime of achievements.

Thoughts of desire, of pure love, of family, of recognition and social acceptance.

Thoughts of contentment.

Thoughts of his legacy.

He opened his diary and poised an imaginary pen over the blank pages, and let images flood his mind.

Images of times long gone.

Images of Erytha.

PART I

THE BOY
FROM ERYTHA

Come from another road – she told him. The night is yellow
With a rosy jab. I prepared
A white shirt for you. Dinner is ready.
Alone I butchered, plucked, and cooked them
The two birds – remember? The little white feathers
That quiver in the night breeze,
And touch your lips and hair, are theirs.
—From "Testimonials" by Yiannis Ritsos

CHAPTER 1

The Chickens of Erytha

"Turn over on your belly," his grandmother said softly. Yanni lay under several thick woolen blankets, shivering and drenched in sweat, too feverish to move. He gazed dully at the wall in the bedroom, covered with icons of Jesus, the Virgin Mary, and Orthodox saints. A small oil lamp illuminated the icons and cast flickering shadows across the room.

"Pneumonia," his grandmother whispered to herself, her voice anxious. "It's his blood. It makes it worse."

Yanni didn't understand. He'd heard his grandparents talking about the bad blood in the family before, something strange that made their blood sick. Something that made other families on the island of Erytha sick also. Something he could not pronounce.

Something that had killed his older brother when he was only an infant. But it couldn't be his blood that was making him sick now. Yanni could barely breathe

7

and his throat was on fire and the coughing hurt so bad that tears came to his eyes with every fresh spasm.

His grandfather sat down on the bed and gently pulled up the nightshirt. Yanni then heard the voice of Anastasia, the old lady who lived two streets over. The cupping lady. She was the town healer, who came with her woven bag full of glass cups whenever anyone in the town had a bad cold or fever. Yanni heard the bed creak when she sat down next to him, and greeted him softly, as she had many times before. He knew what she'd be doing: placing the cup upside down over a small lit candle, to burn up the oxygen, she said, and then quickly sticking the cup on the bare skin of his back. She'd work fast, placing the cups in neat rows and then waiting several minutes before plucking them off with a soft *thwop*, the only reminder a vivid red circle that lingered for days.

Yanni didn't really mind the cuppings. He had them often, prone as he was to colds. All the townsfolk were convinced the cuppings cured their sniffles and sore throats and other ills. He only minded when he had to lie flat without moving for half an hour no matter how the cups pinched.

This time was different, he knew.

"He needs the bleeding," Anastasia said to Yanni's grandparents, and he started to whimper.

"It will hurt a little, Yanni, but only a little," Grandma said. "And it will kill the sickness."

The old lady pulled out a razor blade and made a

tiny cut before she swiftly applied the glass cup. Yanni cried softly each time the razor sliced his skin with a sharp stinging pain, but Anastasia ignored him until his entire back was covered with the cups. Then she placed a blanket over the cuppings and sang a lullaby his grandmother often crooned when he couldn't sleep, tucked into bed beside her and annoyingly tugging on her earlobe for comfort.

"Nani, nani, my little Yanni; come, sleep, make it sleep and sweetly lull it," the old lady was softly singing. "Nani, nani, and wherever it hurts will heal."

Yanni sighed as she pulled the cups off, one by one. He then fell into a fitful sleep, the sound of his grandmother's prayers echoing in his ears.

He'd lost track of whether it was day or night. Every time he woke up there seemed to be different neighbors in the house. Once, he saw his mother's younger brother Nicky leaning over him.

"Hey, sport," Uncle Nicky said with a smile. "How're you doing?"

"I'm fine," Yanni lied. "But I see two of you." He turned his head and saw two grandmas and two grandpas. He laughed in delight even though it hurt his throat and brought tears to his eyes. "I see two of everybody!"

Grandma and her blurry double pressed their hands to their mouths. "It's the fever. Pray God it breaks soon," she said.

Yanni heard the worry in her voice and wondered

what the matter was. It was funny seeing double, and for a few moments he didn't feel sick at all, just sleepy. He closed his eyes and heard Uncle Nicky's voice. "It is in our blood, I tell you," he said. "There's been too much cousin marriage here over the years."

Yanni didn't have a clue what he meant. Cousin marriage? What could that be?

"Hush, Nicky," Grandma said.

"That's why we have arranged marriages," Uncle Nicky went on, ignoring her. "They're supposed to limit the inbreeding to stop the blood disease. But they don't limit it enough, do they?"

"I wish you'd let me arrange a marriage for you one of these days," Grandma said.

Yanni didn't have any idea what they were saying, but something about her poignant tone made Yanni blink open his eyes. He saw his grandmother softly patting Uncle Nicky on the cheek, while Grandpa frowned. Uncle Nicky was their youngest son and her favorite child. Everyone knew she spoiled him. Like they spoiled Yanni.

⚮

Sometimes, when Yanni was feeling contrary for no better reason than he could, he'd refuse to eat. Grandma would fuss and worry, scooping Yanni on her lap as if he were still a baby and spoon-feeding him cajolingly. Yanni loved the attention and clamped his mouth shut.

"Just a few more bites, Yanni," she'd plead.

"Let the boy be," Grandpa would say. "He'll eat when he's ready."

Grandma bit her lip. Any more begging and she risked Grandpa pushing back his chair angrily and going to bed early, turning his back to her and giving her the silent treatment until the first light of morning. One time, though, she couldn't resist.

"You are too easy on him," she recalled.

"And he never wraps you around his little finger?" Grandpa snorted.

"Of course he does. But you are the soft touch here. You have always been too soft on people."

"That's me, a good baker and a bad businessman."

"If you had collected all the money that was owed *then*, we wouldn't have to worry so much about money *now*."

"You always wanted me to get blood from a stone."

Grandma said nothing, thinking back to that conversation, holding Yanni tight. She closed her eyes and remembered the days when they were young and hopeful. Her father was an Orthodox priest, and he thought she was marrying beneath her when Grandpa asked for her hand. "You can marry him if you're in love with him," her father finally said, relenting, "but don't ever come back to me and complain if you're unhappy down the road."

But she wasn't unhappy, not when they owned the two-story town bakery, the rich yeasty smell of the baking permeating through the neighborhood. It was where they raised their five children: Yanni's mother, Silvia; his aunts, Athena and the younger Angela; and his uncles, Dimitri and the spoiled Nicky. The bakery was also near the home of his other grandmother, who showed little interest in her grandson, and the house of her daughter, Aunt Stella, and her husband.

It was where the townsfolk lined up in the morning for a steaming loaf of bread. Occasionally, they would carry pans full of meat and potatoes and vegetables for Grandpa to bake because they had no ovens at home. He would charge them a nominal amount—too nominal, Grandma always said—and go outside to the courtyard to split the wood for the oven with an enormous axe. He'd sweat so much that his lightweight woolen shirt would soon be soaked. Grandma would then hurry outside with a dry one, helping him change and giving him a glass of cool tea to quench his thirst.

But the bakery was no longer theirs. Grandpa was not a good businessman. He was too kindly and extended credit to many people who never paid their debts. The people who rented it now were rude and coarse.

"They should pay more rent for the bakery," Grandma would say.

"How can we ask for more now?" he would reply. "There is no one else to rent it."

The worrisome subject of the bakery often came up in his grandparents' conversations, especially when they were awaiting the monthly letter from their daughter, with dollar bills carefully hidden between sheets of her letters. As soon as that envelope with the exotic American stamps arrived, Grandma's worried expression softened. She hurried to the bank to exchange the dollars for drachmas before returning home laden with groceries.

"We are making do. We should count our blessings," Grandpa said to his wife. "A priest's daughter should know that."

Yanni was confused again. He was not quite five, too young to question the behavior of grown-ups. All he realized was that there were moments when everything felt wrong, especially when he thought about his mother and father. He wasn't like the other children in their town. They lived with parents and grandparents. Yanni's parents were ciphers, silent figures in grainy photographs. His mother was dark-haired and pretty, his father tall and somber, no more real to him than his fleeting, feverish dreams. In these dreams, he spoke with them, but strangely, his voice was silent. They loved him deeply, Grandma constantly told him, but those words meant nothing because his parents were somewhere on the other side of the ocean, far, far away in a place called New York. His father had gone there shortly after Yanni's birth. His mother followed several months later. He wished he had someone he could call Mama, someone who was young, like Aunt Stella, and not as old as Grandma.

"You won't be fine until you're married," Grandma was saying now to Uncle Nicky.

"Not yet, Ma. I want to have more fun first," Uncle Nicky said with a laugh. "Besides, you know Dimitri and I can't marry until Angela has a husband. Worry about getting your youngest daughter married first. And then Dimitri. He's bound to want to settle down before I do."

Settle down, Yanni said to himself as he fell into a fitful sleep laced with vivid dreams. There he was, running around the town's streets with his friends, when he suddenly saw Uncle Nicky in a casket, and a pretty, dark-haired woman crying at his side. Was that the mother he couldn't remember, or Aunt Stella? No, wait, it wasn't Uncle Nicky at all. It was the man whose funeral Yanni had seen before he got sick, when he'd been playing invading armies with his friends. Out they'd go, war-whooping as they zigzagged around the neighborhood, pulling out imaginary swords and holding invisible shields like the statues they'd seen in picture books; dashing in and out of neighbors' yards, ignored by the mamas busy with their chores. They heard the sudden chanting of the priests echoing off the buildings and stopped their game. They watched as the funeral procession slowly made its way up the main street, walking up the gentle slope to the cemetery at St. Ioannis, the Baptist church.

An altar boy proudly walked at the front, holding a cross nearly as big as he was, his vestments so richly colored that Yanni felt a deep pang of jealousy, telling himself he would be an altar boy when he was older. Four men came next, the plain pine coffin balanced on their shoulders, and the priest and deacon followed, softly chanting funeral prayers as the family and friends sobbed behind them.

The man in the open coffin was pale and still, not much older than Uncle Nicky. His moustache was as thick and dark as his hair, freshly waxed and combed till it gleamed, in contrast to the pallor of his skin, curling at the collar of his black burial suit. *Did he have the blood sickness too?* Yanni wondered. *Did his cousin marriage kill him?*

Yanni pushed the thoughts away in his dream. He watched the procession continue up the street, past the houses of the town. They were squat and low, built of thick stones that often made them too hot in the summer and too cold in the winter, with slatted wooden shutters for a modicum of privacy.

But of course everyone in the town knew everyone else's business.

Yanni and his friends walked slowly behind the mourners, shooing away the neighbors' chickens that squawked in protest as a horse and cart passed in the opposite direction.

Chickens, Yanni thought in his feverish dream. *Something about the chickens.*

And then a memory pushed away the sight of the mourners, and Yanni was suddenly standing with his friends in the backyard of Aunt Stella's house. Scratchy, scrabbling sounds stopped him. He turned in their direction and saw Aunt Stella stooped under the back stairs leading to the second floor. Her feet were bare and were holding down a chicken, stepping on its claws and wings. In one swift move she cut off its head with a sharp knife.

"Yesterday my grandma slaughtered a chicken and threw it in our shed," his little friend Eleni said loudly.

Aunt Stella ignored them as she tossed the severed head into the yard. She then reached down for another squawking chicken, again stepped on its claws and wings, and cut its head off just as quickly. As she did, a hank of her thick, lustrous dark hair fell out of her housekeeping scarf and draped across her cheek. She blew wisps of hair away, her lips pursed in irritation, while holding down the scrabbling chicken with her left hand and holding up her bloody carving knife with her right.

As she tossed the second head into the yard, it fell atop the other severed head. The bodies of the chickens at her feet quivered, spurting blood.

Yanni stood transfixed as Aunt Stella slaughtered a third chicken, holding its body down so that the first, strongest rush of blood wouldn't splatter all over. He felt excited and scared and sick to his stomach at the same time. He decided he had to get away quickly. As he turned he felt a sharp stabbing pain in his groin. He began to run and his friends gave chase.

Just as suddenly, in his dream, they were back at

the funeral, and they wound their way along the main street, past the grocery store with its crates of oranges and lemons piled high and smelling sweet in the sun. There were thick glass bottles filled with fresh green oil pressed from local olives. Past the open fields where they played every day. Past the small Greek Orthodox church on the corner, redolent of burning wax from candles and incense, where the locals instinctively made the sign of the cross every time they passed. Past the shoe shop with the man wearing a polish-stained apron, and the sandals made of leather that smelled rank when it rained. Past the yarn lady's tiny shop filled with the scratchy skeins she wound up slowly as she sat in the window. Past the tailor who made clothes to order and who sold thin woolen fabrics. Past the hotza's *taverna* with the pungent strong smell of ouzo and wine. Past more open fields and then reaching the St. Ioannis churchyard, where they could see the mound of freshly dug dirt, inside the cemetery to the left.

Yanni's heart started to beat wildly, and he turned away from the cemetery, looking out instead down toward the sea, to large, expensive homes of the rich families who lived on the island—the ship owners and the captains—that faced the port. The sea surrounded the island of Erytha, and the sea defined all the people who lived there. Water stretching everywhere, west to Athens and east to Turkey, a scant few miles away. Yet there was no running water except for a few hours every third day. Yanni often went with his grandmother to help her fetch the water from the fountain in the town square. He didn't mind. He didn't like baths, anyway, particularly in the summertime. He hated sitting in the cold metal tub and enduring a scrub-down from Grandma. He much preferred swimming in the sea. That's what everybody else did, anyway. Yanni could swim almost before he could walk.

He went with his friends to the beach every day when the weather was warm to splash around in the shallows near the port. And even in the winter, he'd go down by the sea with Grandma and Grandpa to walk around and watch the people sitting outside the harbor café, enjoying a strong black coffee or a glass of retsina. Yanni loved to wait for the steamers to arrive from Piraeus, loaded with goods and passengers and the promise of the world beyond the confines of Erytha.

Everyone managed to make ends meet, barely, but there was no shirking. There was pride of place and pride in appearance. Yanni had already learned that lesson well, from his grandparents. The townsfolk were honest, hard workers, looking out for one another, helping out when they could, living their simple lives in their small stone houses. The mamas scolded their naughty little ones and sat on their doorsteps and gossiped, waiting for their husbands to come home from work. They were families who raised their children and their chickens and goats, prayed in church and cursed the cold rain that fell too heavily in the winter and not at all in the summer. The families who relished the sweet smell of the fresh figs from the trees that grew all over the island.

Yanni's grandfather loved those figs, but not as much as he loved Yanni. Maybe it was guilt that he'd had to rent out the bakery and his daughter had left her infant behind to earn her way. Maybe because Yanni was so young and full of beans, a whirlwind of perpetual motion with knees covered in scabs from his scrambling over low stone fences and climbing the fig trees to steal the fruit and insisting that he was the general in the war games he loved to play with his friends. Or maybe he just loved how Yanni looked up to him, eyes shining as he twirled Grandpa's thick dark moustache.

"Kyrie Eleison, I beg you," Grandma was saying now. Yanni heard her voice so clearly in his dreams.

Far out west, on the mainland, lived Yanni's Aunt Athena with her husband George and their two little children. She, too, was praying for his recovery. As his condition worsened, she became alarmed, then desperate.

"Merciful Virgin Mary," she prayed one night. "My sister only has one child. Please let her keep it. If one child must go, take one of my own!"

Kyrie Eleison, Kyrie Eleison. God have mercy.

"Oh God, please don't take Silvia's only child, I beg you," she kept saying. "You already took her first son. Oh Blessed Mother, please intercede with your Holy Son for Yanni. Oh God, please let Yanni live."

Little did Athena know that, many years later, her prayers would be answered in a most tragic way.

꠹ ꠹

Yanni was burning up. He couldn't stop his shivering, and Grandpa gently placed more blankets over him as Grandma pressed cool cloths to his forehead. He awoke suddenly to the sound of murmuring near his ear. Grandma was kneeling beside him, praying, her eyes shut tight.

In the hazy flickering light of the oil lamp, Yanni watched as his grandmother fixed her gaze on the icon of Jesus and Virgin Mary. His mouth was so dry he couldn't get any words out. Grandma turned back to him and tried to smile as she helped him sip some water. Before he knew it he was asleep again.

When Yanni woke up early the next morning, he knew he was better. He was no longer shivering, and his throat was not hurting as much. Suddenly, he realized he was famished as he looked at his grandmother with a swift tingle of love when he saw her head drooping in sleep, sitting on a chair next to his bed.

"Grandma," he said, the word a croaking in his throat, "wake up, wake up!"

She stirred awake with a start and smiled at him as she stroked his damp hair off his forehead. "You look like you are a little better, my child," she said. "How do you feel?"

"I feel good, Grandma, but I'm very hungry. Could you make me a soft boiled egg?"

"You need *two* eggs," Grandma replied as she hurried into the kitchen, her eyes shining in relief.

CHAPTER 2

Hard Days in School

Yanni sat, staring out the fingerprint-smudged window of his classroom. His teacher, Mrs. Iordanou, called the first-grade class to order with a rap of her ruler on the edge of her desk. Thirty-one heads swiveled to the front of the classroom, and Yanni's reluctantly did too, although he avoided her gaze. He didn't like his teacher. She was squat and stern and droned on and on. She wasn't anything like the lively and gentle kindergarten teacher from last year, Mrs. Xanthopulos, who'd made everything fun; like the day she shuttered the windows, turned out the lights, and then lit a candle. "You see, this is how we measure light," she told the rapt children. "Every light bulb has a number printed on it, the "candlepower." That tells you how many candles it would take to produce the same light as that bulb. Even the dimmest little light bulb has the light of many candles."

As Mrs. Iordanou went to the blackboard and began to do sums, Yanni lost himself in the beginning of a daydream, remembering the events that had taken place several months earlier, on Pure Monday, the beginning of Lent. He'd been busy darting in and out among his relatives crowded into the living room, Grandpa merrily pouring glasses of ouzo for their neighbors and for Yanni's uncles. His favorite, Uncle Dimitri, a petty officer in the Coast Gúard, was visiting from his post in the port of Evroupolis, on the northern part of the mainland. His sister, Aunt Angela, had come with him, and that made Yanni especially happy.

Grandma was busy bustling in the kitchen with her widowed sister-in-law, Great-Aunt Sophie. She'd been preparing savory delicacies for days, cleaning the seafood and stewing eggplant and rolling out the dough for her famous fluffy pita breads. Shooing Yanni away when he tried to stick his fingers in her thick earthenware bowls for a forbidden taste.

She didn't mind all the cooking, even though she'd start following a strict Lenten diet of a little fruit, nuts, and unleavened bread every day afterward until the Easter service forty days later. That's when the parishioners would proudly don their very best clothes and walk eagerly to the front of the churchyard, candles in hand, for the beloved service of midnight mass, after another day of fasting. Yanni would fall asleep with his clothes on, and Grandpa would shake him awake a few hours later, handing him an Easter egg and three almond cookies to put in his pocket. He knew he could eat them only after the service was nearly finished and they heard the priest, swinging his censer as smoky incense plumed out, joyfully announce, "Christ is Risen!"

The delicious smells would make Yanni's mouth water as he'd grab a handful of almonds and run out onto the terrace. Best of all, he thought, no chickens had to be sacrificed for their feasting. No strange fluttering deep in his heart as he wondered why such a simple act had so profound an effect on his psyche.

Still deep in his schoolroom daydream, all thoughts of the chickens flew away as quickly as Yanni's feet took him back into the house, where he tugged so hard on his Uncle Dimitri's sleeve, imploring him to go outside to fly kites together.

A week later, Yanni wished he could fly his kite from the back of the donkey cart slowly plodding up the hill to the Monastery of St. Constantine; Grandma and Great-Aunt Sophie beside him. Below him shone the cerulean-blue vastness of the sea, with the beaches of Turkey across the straits seemingly close enough to touch.

Grandma and Great-Aunt Sophie often visited the island's monasteries and shrines. St. Constantine, with its community of nuns, was their favorite. The only man allowed in, was the priest. Older boys were banned as well, but Yanni was still young enough, especially as God had spared him during his dangerous bout of pneumonia. Prayers of praise and gratitude must be said.

The nuns, with their long black habits cloaking their bodies, fascinated Yanni as much as they terrified him. Their practiced silence, with not a murmur during their meals at long wooden tables in the communal dining room, intimidated Yanni into not saying a word during the meal. He watched, rapt even as he missed the mealtime chatter he usually had, with the nuns keeping their eyes down, focusing on the food they ate quickly. Yanni was glad when the meal was over and they settled into the visitors' cabin near the chapel. He was quickly discomforted, though, as it was the first time he had ever stayed in a strange place. But he soon fell asleep, holding on tightly to his grandmother's hand as she sat next to him.

Two hours later, Yanni woke with a start. He sat up, alarmed by a candle's flickering shadows dancing on the wall, and he suddenly realized he was all alone.

"Grandma!" he screamed in a panic, throwing off the blankets and getting out of bed. He ran barefoot, in his thin pajamas, into the open churchyard. The stars hung brilliant in the clear night sky. Often, Yanni loved to gaze up at them, his grandfather hoisting him up on his shoulders and pointing out the constellations. But now, their immensity in the darkness of the mountaintop was mocking, cold and terrifying.

And then he heard chanting and saw a light spilling out into the night, and he raced into the chapel. The nuns turned to him, their eyes wary, before returning to their chanting. Yanni sobbed harder until he felt a familiar touch on his shoulder and turned around to see his grandmother. Still shuddering with sobs, he buried his face in her skirts and wrapped his arms around her legs.

"There, there, Yanni. Everything is all right," his grandmother whispered. "But we cannot stay in here."

She took his hand and led him quickly back to their cabin. The evening service was not yet finished, but Yanni was so inconsolable that his grandmother stayed with him, even after he finally fell asleep again.

Yanni didn't know it at the time, but that memory of awakening in the dark, then running out into the night, alone and terrified, the stars coldly twinkling above, would become one of the enduring memories of his childhood. He would always feel uncomfortable, if not outright scared, every time he found himself alone at night in an enclosed area.

⁘⁙⁘

The long, involved daydream disappeared in a flash. Yanni sat up with a jolt, realizing that he was far from the chapel on the mountain, and his boring teacher was still doing boring sums and calling on his classmates. Dimitris, one of the teacher's favorites, waved his hand, begging to be called on. *This is the only good thing about sitting in the back,* Yanni thought. At the start of the second semester, after Epiphany, Mrs. Iordanou had announced that her students would be seated according to their grades. Now it was mid-February and Yanni was sitting in the very last row with three other boys. One of them was a year older and repeating first grade. Mrs. Iordanou usually ignored them.

"You're the class dunces," she would rudely say to them as the other students laughed.

Yanni sighed again, wishing he could see the ocean. More than anything, he wanted to be a sea captain when he grew up. Nothing was more exhilarating for this little boy than stepping onto the small steamboat with his grandparents every summer for the long trip to the hamlet of Keramos. The hamlet was nestled at the northernmost tip of Erytha and was famous for the hot springs Grandpa soaked in all morning while Yanni tried to fish from rocks on the shore with a little wooden rod.

His heart would thump in excitement as the deep horn sounded and the boat slowly pulled away from the harbor. From ancient days, steeped in the myths of the gods and goddesses, the island of Erytha had always been known for its fearless sailors and captains and traders. They'd sail off to explore the Mediterranean, hoping for a smooth sail and a swift journey to their destination while praying to the three sisters—the Fates themselves, Clotho, Lachesis, and the fearsome Atropos. They were the ones who cut the thread of life to send mortals to their doom.

Yanni knew nothing of the Fates. He didn't know that his fellow Erythans were seen by other Greeks as naïve and gullible, traits cultivated by the islanders themselves to give them an edge in their business dealings with those from the mainland. "Why, those silly Erythans!" the mainlanders would crow. "They actually believe that the moon has fallen down into their wells because, when they look down, they see its reflection staring back up at them! They're so easy to fool!"

And then the Erythans would move in for the kill.

Yanni sighed deeply as his teacher droned on and quickly fell into another daydream. In the lovely images that floated into this head, he was back in the previous summer when he'd taken an overnight voyage to Patras on a much larger ship. He was with his grandparents on a visit to his little cousins, Costas and Maria, and their parents, Aunt Athena and Uncle George, who was a captain in the Greek army and commanded a mountain artillery battalion.

Yanni followed that daydream with another one: an even longer trip to the island of Thermy for the wedding of Grandpa's nephew Michael to Nelly, a local beauty. There, they stayed at Nelly's spacious home. At the end of the large yard behind the house, five chickens were cooped up in readiness for their demise. After lunch, the day before the wedding, everyone was taking an afternoon nap in the sultry August heat. But as tired as he was, Yanni was too anxious to nap, because he'd heard the hired cook say she was going to kill and clean the chickens that afternoon. He quietly got out of bed and tiptoed to the rear balcony of the house, facing the backyard. The chickens clucking quietly inside their coop were too dazed by the blazing heat to peck for food.

Yanni waited for what seemed like hours, crouched down in the shadows behind the balcony railing. Several times he nearly gave up to hurry back into the cool depths of the house for a nap, he was so sleepy. But a mix of excitement and fear stopped him.

Finally, he saw the cook walk out of the house into the garden. She was barefoot and carried a large basket and a sharp, thin knife.

Yanni quickly ran downstairs, stumbling slightly as he stopped in the middle of the yard, his heart thumping wildly. He was caught between a powerful urge to see the slaughter and an equally powerful urge to run far, far away.

The cook didn't seem to notice or feel his presence. She was bent on dispassionately and methodically lifting up a chicken, ignoring its protests, stepping on its feet and wings to hold it still, and then bringing down the knife in expert swings. She waited stoically as the chicken shuddered and sputtered out its lifeblood. When it was still, the cook moved on to the next one, and the next.

"Poor chickens," she said, mid-slaughter, that Yanni jumped. As soon as all five chickens lay in a headless, bloody pile, he raced back up to his room and leapt into bed, pulling the covers up over his head and shivering in the dark despite the heat, his heart pounding too wildly for him to sleep.

Yanni pushed the thoughts away and sailed off into yet another daydream, musing instead about the yacht he would own someday so he could take his mother sailing. He tried to imagine what she would say to him but all he could hear was the faint echo of Grandma murmuring, "Your mother loves you with all her heart and soul. Her letters are filled with nothing but questions about you."

Then why wasn't she here in Erytha to take care of him, or why wasn't he in America with her?

A harsh, loud sound jolted Yanni out of his reverie, and he jumped in fear. The metal edge of Mrs. Iordanou's stout wooden ruler had come down with such force that it left a deep nick in the edge of Yanni's wooden school desk.

"How much is four minus two, Yanni?" she demanded, looming over him like a Gorgon.

"Um, six?"

"That is four *plus* two, not four *minus* two," Mrs. Iordanou said, shaking her head. She still wasn't quite sure whether Yanni was refusing or unable to learn, merely stubborn or intractably stupid. "So then, what is five minus three," she asked, sighing dramatically in exasperation.

"One," Yanni said quickly.

"No! Five minus three is *two*. At the beginning of the year I thought you were going to amount to something. I never expected a child from your family to be so hopeless." Mrs. Iordanou stamped her foot. "This was all on yesterday's arithmetic homework. Show me your homework."

Yanni's face went blank. "I lost it," he told her as the class tittered.

Mrs. Iordanou's cheeks flushed bright red, and she told him to stand up and hold out his palms. He felt the flat of the ruler thwack, hard, three times on each palm. "If you keep on like this," she said, her voice hoarse with rage, "you're going to have to repeat first grade. You know what you are? You're a *dunce.*"

As she stormed up to the front of the classroom, Yanni sat down, determined not to let a single tear spill out of his eyes.

⊰⊱

After school, Yanni's friends were waiting for him as he trudged out of the building and put on his school cap, then hiding his hands deep in his jacket pockets. His palms still smarted painfully, crossed with thin red lines as a souvenir of his teacher's rage.

"Wow, Yanni, she really let you have it," Andreas said.

"It doesn't matter," Yanni said. He was in no mood for conversation.

"But what if you have to repeat first grade?" Andreas asked.

"She can't do that," Yanni said, clenching his hands into fists even though the jolt of pain nearly made him cry out. "When I sail to America on my yacht, I'll go to school in New York and I won't have any homework."

He glared at the boys, and was satisfied by their admiring looks. Except for Dimitris. His face suffused with an expression of pure sympathy. It made

Yanni so uncomfortable that he rudely turned away and ran all the way home. As soon as he got to the house, he grabbed a snack and lied to Grandma that he didn't have any homework before hurrying back out to play. He didn't want her to see his hands. He didn't want her to know he was a dunce.

"Are you sure you don't have any homework?" Grandpa asked as they slowly ate beef stew at dinner a few hours later.

"I did it already, Grandpa, just like I told Grandma," Yanni replied.

"How can you do your homework so fast?" Grandpa persisted. "You were out playing all afternoon. Andreas's grandfather says it takes him an hour to finish his, and both of you are in the same class."

Grandma and Grandpa were staring at him, expectant, and he turned his eyes back down to his meal. "Oh, that is because I am the best in the class," he lied. "When I get home late, it is because I am helping the other kids with their homework. Today I was helping Andreas with his arithmetic. He is having a lot of trouble with adding and subtracting."

"Is that really so?" Grandma asked softly.

"Of course. I would never lie to you and Grandpa. Lying is bad. I know that."

Yanni focused even more intently on his dinner, knowing that Grandpa was frowning, and he quickly changed the subject. "I want to be an altar boy," he said.

Grandma smiled and answered as she always did to

this familiar refrain. "That is good, Yanni. But you must wait until you are a little older."

"How much older? I don't want to wait. I can carry an icon or a big candle now."

"You must be patient for a while," Grandpa replied. "You already know that the altar boys are older than you."

"Why does that matter?"

"It is just how things are, Yanni."

Yanni found out precisely how things were, during recess the next day at school when he was busy skittering small black pebbles around the yard, while his friends played tag.

"Hey, Yanni!" Andreas called out as they ran over. "Tell us about your parents in America."

"Oh, is that all?" Yanni said, smiling smugly. Several of his classmates had relatives who'd left for the golden shores, but no other child had parents who'd left the island for good. Had he known his friends would have been so interested, perhaps he would have brought the topic up sooner; but then he realized it was still too painful and too strange to discuss. He often wondered what it would be like to live with someone he could call Mama, or how his father combed his hair, and what their voices sounded like and how they would talk to him. Whether or not they relished fried fish fresh from the sea, sprinkled with lemon, as much as he did, and if they were kind and would love him as much as Grandma and Grandpa did. He was so surrounded and protected by his grandparents' love that he didn't feel particularly abandoned by his parents, only curious about what it would be like to live with them. Sometimes Grandma would pull out their photos and talk about them, especially when the monthly envelope arrived from New York.

"What is your father's job in America?" Paul asked.

"Oh, he is a big businessman," Yanni replied, lying easily. "He sits in his office and tells everyone else what to do."

"Does he own a restaurant?" Mark asked. His great-uncle was a legend in their extended family because he owned a coffee shop in Pittsburgh.

"Sure," Yanni said. "He owns lots of restaurants, department stores, newspapers, a bank, and a steamship company."

"What does your mother do in America?" Paul asked.

"She is busy managing the servants in their big house."

"Do you have brothers and sisters there?" Mark asked.

"Oh, no. I am the only child."

"Why aren't you with them?" Andreas said.

"I will see them in the summer. As soon as school is out I will sail to America in my yacht."

"Your *yacht?*" Mark said as he looked at the other boys in disbelief.

"The yacht my father gave me," Yanni went on. "It is called *Sea Eagle*, and it has a crew of five. Right now the engine is broken and they have to fix it. In Piraeus. They need a lot of people to do the work because the yacht is so big. When it is ready, I will take you for a cruise."

"I want to go too, Yanni," Andreas said.

"Me too," clamored the other boys, except for Dimitris. He was looking at Yanni with a doubtful expression.

"Of course. Everybody can go," Yanni said.

"Do you speak American?" Paul asked.

"I learned it two years ago."

"Say something in American."

"Let me think of something good," Yanni said, stalling as his friends looked at him expectantly. "Oh, I know: 'Malan, poh radda, shabik flom.'"

"What does that mean?" Mark asked.

"It means, 'Slow down. We're coming up to the port,'" Yanni replied.

Mercifully, one of the teachers began ringing the end-of-recess bell, putting an end to further questions. Until the next day, when Andreas came over to Yanni with Philip and his cousin Matthias, a fourth grader.

"Speak some American with Matthias, Yanni," Andreas said. "He knows some, too."

The confident expression on Andreas's face made Yanni's heart sink. "I don't feel like it right now," he said. "Maybe later."

Matthias elbowed Andreas aside and said, "How do you say 'good morning' in American?"

Yanni could feel his cheeks turning scarlet. "Belasa dool," he stammered.

"Ha!" Matthias said, his voice dripping with disdain. "That's nothing but gibberish. My uncle Stavros was here from America at Epiphany. Before he went back he taught me how to say a bunch of stuff in American. I know 'good morning,' 'good afternoon,' 'good evening,' 'hello, sweetheart,' 'what's your name,' and 'how about a kiss.' He was going to teach me more, but my mother got mad at him. You're just making things up."

"I am not!" Yanni said.

"Okay, then, say something else in American," Matthias shot back.

"I don't want to."

"Don't want to because you *can't*," Matthias said as he turned to Andreas and told him, "Your friend is a big fake."

"No, no, his father is a rich man in America. He's going to take us for a cruise on his yacht," Andreas said.

"You're a liar," Matthias said as he turned to Yanni. "If your father is so rich, you must have all the spending money you want for candy and stuff."

"That's right, I do," Yanni said.

"Oh, yeah? Show us how rich you are and treat us to some candy."

"I don't have to show you anything."

"And you must live in a big house here on Erytha with servants to do the cooking and cleaning. Where is your house?"

"He lives near me with his grandparents," Mark said. "They used to run the bakery downstairs and now they rent it to Mr. Vlahos. But they don't have any servants."

Matthias rolled his eyes as the bell rang. When Yanni got in line with his classmates, he saw Matthias pointing him out to another fourth-grader and whispering in his ear. Both boys started laughing, but stopped abruptly when a teacher sauntered by. Yanni kept his head down as he trudged back into class, wishing he really did have a ship so he could sail far, far away from Erytha and never come back.

Classes that afternoon passed in a blur, and after the last bell rang, Yanni hung back in his classroom as long as he could, hoping the other kids would be gone by the time he got outside. He slowly walked down the school steps, then froze when he saw Matthias stick his head out from behind the corner of the school building, along with the fourth-grader he'd been laughing with, and Yanni's friends Mark, Paul, Andreas, and Dimitris.

"Hey, rich kid," Matthias yelled. "We want you and your grandparents to tell us all about your big-deal father in America."

Tears sprung into Yanni's eyes and he quickly blinked them away; then he took off as Matthias shouted, "Get him!" He knew he couldn't outrun the fourth- graders for long as he turned left at the first corner and sprinted down a winding passageway into a narrow alley. It was a dead end. Yanni crouched behind a little shed and tried to catch his breath. *Don't let them find me. Please, God. I'll never lie about my parents again,* he said over and over to himself. *Don't let them find me.*

"I'll look this way," Matthias called out. "You guys go in the other directions. The first one to see him, lemme know."

As Yanni scrunched down and tried to make himself smaller, he heard footsteps approaching the shed, and then he recognized the brown leather sandals. It was Dimitris. His classmate leaned down and put his fingers to his lips then called out, "He's not here. He must have gone the other way," before running off.

Yanni slowly counted to a hundred before peeking out from behind the shed. Nobody was in sight. His heart thumping so hard he felt as if it would burst from his chest, he got up and ran and ran and didn't stop until he was safely home.

The next few days at school were a living hell of taunts and accusations. "Your yacht is sinking," Matthias said with a sneer. "But don't worry, we'll throw you a life preserver so you don't drown. *Faker.*"

Of all his friends, only Dimitris tried to talk to him, but Yanni was too upset to thank him. The taunts soon died down but the humiliation burned so brightly that Yanni stopped playing with everybody as he usually did after school. His grandparents fussed and worried but all Yanni would say was, "Nothing's wrong. I just don't feel like playing with anyone. I'm fine by myself." Each morning before school, Grandpa would say, "Don't be shy, Yanni. Patch things up with Andreas and Mark. Make other friends. Don't be shy."

The only good thing to come of Yanni's distress

was that his grandparents stopped asking about his homework.

⊰ ⊱

Over the next few weeks, Yanni was sure he would never have friends again. He thought life couldn't get any worse until he came home from school to find Aunt Angela, who had just arrived from the mainland, deep in conversation with his grandparents.

"When the coup failed last week, on the very day it started, Dimitri and I thought it was all going to blow over quickly," she was saying, "but then he heard that they are purging all the Venizelist and anti-monarchist officers, even those who had nothing to do with the coup. Dimitri has never been political, so he should be all right, but we decided it would be better for me to come here until things quiet down. Of course, the one we are really worried about is George, who is stationed in Patras. You know how outspoken he is."

That must mean Uncle George, Aunt Athena's husband, Yanni thought, looking at the worried faces in the kitchen. "What does 'purging' mean?"

Aunt Angela frowned. "It means getting rid of," she told him. "The people who control the government are throwing some officers out of the military."

Grandma quickly crossed herself. "Pray God it is only that," she muttered.

"But why are they throwing officers out of the

military?" Yanni asked. Even for a six-year-old, that didn't make sense. He knew the army needed its officers and soldiers to keep them safe.

Aunt Angela's frown deepened. "For stupid reasons, Yanni, because they disagree. Or because that's a convenient excuse for attacking people they don't like."

"What is a Veni—, a Venizelist?" he asked.

"Venizelist. It means someone who supports Venizelos, a man who used to be prime minister. And an anti-monarchist is someone who thinks we shouldn't have a king."

"Is Uncle George in trouble for being one of those?"

"We hope not, Yanni. Your uncle George is a loyal officer who loves his country." Aunt Angela drew a deep breath. "But we can only talk about these things here at home, so you must never breathe a word about them to anyone else. Not a single word. People will use any excuse to get at someone, and it could be very bad for us if people think we are on the wrong side. Do you understand?"

Yanni nodded. The last thing he wanted was to make trouble for any of his uncles. Aunt Angela's face relaxed into a familiar smile, and she gave him a long hug. They spent the weekend playing cards and cooking, Grandpa and Grandma bustling happily around the house, thrilled to have their youngest daughter home, even in fraught circumstances. Yanni almost forgot about school and how much he hated it.

When Yanni got home from school on Monday,

Aunt Angela was sitting in the living room with his grandparents, and the looks on their faces stopped him cold. "I think I'll go outside for a little while," he quickly said.

"Okay," Aunt Angela said. "When you come back, I'll help you with your homework."

"Um, I don't have any homework today."

"Really? There must be something you have to do for school."

"No, no, nothing," Yanni said as he darted out the door. For the next hour he kicked around aimlessly in the empty field behind the house, dreading what he knew awaited him. After dinner, the battle commenced.

"Time to get out your school books, Yanni," Aunt Angela said, her voice chirpy.

"I left my books at school," Yanni told her. "You can check in my book bag and see."

"What about your homework?"

"I don't have any."

"How can that be? Show me your notebook."

Yanni slowly pulled it out of his bag and handed it to her. She leafed through the first few pages, then stopped, holding it up, so Grandpa and Grandma could see that most of the pages were blank. "Today is March eleventh, Yanni," she told him, "yet there is no homework in here since the middle of November. What's going on?"

"I told Grandma and Grandpa already," Yanni said stoutly. "I am the smartest in the class and I get all my homework done before I come home. Plus sometimes the teacher doesn't give me homework because I am so far ahead of everybody else."

"I don't believe you," Aunt Angela said. "No one here believes you. You need to stop telling stories."

"No, I'm not! It's the truth!" Yanni shouted. "School is stupid! The other kids are stupid! The teacher is stupid!"

He began trembling with such alarming vigor that his grandmother put her arms around him. "There, there, calm down," she crooned. "We are trying to help you."

"I don't need any help. I just need to be left alone."

"Listen to your grandmother," Aunt Angela said, her voice stern. "We all want what is best for you. You must not lie to us anymore."

"I'm not lying!" he screamed, pulling away from his grandmother and stamping his foot.

"That's enough. Let the boy be for now," Grandpa said.

"But that's the problem, Papa," Aunt Angela said. "You've let him be for too long. You've spoiled him." She sighed. "We'll figure out what to do tomorrow."

A knot of worry formed deep in Yanni's belly. It gave him a restless night and ruined his appetite for breakfast and deepened into a sharp throb when he saw Aunt Angela walk into his classroom just as the bell for recess was ringing. She shook Mrs. Iordanou's hand and was still engrossed in conversation when the class trooped back into the room twenty minutes later. Aunt Angela gave Yanni a brief nod, and Mrs. Iordanou looked at him searchingly before ignoring him for the rest of the day.

Thoughts jumbled in Yanni's head as he slowly walked home after school. Maybe there would be a miracle and he'd be left alone. Or maybe his teacher told his aunt that he really was a dunce and deserved to be held back, like Spyros, who was sweet-tempered and helpful but very slow. Yanni knew he was much smarter than Spyros. Or was he? Why did he have to endure such humiliations? It was all his mother's fault, he decided. If she hadn't left him with his grandparents, none of this would be happening.

Aunt Angela was alone in the house when Yanni trudged in, and she handed him his favorite snack of fresh yogurt, apples, and honey. As he slowly licked his spoon, she said, "Mrs. Iordanou has explained the situation to me. Your grandparents and I have talked it over. If you don't apply yourself and do your homework and learn what you are supposed to, you are going to be held back in first grade for another year. You don't want that, do you?"

"I don't care."

"That attitude is exactly what has to change, young man. This family is not going to let you ruin your life before it starts."

"I don't care, and I'm not doing any homework," Yanni yelled. "School is stupid."

"School is not stupid and neither are you," his aunt replied, her voice calm. "You don't belong in the dunces' row."

"Maybe I do."

Aunt Angela sighed. "I'm warning you, Yanni. You can wrap your grandparents around your little finger, but not me."

Yanni crossed his arms, clamped his jaw shut, and stared straight ahead. He would just sit there until she gave up on him, like Mrs. Iordanou had.

The next thing he knew, Aunt Angela yanked him up out of his chair, held him with one arm, and with the other switched his bottom three times with a long, thin stick from one of the bushes in the field. Yanni howled in pain and tried to wrench free as she gave him two more switches and then let him go. He stood there crying and rubbing his bottom as Aunt Angela went into the living room. She returned with a large sheaf of papers in one hand, the switch still held firmly in the other. She sat down and neatly arranged the papers in a pile, then put the switch at her feet.

"Mrs. Iordanou has given me the homework from the last three months," she said. "We'll start with the vocabulary list." She looked up at Yanni. "If you're not ready to sit down and study, pick up that switch and hand it to me." Even though his bottom still stung, Yanni gingerly sat down. When his grandparents walked in twenty minutes later, he barely glanced up to see the happy smiles on their faces.

Every day for the next month, Aunt Angela worked with Yanni on his homework until he was caught up. At times he wanted to scream in resentful frustration, and he exerted himself only enough to avoid being switched again. Still, he had to admit to himself, the humiliation stung worse than the switch ever did.

Mrs. Iordanou's teaching was as boring as ever, yet Yanni was surprised to find that he actually relished her nods of approval when he answered questions correctly. And he was secretly overjoyed when she ultimately moved him out of the dunces' row. Best of all, his friends seemed to have forgotten all about his lies, and he and Dimitris had become close friends. He knew it would be hard to see Dimitris over the summer because he lived on the other side of town but that didn't matter.

Having an ally who understood him warmed his heart.

CHAPTER 3

Coming Into His Own

Heaven must be a little bit like this, Yanni thought as he lay in the grass of a field near his house, staring up at the clouds. Andreas and Mark were at his side. The sky was blazingly blue and a light sea breeze tickled their bare toes.

"I wish it could be summer all year round," Yanni said dreamily. "Just think. No school."

"No teachers," said Andreas.

"No homework," said Mark.

"No one hitting you with a ruler," Yanni added.

They sighed happily.

Yanni was in an even better mood as he walked into the house for lunch and inhaled the luscious aroma of lamb simmering with garlic. This mingled with the sweet, rich scent of his favorite almond cookies just being taken off the wood fire by his beaming grandmother.

"Wow, what a feast," he said, his mouth watering.

"What's so special today?"

"How could you forget? Aunt Athena and Uncle George and your cousins Costas and Maria are coming today," she replied.

"Oh, right." His lazy days had pushed all thoughts of their visit out of his mind. But he was thrilled they were coming, especially his cousins. Yanni was much more accustomed to the visits of Uncle Dimitri—who seemed more like an overgrown kid, eager to fly kites and roam around outside with his nephew—than his sternly taciturn Uncle George, bristling with army discipline and strong opinions. Yanni, awed and admiring, never dared misbehave around him.

Soon, Yanni heard his name being called and he eagerly ran outside to embrace his relatives. As soon as Costas and Maria put their bags in the living room, the happy cousins all ran outside to play. After a leisurely, laughter-filled dinner, Yanni got down on the living room floor with Costas and Maria to play cards. The grownups sat around chatting. Engrossed in the game, Yanni paid no attention to them until he heard Aunt Angela ask her older sister Athena, "How is that house going to suit you long term?"

"It should be fine," Athena said, her tight smile vanishing. "I'm glad it's only about ten minutes' walk from here."

Angela nodded as she turned to her brother-in-law. "What they've done to you is really horrible," she said, her voice thick with anger. "To have your career ended now, because of politics. I mean, you're only forty-three. That's not fair! And officers like you are the backbone of the army."

Yanni was so startled he dropped his cards, then sheepishly picked them up as he glanced at Uncle George. His features were set blankly as he shook his head. "Not everyone thinks so," George said, his voice heavy.

Last summer, when they were visiting Patras, Yanni remembered he'd been thrilled at the sight of Uncle George's artillery regiment on parade. He recalled the flags flapping with a crisp snap and the uniforms sharply khaki with sumptuous crimson sashes tied just so, as the soldiers marched in perfect unison. Yet he thought he'd still prefer to sail the seas when he grew up, just like Uncle Dimitri. Commanding an artillery battalion was a close second. What had gone wrong for Uncle George?

"Can't you ever go back to the army, Uncle George?" he asked.

"Not for a while, Yanni."

"Why won't they believe you when you tell them that you really love Greece?"

"It doesn't matter what I say anymore," he replied, his voice flat. "Too many people have heard me say over the years that Greece does not need a king."

"But, we *don't* have a king." Yanni was perplexed. He was learning all about Greek history in school. "Do we?"

"No, we don't. But we've had one before, and we'll

have one again soon, mark my words."

What Yanni was too young to understand was that Uncle George had been retired against his will in the latest coup to roil the already unstable government. Uncle George had not wanted to retire at his age. He was still strong and vigorous, a career soldier, well-liked in his regiment until the political climate in Athens shifted and forced him out. There would be no going back.

Yanni glanced at Costas and Maria, who kept their heads down. They'd heard this situation discussed endlessly in the weeks leading up to their arrival in Erytha, and were dreading yet another outburst of rage from their father. As well as more tears from their mother.

Yanni was too confused and curious to keep silent. "What are you going to do now, Uncle George?" he asked.

"That's enough, Yanni," Aunt Angela said sharply.

Uncle George shrugged. "I don't mind. It needs to be said," he replied. "Perhaps I will become a carpenter and cabinet maker, like your father's brother, Uncle Emmanuel."

A spasm of pain flashed across Aunt Athena's features, and she blinked back tears. Glancing at her older sister, Aunt Angela quickly said, "That might be just the thing. Anyway, Yanni, isn't it nice that Costas and Maria will be living here all the time?"

Yanni nodded happily, but his mind was racing. Something big and grown-up and ugly had happened to Uncle George. He was too young to understand it all but old enough to promise his grandparents, later that night, not to talk to anyone about his uncle leaving the military.

He remembered how the stories about his parents had quickly spun out of control that humiliating day in school, and he certainly didn't want that to happen to his uncle.

⚶

As the lazy summer days melted into one another, and school started again, life followed an easy, regular rhythm. No one nagged about homework and Yanni worked just enough, always remembering the stern look on Aunt Angela's face and her heavy hand with the switch. Whenever those memories crept into his mind as he struggled with arithmetic, trying to hurry through his sums to get them over with as quickly as possible, he was glad she'd gone back to Evroupolis with Uncle Dimitri. A young, beautiful woman, Aunt Angela was busy trying to land herself a marriage proposal from the many suitors clamoring for a chance to live with someone as smart and pretty as she was.

If only Uncle George were as carefree. On a chilly November day, he hurried into Grandma and Grandpa's house just before dinnertime, a newspaper in his hand and a bitter smile on his lips. "I said mark my words, didn't I, and look what has come to pass," he said to Grandma, who was sitting on the sofa with Yanni, before throwing the paper on the floor and stomping back out. Grandpa picked it up and read the headline: NATIONAL REFERENDUM: THE MONARCHY IS RESTORED AT LAST.

The following year, Uncle George obsessed over the news coming out of Europe. His mood had already been dark when, the year before, Metaxas and his cohorts took over the Greek government in a coup, installing himself as prime minister. "A puppet king and a dictator. No country could ask for more," Uncle George said sarcastically at the time. Now, his mood was positively black.

As he so often listened to his uncle's discussions, Yanni began to dream of dictators who looked worryingly like Hitler, the noisy, fearsome man in Germany that had Uncle George so concerned. Hitler's tiny moustache bothered Yanni to no end. He much preferred the luxurious thick moustache of his beloved Grandpa, the one that still tickled his skin when he bent down to kiss his grandson good night.

But Yanni didn't mind everything that the new government did as much as his uncle. Fortunately, he was still too young to understand the harsh mindset behind the abolition of the Boy Scouts and their replacement with new fascist groups, mimicking those already set up in Italy and Germany. Although membership was voluntary on paper, Yanni and his friends joined EON, the National Youth Organization. They were taught rousing songs praising the fascist system, sitting in rows under posters plastered on the walls emblazoned with patriotic slogans and enormous photos of Metaxas and his ministers. Yanni was oblivious to the fascist slogans, especially "One Nation, One King, One Leader, One Youth." He enjoyed, instead, their hiking, camping, and treks to the forest, especially as they allowed him to be outdoors and spend even more time with his closest friend, Dimitris. One of his favorite adventures was spending several days with his friends, digging holes on a barren hillside and planting seedlings for a new forest. And at Christmastime, visiting the poor section of town and offering food and words of encouragement to the elderly.

Christmas that year was memorable for another reason. Uncle Dimitri, still in Evroupolis, sent his parents a live turkey for the holidays. The poor bird was tied up in the kitchen, near a drain, fussing and squawking and doing its utmost to escape.

As soon as he saw it, Yanni got the familiar, odd feeling of excitement, his heart fluttering, reminiscent of the chicken slaughter he witnessed in Thermy. Aunt Angela, visiting the island for Christmas, was given the task of slaughtering the hapless bird later that night. Yanni was torn between an intense desire to watch the killing and compassion for the animal about to die. The turkey had been staring at him seemingly for hours, imploring, with a piercing look that filled Yanni with pity. He couldn't tear his eyes away as Grandma busied herself in the kitchen, walking around barefoot. So hypnotized was he by the round, staring eyes of the turkey that he soon found himself nodding off and Grandpa scooped him up and took him to bed.

At breakfast next day, he heard Grandma admonishing Aunt Angela for shirking her turkey-killing duties. "I just couldn't do it," Aunt Angela said as Yanni put down his spoon and listened intently. "The poor thing knew what was coming, didn't it."

Grandma shook her head. "After I cut off its head," she said blithely, as if turkey-head-chopping were something she did every day, "holding it down under my feet, it bounced free and started running around the kitchen, flapping its wings. I tried to finish it off, and poured some hot water on it." She took a sip of tea. "That just made it crazier, and it kept fluttering around with blood gushing everywhere, and made a huge mess in my kitchen."

Aunt Angela shuddered. "Stop it, Mother, please," she begged. "There's no way I'm eating that turkey now."

Grandma laughed. "Don't be so silly," she said. "Of course you'll eat it. That's what it's there for, isn't it?"

She did eat it. So did Yanni. It was so perfectly delicious.

As the school year went on, Yanni received the inevitable lecture from Aunt Athena about his below-average grades and perfunctory attitude. "You think third grade doesn't matter, but your whole future is at stake," Aunt Athena warned him. "Before you know it, your class will be split into two. Only the top twenty-five percent will be allowed to study for a profession. The rest will have to learn a trade or be a laborer. Which group do you want to be in? You must apply yourself to succeed in life."

Yanni briefly thought that of course he wanted to be in the top quarter. Dimitris, one of the best students in the class, was firmly entrenched at the top, and he'd hate to be separated from his friend. He still loathed school, though, and was about to shrug with disdain at applying himself to his studies when Aunt Athena said, "You can forget about being in the Coast Guard like your uncle if your grades are poor."

Yanni paused but he soon rationalized by asking himself, what did the Coast Guard matter when he could just run away to join the merchant vessels? As long as he could spend his life at sea, bliss was sure to follow.

And summer was quickly approaching. More bliss.

⊰ 🙢 ⊱

That summer became an unexpected turning point for Yanni. Years later, he would look back at it and remember it being the dividing line between his life as a little boy, and of his finally beginning to grow up and understand more of the world around him; of responsibilities, of discipline and hard work, even of life and death.

The first Sunday after school ended, the entire family

met for lunch after church. As usual, Yanni was happily sprawled on the living room floor with his cousins, intent on beating them at cards, when his contented mood flew off like a kite that had come undone from its strings.

"It's time for Yanni to get his own bed," Uncle George said suddenly. "He's too old for this."

Yanni's head jerked up and he saw Uncle George sitting with his arms folded in front of his chest—never a good sign—and Aunt Athena nodding vigorously in agreement. Grandpa opened his mouth to speak, but Grandma beat him out. "We don't need to change yet," she said indignantly. "He is fine with us. It's not an issue."

Grandpa pursed his lips and frowned, but remained silent.

"It is an issue. It's unhealthy," Uncle George said. "Unhealthy for everyone."

"Nonsense," Grandma snapped as she got up and went into her already spotless kitchen. She began scrubbing the sink in frustration.

Behind her back, Grandpa raised both hands, palms up, and looked at Uncle George with a poignant expression of exasperation mingled with gratitude. Uncle George quickly nodded, then looked pointedly at Yanni, who ignored him. His stomach was churning. He wasn't sure what he wanted. He couldn't imagine not sleeping beside the warm bodies of his grandparents, feeling safe and secure and encased by their love. It was all he had ever known.

But all of his friends had their own beds and he didn't want them to think he was still a baby.

Later that week, Uncle George and his family came over after dinner. He was holding a large bundle and when he unwrapped it Yanni saw a small, rough-hewn wooden bed frame topped with a thin mattress.

"Your bed has to be getting awfully cramped with two adults and a growing boy, Mother," Aunt Athena said. "George made this specially for Yanni, in his workshop."

Grandma looked at the bed with obvious distaste. "You can take that back home with you," she said. "There is plenty of room where he sleeps already. Yanni is small for his age, after all."

"No I'm not!" Yanni shouted. He'd just been about to agree with Grandma, but her comment hit his sorest point. Although he was not the shortest boy in his class, he was among the smallest, and it rankled him deeply. "And I like the new bed. My uncle made it just for me."

Uncle George smiled. "Very well, then," he said. "I'll put this across from the big bed."

By the time everyone left, Yanni's anger had dissipated along with his good mood. Anxiety gnawed at him. He wanted to sleep between Grandpa and Grandma, like always. He wanted everything to stay the same. But at the same time, Grandma's comment about his size still ate at him. She hadn't apologized. *I'll show her,* Yanni said to himself. *I won't say anything, until she asks me where I want to sleep.*

That resolution faltered as he saw Grandma fixing

up the cot with soft clean sheets and a little pillow, her face set in sadness. He even thought he saw her wipe a tear away, but he said nothing, waiting for an apology that didn't come.

"It looks so comfortable, doesn't it?" Grandpa said. "Now you'll have room to stretch out."

Yanni nodded in reply, still hoping for Grandma to say something. When she didn't, he slowly clambered onto the bed. The legs were slightly uneven, and it rocked a little. He lay back, wondering how long he could stand it. A few minutes later Grandpa got into the big bed with a huge sigh of satisfaction. Grandma turned out the light and lay down beside her husband.

Every time Yanni shifted in the cot, it rocked on its uneven legs. *This stinks*, he thought, tossing and turning and staring up at the dark ceiling as Grandpa began to softly snore. He was mad at everyone: at Grandpa for wanting him out of the bed, at Grandma for saying he was small for his age, and at Aunt Athena and Uncle George for meddling. *To top it off*, he thought, *Uncle George is a lousy carpenter! Why couldn't he make the legs right? I can't stand this one more minute. Wait—I know what to do. I'll go sleep in the living room, like Aunt Angela does when she comes to visit.* He was just about to sit up when he realized that if he snuck into the living room, he wouldn't be able to see or reach out to Grandma and Grandpa. He didn't want to feel as he had on the mountaintop monastery, where he'd woken alone in the dark, the shadows deep and dancing around him. He dreaded feeling alone.

A few long minutes passed, and Yanni yawned deeply. He was so sleepy. It had been such a long day.

Several minutes later, Grandma lifted her head and whispered, "Yanni, are you all right there?"

He was fast asleep.

Moving into his own bed wasn't the only shift in Yanni's routine that summer. As autumn approached, another family conclave took place. The subject, as usual, was Yanni. Aunt Athena decided it was time for him to come stay with her family. To move in with them; to live, study, and go to school together with his cousins. Eventually, they all agreed that this was for the best.

Yanni's heart felt a sharp pang when he realized the decision was made. His joy at being with Costas and Maria was tempered at the sight of Grandma weeping, bereft at the idea of her adored grandson being taken away, no longer underfoot to fuss over. He loved his grandparents dearly, and especially relished how they spoiled him rotten and let him get away with all sorts of naughtiness. Aunt Athena wasn't a soft pushover like Grandma; she was a matter-of-fact kind of mother to her children, detached and demanding. And Uncle George, he knew, was a stern disciplinarian.

Even though the two homes were separated by a walk of no more than ten minutes, they had little in common. As he looked at Grandma's lined and worn face, and at Grandpa's stooped shoulders racked with rheumatism, he realized it was time.

They're really getting older, he said to himself, *and*

I am getting bigger.

When it was finally time to leave, Yanni was smothered in Grandma's kisses, her cheeks wet with tears. Grandpa cleared his throat gruffly.

"Don't worry, I'll be visiting all the time," Yanni said to appease them. "So please make me lots and lots and lots of almond cookies."

⇥⇤

Ambivalent feelings consumed him as he walked out of his home silently, following Uncle George and his family down the familiar street that somehow looked different that night. He wasn't scared, just wondering what it would be like, mingled with a sense of discomfort that his uncle's strict regimen might chafe. But his cousins would know how to manage it. They'd guide him through.

It's going to be fine, he kept thinking as he made up his bed in a small room next to the dining area. Costas's bed was pushed up against the other side of the room, a tiny window facing the street below. *Besides, my parents will send for me one of these days. And then I'll leave here for America and everyone will be so jealous.*

It did take some adjustment, though, as Uncle George ran the house like the barracks. Every morning, he'd stand in the doorway of the boys' bedroom, clap his hands sharply, and shout out, "Reveille!" Even if Yanni needed a minute to wake up, especially in the cold winter mornings, Uncle George paid no mind. He'd yank the blankets off the beds and demand obedience. And at night, when it was time for bed, Uncle George would call out, "Taps!" That signaled the end of any conversation or playtime, and the cousins hurried to their rooms as the lights went out.

Chores were regimented as well. The cousins rotated who set the table and served the food and did the cleanup. Anyone who expressed even a hint of displeasure at the food would be certain to see an even larger amount on their plate the next day.

"Iron discipline," was Uncle George's favorite phrase. "This is the only thing that makes sense. It's how you must practice all your life," he'd thunder. "Iron discipline, or you'll wind up failures and garbage collectors."

Costas and Maria merely nodded when their father went off on his daily tirade, as they'd heard it so many times already it barely registered anymore. They warned Yanni about their father's moods, and how to gauge them, especially as their mother was equally rigid and unbending. Yanni had no idea that his aunt took the responsibility of looking after her younger sister's little boy very seriously, and that she often wondered if Yanni would ever be able to leave the island to live with his parents. Could his relationship with them withstand the years of separation?

Much to his surprise, Yanni quickly thrived under the new rules. He might not have liked the orders being barked at him, and he often inwardly chafed at his aunt and uncle's autocratic attitude, but having such iron-clad rules actually made life much easier. He knew what was expected of him. He knew he had to make his bed with such tight corners that Uncle George could bounce drachmas off it. He knew he had to be home for dinner or he'd be sent off to his room with nothing to eat. He knew that all homework had to be done and checked before he could play games with his cousins, usually with the pebbles he kept in a little bag. He knew that if he dared to ask "Why?" about anything at all, he would be shouted down immediately with no explanation. Uncle George was so consistent with all three of the children that it made life run quite smoothly.

Only once did Yanni catch his aunt trying to repress a smile when he dared question his uncle. *Maybe she's on my side after all,* he thought. He had no way of knowing that she was secretly disappointed with her children's submissiveness, and relished Yanni's restlessness and marked spirit of independence even as she scolded him. *He needs to be tough if he's going to be a foreigner in a strange country, living with his parents as he should be,* she'd tell herself. *He needs to find his voice.*

Where the military-style discipline helped Yanni the most was at school. Long gone were the bored, dreamy days where schoolwork was avoided and lies spun to impress his friends. Instead, there was a keen sense of competition, as Yanni simply could not bear the thought of being inferior to his cousins. Costas and Maria were top students who enjoyed learning. Yanni soon discovered that schoolwork could actually be fun if he paid attention in class.

He especially loved learning anything about the sea and Greek history. It was far more interesting to study the Peloponnesian Wars or the Byzantine period or the horrors of the Turkish occupation or the wonders of the Greek Revolution of 1821. More so than to think about the heated discussions Uncle George would have with his friends. There was an undertone of anxiety and anger fueling their conversations, which would stop short as soon as Yanni walked into the room.

"Mussolini is a buffoon," he couldn't help overhearing. "But he is way too close to us for comfort."

"Hitler is no buffoon," someone else would say. "He's far more dangerous than we know. Nothing good will come of it. Nothing at all."

Uncle George frowned and shook his head. More than most, he could read the signs of impending war in Europe, and seethed with resentment that he'd been summarily retired from the battalion he'd loved. He was still fit and strong and desperately needed to keep himself occupied, but woodworking wasn't the answer. He simply didn't have the knack and became so stressed with worry that he broke out in painful hives.

Luckily, an opportunity appeared when Aunt Athena found an elderly man looking to share his fabric store in the main shopping district. It was a great location, on the busiest street, and the couple decided to open a haberdashery. Uncle George busied himself buying household items: wool for knitting, perfume for the ladies, and socks for the men. Much to his amazement, he found that he enjoyed running his own store, talking to the customers and helping them find just the items they needed from the shelves that he took great pains to keep well stocked. They looked up to him, and the shop became a gathering point for conversation and the sharing of news, especially once the original owner retired and Uncle George was able to take over the entire shop.

He had no idea how important that little shop would become to the family's survival in only a few short years.

Everyone in the family was working hard, and Yanni was thrilled when he managed to pass the entrance exams for the junior high school.

❦

Yanni spent most of the following summer recess in Evroupolis, under the watchful eyes of Uncle Dimitri and Aunt Angela. There were long glorious days of playing by the shore with local friends under the shadow of the town's famous lighthouse; of fishing excursions; of Uncle Dimitri regaling him with tales of the Coast Guard; of church festivals and feasting and fun.

There were only two blots on the otherwise indelible sun of that summer. One was the worried expression on the faces of his aunt and uncle after they heard from Grandpa that his asthmatic cough had taken a sudden turn for the worse.

The other was the even-more-constant conversation, long into the night, of the grown-ups. Yanni would sometimes pinch himself to stay awake, listening and wondering if war would really happen. Their voices rose and fell, and the anxious tone was palpable. Sometimes he felt as worried as they obviously were; other times, he felt almost an unbearable sense of excitement. What was a little bit of war, anyway? How bad could it be?

And then he heard Uncle Dimitri saying that Hitler's army was massing. Mussolini had already invaded Albania, and had signed a Pact of Steel with Hitler a few months before. Italy was worryingly close to Greece. How vulnerable were they? What would happen to Uncle Dimitri and his position in the Coast Guard? Was he in danger?

The first of September dawned hot and sultry, just as it had been the day before, and the day before that. Yanni hurriedly gulped his breakfast and went outside as he always did, eager to find his friends down by the harbor. This morning he recognized a girl who was the older sister of one of his friends and a student at the local sewing school. Her name was Eleni. She had a knife in one hand and a squawking chicken in the other. Before Yanni could blink, she stepped on the chicken, squeezed her eyes shut and brought down the knife on the neck of the hapless bird. Blood spurted everywhere and as Eleni opened her eyes she started to cry. Yanni stood frozen as the sewing teacher came storming out of her house, shouting in frustration before quickly placing her foot on the still-flapping chicken and finishing the job. Then she wagged her finger at Eleni and told her to clean up the mess.

Yanni's heart was thumping as it always did whenever he saw a chicken meet its demise. But this time, for some reason, he felt differently. A wave of pure anxiety splashed over him. *It's a bad omen,* he said to himself. *Something is very wrong. Something bad is about to happen.*

He pushed the thoughts away as he found his friends and they started playing. It wasn't long afterward, though, when they heard screams coming from outside a house near the harbor. He recognized the harbormaster's wife.

"It's war! God save us! Hitler invaded Poland! We're done for!" she shouted, collapsing in hysterics as her neighbors ran outside, surrounding her in consternation. "God save us! It's war! God save us!" she wailed, over and over.

Yanni ran back to the house, the image of the harbormaster's wife's prone body mingling in his mind with that of the bloody chicken butchered so ineptly at Eleni's hand. No one was home, and he was glad for the silence as he splashed cold water on his face and calmed his ragged breathing. By the time Aunt Athena came, calm and serene, the bad feeling had gone.

"My God, did you hear that crazy woman?" she exclaimed about the harbormaster's wife. "She got the whole neighborhood in an uproar." She looked at Yanni pointedly, then smiled. "There's nothing to worry about.

Poland has nothing to do with us."

Yanni nodded and got up to help her with dinner, glad it wasn't going to be chicken. A few days later, he sailed back home and was quickly immersed in his studies. Despite the fighting in Europe, life on the island continued as it always had, slow and safe and serene. As the months flew by, the grown-ups stopped talking so much about their worries. They wanted nothing to do with Hitler or Mussolini. They just wanted to be left alone.

The specter of war did little to change Yanni's thoughts about his parents. He wondered about them, imagining what they looked like and how their voices sounded and what they liked to wear and eat. If they spoke good English and how they behaved in America and whether or not they missed him and thought about him, too.

⊰ 耳 ⊱

On the Sunday after Easter, when he was finally clad in the adored vestments of the altar boy he'd always wanted to be, he was carefully holding a heavy cross, walking in a stately processional past his old house. He realized Aunt Athena was running toward him. "I have wonderful news," she said excitedly. "You have a new baby sister! In America! Isn't that lovely?"

Yanni nodded soberly, not wanting to lose step with the processional, and then pushed the thought out of his mind. A newborn little sister was no more real to him than his own mother and father.

Routine suited Yanni. Up at reveille and off to school. Back home for lunch at two-thirty in the afternoon and time for homework when the grown-ups had their daily nap. When he was done, he'd go to the local library to read poetry or short stories. The little boy who hated school had surprised himself and thrilled his relatives by discovering an insatiable love for reading. His head still in a book, he'd often walk a few blocks to Uncle George's haberdashery to help out with the customers. Yanni's transformation was complete.

He adored his cousins and wanted them to be proud of him. Costas, three years his senior, was serious, somewhat timid and aloof, but always unobtrusively protective. Maria, two years his senior, was a beautiful and vibrant young lady, who was especially obedient and proper as her mother was fond of saying.

One afternoon, however, she shocked Yanni when they were alone in the house after school and she asked him to come into her small bedroom. "Do you know how babies are made? Are you curious?" she asked coyly, before adding, "Two girls from school showed me these photos in a book, and they made me want to know more. Let's try to find out!"

She pulled out two small photographs of naked boys and girls from her wallet. Yanni could not figure out why the kids were photographed like that. He was puzzled and confused. Especially when Maria asked him to take off his pants. He hesitated, but then the thought of disappointing his cousin flashed through his mind, so he pulled down his pants. She took off her panties and asked him to lay down next to her on the bed. When he did, she looked at Yanni's penis, examining it carefully for a minute, then softly took it and tried to push it into her vagina. *What a silly thing,* Yanni thought. *What on earth is she trying to do?* He was too young to have an erection and couldn't figure out what she found so interesting about it. She just kept asking him to push it into her vagina. When his penis eventually slipped inside, Yanni became alarmed and pulled it out quickly.

"Don't take it out," Maria said soothingly. "Nothing happened. I just wanted to know how it felt. It'll just be our secret, right?"

They lay in bed next to each other, silent, for a few more minutes. Deep inside, Yanni felt a mixture of guilt and shame. He knew enough about her parents to realize that if she got caught trying to do this same thing to anyone else, her life would literally be at risk. He got out of bed, nodded to his cousin, pulled up his pants and hurried out into the safety of his own room, scarcely daring to breathe.

Later that night he overheard his aunt scolding her husband in their bedroom. "For shame," she said. "How could you not trust your own nephew?"

Yanni felt a sharp jolt of adrenaline at those words and quickly sat up on his bed, glancing over at Costas, who was fast asleep. He got quietly out of bed and stood by the door, listening.

"Well, I did it for his own protection. He's a young man and could make a mistake. He claimed he was going to the library every day and I wanted to be sure," Uncle George said petulantly.

"For God's sake, he's only eleven years old. He's not interested in girls. Thank goodness. He likes to read. You should be glad of that. Remember when he hated school so much? He's quite the young scholar now."

"All right, all right. Forget it."

Aunt Athena laughed. "I still can't believe you paid someone to follow your own nephew to see if he was actually going to the library."

"And now I'm never going to hear the end of it, am I?" Uncle George said, but Yanni heard the teasing note in his voice and relaxed. He was astonished that his uncle thought he'd been lying about his jaunts in search of a good book to read. Yet he was also proud that his uncle evidently considered him a young man rather than a little boy. Still, girls were disgusting creatures. Honestly, who would want to sneak off to see one when a good book was so much more interesting?

He remembered Maria's cajoling tone and soft fingers as he crept back into bed, and he lay there for a few minutes, thinking hard. Grown-ups didn't make any sense sometimes, and teenagers even less so. Life was getting complicated when he didn't want it to be. *And you know what? Uncle George should be paying more attention to his daughter than to me,* he thought with not some little satisfaction as he drifted off to sleep. *She's the naughty one!*

PART II

THE GERMANS ON THE ISLAND

Idealized voices and dear
Of our dead, or those that
Like dead to us are they now.
At times, we hear them in our dreams;
At times, they talk in our thoughts.
And with their sounds bring to our minds
Sounds from the early poetry of our lives,
Like a distant music, in the night, that dies.
—From "Voices" by Konstantinos Kavafis

A loud knock at the door of the house shook the old man out of his reverie. His wife was still out visiting local relatives. He opened the door to see a delivery boy dwarfed by an enormous bouquet of fresh flowers. Yanni knew who'd sent them without even looking at the card. Dimitris, his lifelong friend. He always sent Yanni a welcome-home bouquet whenever he arrived on the island, and he was always the first to call.

The old man tipped the delivery boy and carefully arranged the flowers in a vase, thinking with pleasure about Dimitris' loving heart and endless generosity. Then he slowly walked back to the veranda. His neighbors' grandchildren were playing by the pool, and their giddy shouts filled his ears.

As the old man stretched out on the chaise, the sky suddenly darkened. He glanced up at the thick clouds, expecting them to burst at any moment. A distant clap of thunder rolled, and it reminded him, in a flash, of the sound of bombs that exploded on the island when Allied planes came to hit the Germans in the dark of moonless nights.

How did we survive it, he asked himself, *without surrendering to the fear?*

We are survivors, we island people, he realized. We are always surrounded by openness, and we need to find our own way.

CHAPTER 4

War and Death

August 15, 1940, dawned hot and clear. It marked the feast day of Theotokos Dormition, a holy day widely observed in Greece. On the island of Tinos, the Church of the Virgin Mary was revered as one of the most sacred centers of worship in the country. Dignitaries and government officials arrived on the island every year, resplendent in their stiff new uniforms or softly draped bright dresses, to venerate the miraculous icon of the Theotokos.

This year was horribly different, however. A destroyer, sent to the island by the Greek navy to honor the holiday, was torpedoed by a submarine of unknown nationality. It swiftly sank. Several sailors and officers died, and all of Greece began the countdown to war that they now knew was inevitable.

Several months later, Yanni woke to the pealing sound of church bells. He shook the sleep from his eyes and sat up in the dark. Something was very wrong, he quickly realized, when he heard the low voices of his aunt and uncle mingling with the rapid, jumbled speech of someone on the radio. He got dressed and joined everyone in the kitchen, but the anxiety was so strong that he walked with his family to the town square. Many of their friends and neighbors were there, milling about, too worried to stay at home or to stand still. They all waited for news. It soon arrived. Over the square's loudspeakers came static, and then the clipped tones of King George.

"Today at dawn, we were attacked by the Italian fascists," the king said, his voice strong, clear, and decisive. "We must now defend our homes. We shall fight for our country. We shall never surrender. We shall prevail. God and justice are on our side."

The crowd cheered, and the town's band hastily assembled and started to play the national anthem.

Women began sobbing as men threw their hats in the air when the band switched to rousing military marches. For a moment, Yanni recalled how he used to play soldiers with his friends in the fields behind his grandparents' house. He would wield a small wooden sword, shouting "I am victorious, like the mighty Achilles!" while dashing in and out of imagined forts, certain that he was strong and brave and all was good with the world. And there he was now, several years later, standing in the town square with his aunt and uncle and cousins, thrilling to the sound of the music and the excited voices of the townsfolk and the cries of the women. For a moment, he heard a tiny nagging voice inside him that said, *"This isn't a game any more. This is going to be very, very bad."*

He put his arm around his uncle's shoulders to stop his trembling.

The townsfolk were soon told that Greece had been attacked from the north by those who had conquered Albania a few years earlier. Soon the entire country was enveloped by war fever, together with patriotic enthusiasm. As a mandatory mobilization was declared, Uncle George was called back to the army and sailed off for the mainland. Aunt Athena took over the haberdashery, keeping herself busy to dampen her worries over the safety of her husband and the rest of the country.

As the months came and went, the family veered from elation to sadness, from pride to fear. They followed the news closely. After the first sudden attack, the Greek army regrouped and surprised the Italians with their courage and ferocity. The family rejoiced with every news bulletin showing Mussolini puffed up like a peacock with his own self-importance. How could such a fool possibly prevail over the power of the Greeks, they thought.

Every day, they heard the radio playing the teasing tunes sung by the Songstress of Victory, Sophia Vembo.

Hey, Italians/Forget the war
Tanks and cannons are not spaghetti.

Every chance they had, Yanni and Costas tried to find a radio to listen to the news. The Greeks kept fighting into Albania, they heard, freezing on the snow-drifted mountains, furiously driving back the Italians, one hill at a time. Jokes about the Italians and Mussolini were rampant. One Yanni kept repeating to his friends went: "Hitler called Mussolini on the phone. 'Benito,' he said, 'aren't you in Athens yet?'

'I can't hear you, Adolf.'

'I said, aren't you in Athens yet?'

'I can't hear you. You must be calling from too far away. Are you in London?'"

Yanni would burst into laughter, together with his friends, every time he told it.

Late one afternoon, when a tired Aunt Athena came home from the haberdashery, Yanni tried to cheer her up. "Did you hear what Churchill said?" he asked her excitedly, before quoting, 'From now on, we will not say that Greeks fight like heroes, but that heroes fight like Greeks.'" He was proud and thrilled.

"Aunt Athena," he continued, "I just heard over the radio, our soldiers were called the eighth new wonder of the world!"

"That's wonderful," she replied. "And this should make you happy, too." She pulled out a letter from Yanni's mother. "Read it to me while I make dinner."

Costas and Maria sat down next to Yanni as he eagerly tore open the letter and read her greetings and hopes that all was well. "Let me tell you what is happening now in New York," he read aloud. "Suddenly, it is an honor to be Greek. Strangers who overhear us talking in Greek are stopping us on the street! They ask us what language it is, and when we tell them Greek, they embrace us and sometimes even give us a kiss in gratitude! Our church told us about the Greek War Relief. It's a new organization to raise money for the fight. They just had a fundraiser at Radio City Music Hall. Lots of celebrities went. Singers and dancers and famous people. We Greeks are so popular that all six thousand seats were filled, and people were standing in the aisles. Can you imagine!"

"I wish I could have been there," Maria said wistfully.

"Me, too," said Yanni.

"Is there more?" Aunt Athena asked.

"Yes," he replied, clearing his throat. "Let me tell you another story," he read on. "We have a friend named Ted. He works in the shipping business. One of the company's ships arrived in New York from the West Coast. The captain told Ted that one of the pumps was broken, so Ted took it to a small shop in Jersey City to get it fixed. The store's owner looked at the pump and said it would cost $200 to get it fixed. So Ted said fine. He went back a few days later to pick up the pump, and thought he'd ask for a discount, hoping for the best. The owner refused. Ted wrote out the check and gave it to the owner. The owner looked at it carefully, then handed it back to Ted. 'Take it,' he said. 'Give it to the Greek War Relief. Give it to those who are fighting against the fascists. You Greeks are my heroes.'"

"Wow," Costas said. "We're heroes even in America!"

⧩⧨

The euphoria filling the hearts of the islanders with pride and joy was tempered for Yanni and his family, as his cousin Maria began having problems walking, dragging her feet in an unsteady gait. She was in such constant pain that Aunt Athena had to find a way to take her to Athens so she could consult with specialists. They discovered that one of her vertebrae was damaged, and her only options were a risky operation or complete bed rest and treatment in a hospital outside of Athens, for several months. They hoped that treatment, together with bed rest, would help her get well again. They decided to take the bed rest in the hospital, and Aunt Athena came back to Erytha, her face lined with worry and exhaustion. She asked her younger sister, Aunt Angela, who lived in Athens at the time, to look after her niece.

Athena's worry lines soon deepened because her father's health was suddenly deteriorating. Grandpa had always seemed so strong and indestructible. Now, Yanni didn't know what to do. He got up early with Costas and hurried over to Grandma and Grandpa's house for a short visit before school started. Then he'd rush home to their house again, after his classes were finished to do his homework in the familiar living room. Grandpa smiled at the sight of his grandson working so diligently, his books spread on the table and his pencil skimming over his papers. It made him remember all the old fights about school when Yanni used to live there. The little boy who'd lied so stoutly about his homework was growing up into a fine young man. More than anything, right then, Yanni wanted to make his grandfather proud of him.

But Grandpa wasn't getting any better. He had a constant cough due to the emphysema he'd ignored for years, and his breathing was getting more ragged with every long day that passed. He'd smoked all his life, and his work in the bakery, with the heat of a stuffy oven in the cold winter months, together with the smoke from the wood and coal, had damaged his lungs. Now he sat by the window, hoping for a bit of the soft spring breeze on his face to help clear his lungs, struggling for nearly every breath. Grandma sat next to him, trying to hide her tears as she patted his hand and tenderly wiped his cheeks, bringing him tea he barely had the energy to drink. While the good news from the front— the Greek Army was advancing into southern Albania— arrived regularly, filling the hearts of the townsfolk with jubilation, the bad news in Grandpa's house grew alarming. Soon, Grandpa could no longer get out of bed.

The town doctor came often, and left shaking his head. There was nothing he could do for Grandpa. Yanni tried his best to be brave every time he visited his grandfather. He was grown-up enough to take his cues from Grandma, even as he heard Aunt Athena sobbing in her bedroom every night. He knew the end was close, and prayed that it would be swift and painless. He couldn't bear the thought of his beloved grandfather suffering so much.

One day, the local priest arrived. Yanni was in the room, together with his aunt and cousin. He looked at Grandma's tearful face, and he bit his lip so hard to stop his own tears that it started to bleed. The priest went into Grandpa's room and Yanni could hear their low voices as Grandpa shared his last, private confession. All the poignant memories of his long, hard, loving life flooding his consciousness and spilling out in his last, peaceful moments.

Yanni heard the priest's voice get louder as he gave Grandpa holy communion. Then he came out into the living room and asked that everyone join him in prayer. Grandma, Aunt Athena, Costas, and Yanni knelt around Grandpa's bed. He managed to smile at them as he crossed himself, his face relaxed. *He was at peace,* Yanni realized as he closed his eyes to pray, *and that, at least, was a small comfort.*

"Lord Jesus Christ, who suffered and died for our sins that we may live, if during our life we have sinned in word, deed, or thought, forgive us in Your goodness and love," the priest said, his tone soft and even as he recited the prayer for the dying. Grandma repeated the words after him, her lips moving as she gazed at Grandpa lovingly. "All our hope we put in You; protect your servant Michael from all evil. We submit to Your will and into Your hands we commend our souls and bodies. For a Christian end to our lives and to the life of Michael, peaceful, without shame and suffering, and for a good account before the awesome judgment seat of Christ, we pray to you, O Lord."

Yanni looked at Grandpa, who had fallen into a deep, lethargic slumber. His mouth was slack, and Yanni realized with a terrible feeling that Grandpa really was dying, that he would never ever wake up again.

"*Kyrie Eleison,* bless us, be merciful to us, and grant us life eternal," the priest intoned, and closed his prayer book.

"Amen," they all whispered.

Grandma sat on the edge of the bed, holding Grandpa's hand. Several of the neighbors arrived and set up chairs in the living room. The deathwatch was, thankfully, brief, and Yanni was glad that he had been in the room when Grandpa's spirit left his body, a moment nearly elusive as Grandpa's face suddenly relaxed and his tortured breathing stilled. Grandma began to cry inconsolably as Aunt Athena tried to comfort her. Costas and Yanni sat, frozen as statues, gazing at their beloved grandfather and wishing that, somehow, a miracle would take place and that Grandpa would suddenly sit up again and be himself, alive and full of happiness and love, ready to spoil them and forgive their naughtiness.

But that was not to be.

Yanni sighed deeply, gave his aunt and grandmother

a hug, and went to sit outside for a few moments. He needed to be alone. *Grandpa really was dead,* he told himself over and over, disbelieving as he ran his fingers over the rough bricks of the wall outside the house.

He recalled the stories Grandpa had told him over the years. This was where Grandpa and Grandma had started a family together, where his children had been born, where life had been sweet sometimes and heartbreaking at others. Especially when two of his children died young of a strange, unknown disease that tainted their blood and doomed their future. When long ago, he was young and strong and ambitious, he had made a booming success with his bakery, his breads soft and fresh and delicious and his almond cookies famous all over the island. Along with Grandma, his loyal and loving wife, he was always seen as honest and proud, respected and held in high esteem by friends and neighbors. He'd seen two of his daughters married. He'd been blessed with grandchildren. No doubt, Yanni thought, Grandpa had years of unexpected, great joy, his young grandson Yanni tickling his moustache and filling his heart with so much love that he spoiled him rotten.

Yanni had to laugh at the thought. He remembered how safe he'd felt in the big bed in this house, nestled comfortably between Grandpa and Grandma, reaching out to tug on her earlobe as Grandpa's soft snores gradually filled the room. And now Grandpa lay in that bed, gone forever from this world. Tears flowed down Yanni's cheeks. He sat outside in the balmy late afternoon and cried until the tears left him, and then he wiped his eyes and his nose and went back into the house. Grandpa had been laid out in a plain pine coffin in the living room, thick white candles in standing holders on either side. Grandma sat next to him, bereft and silent, as family, friends, and neighbors kept vigil, handing Yanni and Costas the black bands of mourning that they somberly wrapped around their sleeves.

Later, someone from the church placed the coffin cover, emblazoned with a large black cross, up against their building so that the neighbors would know it was a house of mourning. Many of them came that evening, crossing themselves, to pay their respects. Yanni was grateful for their company. There were dozens and dozens of them coming to say their farewells and trying to comfort Grandma. He knew Grandpa would have been incredibly touched to realize how many townsfolk looked up to him and remembered his kindness and generosity when he handed them loaves of bread he knew they couldn't afford.

Yanni spent a fitful night, barely sleeping. As an altar boy, he'd already been to many funerals, and he knew that the highly structured rituals and the prayers for the dead were meant to help the mourners with their burden. But this was the first time it was for a member of his own family, someone he loved so dearly. Eventually he got up and joined his aunt and cousin as they walked slowly to the house, realizing with a heavy heart that this was the last time Grandpa would ever be in it.

The priest, the church sexton, and the altar boys carrying large crosses soon arrived. There was a short service by the coffin, and four pallbearers then lifted it up and carefully carried Grandpa down the steps toward the street. Grandma burst into loud, heartrending sobs, knowing that this was the final, irrevocable ending to their life together. *"Ame sto kalo."* "Go to a happy place," she said over and over between sobs, bidding a last farewell to her beloved husband. "Please, please, go to a happy place."

It was not appropriate for the widows of the town to join in the funeral procession, so Grandma stayed home, tended by several of her neighbors. Yanni and his relatives walked slowly behind the pallbearers until they reached the church. After a longer service, Grandpa was taken to an open grave, where the lid was placed on his coffin and he was placed in the grave.

Yanni stood there for quite some time, in silence, with Aunt Athena's hand on his shoulder, Costas at his side, as the gravediggers slowly covered Grandpa's coffin with dirt. Nearby stood his other grandmother, Barbara. Yanni was surprised that she lingered. She'd barely been a presence in his life even though she lived across the street from the house where he'd grown up. Her indifference was so obvious that Yanni often forgot he had two grandmothers. One loved him so fiercely, and the other barely acknowledged his existence. Yanni didn't mind, though. Once in a while, when he saw

Grandma Barbara on the street and said hello, he would receive a curt nod and a frown. He often wondered if her aloofness was the result of her son having left the town so long ago, and that he hadn't yet returned for his own son—or to see his mother. Perhaps she had closed her heart to the pain.

Yanni glanced over again, but Grandma Barbara was gone. The rest of them made their way back to the house where Grandma awaited them.

⌖

In the following weeks, Yanni tried to spend as much time with Grandma as he could, but the town was soon preoccupied with devastating news. The Greek miracle was seemingly no more than a brief shining moment. Hitler's troops intervened in the war against Greece. The mechanized German army, disciplined and well trained, marched down from the north, quickly taking one town after another and slaughtering anyone who resisted. As the Germans approached Athens, the king and his government escaped to Crete, which was held by the British. The radio station in Athens played the Greek national anthem, then went silent.

The German onslaught took only two weeks to conquer the rest of the mainland.

Once in Athens, the Germans went to the Acropolis and ordered the guardians of the Greek flag flying high over the "sacred rock" to pull it down and replace it with the swastika. One brave soldier who followed the orders wrapped the Greek flag around his body, and leapt off the cliffs of the Acropolis to his death.

This was the story Yanni heard from Uncle George, who had silently returned in the middle of the night and shocked Yanni and Costas the next morning when they saw him sitting at the breakfast table. Aunt Athena was hovering nearby, her eyes swollen from thankful tears. She'd brought Grandma over to rejoice in Uncle George's homecoming. They all sat quietly around the table, listening as he told them how he'd escaped from the mainland just ahead of the Germans, when his unit was asked to disperse—and disappear.

"I still wish I had been with my old unit," Uncle George said, his voice hoarse. He was exhausted and dispirited; he'd lost weight and had dark circles under his eyes. His thick dark hair was laced with silver, seemingly overnight. "Even though nearly everyone was killed," he admitted.

Yanni knew that those soldiers in Uncle George's mountain artillery unit had the difficult task of transporting weapons in inhospitable terrain. Disassembling the cannons, overseeing the mule trains that slowly hauled them up on hidden paths into the rugged hills of the countryside, and then reassembling them while waiting for orders.

Aunt Athena's eyes filled with tears again, but she knew better than to contradict her husband. He'd been assigned to the anti-aircraft artillery, which kept him in a safer place. He had been so grateful to be doing his duty, back in the army he loved, that he didn't harbor any hard feelings. At the end, he followed orders to disperse, as everyone else was told to do, in the face of certain death had their unit been captured by the Germans.

"Where's Uncle Dimitri?" Yanni asked, suddenly worried that Dimitri might have been captured by the enemy.

"He's on his way back, too," Uncle George said, as Grandma said a prayer of thanksgiving. "He should be here tonight or tomorrow. Luckily, the Coast Guard knows these waters so well that they can move from the mainland to the islands with less risk of getting caught. Don't worry. They know what they're doing." He looked at the boys somberly. "But you know nothing, remember. When the Germans come, they must not know I've been fighting. Let them think I am a simple man who runs a haberdashery."

"What do you mean, *when* the Germans come," Grandma said. "Why would they want to come here? There's nothing for them on Erytha."

"They want everything," Uncle George said, his voice so fierce that Yanni got scared. "They want to rule the world and they don't care what they have to do and how many people they have to kill and how many things they have to destroy to get what they want." He sighed. "They're coming to all the islands. So are the Italians. If we're lucky, we'll get the spaghetti army to tell us what to do. If not, just do as you're told. It's merely a matter of time before they set foot here and start—"

"That's enough," Aunt Athena said quickly as Uncle George nodded, glancing at the terrified look on Grandma's face. "We have a lot to do today, to get the house ready for Dimitri, don't we, Mother?" Grandma nodded and brightened noticeably. The house would be much less lonely for her with her son for company.

Dimitri arrived the next afternoon along with his longtime girlfriend, Anna, and her older sister, Linda. They had no one to stay with back in Evroupolis, where he'd been stationed, and Dimitri announced that they wanted to get married as quickly as possible. Grandma's joy at seeing her son back safe in Erytha disappeared. She was sorely disappointed.

Aunt Athena was particularly unforgiving. "How could you think about marriage?" she scolded her brother when he came to her house for a visit. Anna and Linda were still with Grandma. Athena was busy frying potatoes and shook the pan angrily. Yanni and Costas were already at the kitchen table, and they looked at each other, worried. "Papa is newly dead in his grave," she went on. "We haven't even had his forty-day memorial. We are still in mourning, and you bring in your girlfriend, ready to get married!"

"Of course I know we're in mourning," Uncle Dimitri said, keeping his voice even. "Do you think I don't grieve for him? I still can't forgive myself for not being able to get here for the funeral."

Aunt Athena continued stirring the potatoes as she listened to her brother, her demeanor unimpressed.

"And what do you think I should have done? Left Anna and Linda to the Germans? The enemy is in Evroupolis now. They have no one else in the world," he continued. "And no money. There's no way I could leave them there." He got up and poured himself a glass of water, then stood near his sister. "I love her, and I want to marry her," he said softly. "We're at war. These are extraordinary times, and need extraordinary action. Our father would be happy for me, I know it. He would want me to be married, and for Anna and her sister to be safe here. And you know it, too."

Yanni saw Aunt Athena wipe her eyes, and his heart melted for her. Lately, he realized, she'd been in tears most of the day. Who could blame her?

"What about Angela?" Aunt Athena said in her last protest. It was the duty of every brother not to take a wife until all of his sisters were married. This was the unwritten law of Erytha.

"She'll understand. She'll be happy for me, I know," Uncle Dimitri replied. "She knows about Anna from the time she was with me in Evroupolis. Everything will work out. You'll see. Who knows what's going to happen. We need to stay together."

Aunt Athena said nothing, concentrating on the potatoes. Yanni knew how desperately she worried about her daughter, whose spine was no better. And now the Germans would make it that much more dangerous for Aunt Athena to travel to see her child.

Not every battle takes place with guns and soldiers during a war, Yanni realized. Sometimes, the battles take place in a tiny kitchen of a small house on a Greek island.

The wedding took place a few days later. It was small and private and unlike all the other weddings Yanni had been to. The priest from the local church came to the house and performed the service in the small living room, where Grandpa had laid only a few weeks before, lifeless, candles burning at either side of his coffin. It was a somber, quiet ceremony. There was no honeymoon. Grandma and Linda offered to stay with Uncle George and Aunt Athena for a few days to give the loving couple some time alone.

⊰⊱

The war news was ominous, foreboding. The Germans were taking one island after another. The local folks were desperately praying that their island was too small and insignificant for the Germans to invade.

Alas, nothing was too small for the Nazis. On an early May afternoon, Yanni stood on a bluff with Costas, watching as a German troop carrier, together with two destroyers, approached the harbor. They stood, frozen in silence, as they saw a German speedboat come ashore. Less than an hour later, the boat returned to the troop ship, which slowly started to move into the harbor. Not long afterward, hundreds of soldiers disembarked. Not a shot was fired for the takeover to be complete.

The German officers commandeered all the bigger homes near the harbor, kicking out the residents and ignoring their protests. The soldiers set up a large garrison near their officers' homes, surrounded by barbed wire and with sentries on constant duty. As this new German Quarter had an irregular V-shape, it was soon referred to by the locals as "The Triangle." There, isolated from the rest of the town and its people, the invaders made themselves at home.

Two Jewish families living near Grandma's house, were quietly taken away by the Germans and no one ever heard from them again. One of the families had a little girl who was Yanni's age. Everyone in the classroom stared at her empty desk every day, until the teacher finally pushed it against the back wall. It was too stark a reminder that they really were a conquered people.

The Germans thrived on their endless rules, Yanni and his family quickly learned. There was constant regimentation imposed on the locals, made much more difficult by arbitrary rulings. Every other day, it seemed, a new notice would appear, handed out to all the town shopkeepers and in the villages. It was impossible to not see them as everyone walked by. The one that scared Yanni the most read: "Anyone who does not turn in any guns in their possession will be executed without appeal within 24 hours." He knew that Uncle George would never give up his gun, and had hidden his weapon deep under the chicken coop, hoping no one would ever think to look beneath the dirt.

Germans constantly patrolled the town, rifles in hand, walking slowly with a great air of authority, their boots highly polished and their olive drab uniforms stiff and clean, the buttons gleaming. They threatened everyone of being shot on the spot if he questioned their authority or hiding any Jews. The townsfolk scurried inside or kept their heads down as the soldiers passed, trying to keep their distance and not be noticed in any way.

A strict curfew was imposed. Everyone had to be home soon after darkness fell or risk immediate arrest. No lights were allowed in the streets, and everyone had to cover their windows or put up shutters so no light would escape.

"What fools they are," Uncle George muttered one night at dinner. "The cover of darkness makes it easier for people to slip away. And we know these streets better than the Germans ever will."

"What do you mean, Papa?" Costas asked.

"Nothing," his father replied with a heavy sigh. "Nothing at all. It's just the soldier in me. Forget I ever said anything."

Yanni wished he could forget. Life in the town had been transformed. It was no longer a haven, a friendly environment where everybody seemingly knew everyone else's business and shared the good times with the bad. Now, no one stopped to talk to their neighbors. They did their errands as quickly as possible and hurried home to shut the windows and lock the doors. The fear was clear whenever a German soldier walked down the street. No one laughed anymore. Terror was lurking in the dark.

No one trusted anyone, either. Some of the locals who turned out to be secret Nazi sympathizers were hired to help the Germans with their daily duties, much to the shock of their neighbors. During the day, they were the only locals roaming around the town as everyone else once did. They helped the Germans confiscate whatever they wanted to plunder. At night, German soldiers patrolled the streets to enforce the curfew and make sure the whole town remained dark. If an accidental sliver of light spilled from someone's window, the soldiers would bang at the door, terrorizing the inhabitants as they shouted, *"Raus licht, raus licht, schnell!"* until the offending light disappeared.

After school one afternoon, as Yanni and Costas were walking home, they heard shots by the harbor, and they jumped in fright. A notice appeared the next day: "Thieves will be executed without appeal within 24 hours."

A month later, several young men from a nearby village were hanged during the night, their bodies swaying to the screams of the locals who awoke to find them. Signs had been draped around their necks. THE PUNISHMENT FOR SABOTAGE IS DEATH.

Uncle George was in a fearsome temper that night. "Those boys did nothing wrong," he said. "There was no sabotage. It's all lies."

Yanni never got used to the terrible sound of shots suddenly ringing out by the harbor. The next day, the church bells would toll out their mournful sound signifying yet another execution. He was scared; he was angry; he was sad for the families.

And mostly, like everyone else on the island, he was helpless.

Those who had clandestine radios knew that trying to listen to them was increasingly dangerous; worse, reception had become nearly impossible, and the only news coming out of Turkey was laced with static. Not that it was news they wanted to hear.

It was a triumph of terror.

Yanni thought nothing could be worse than fear. Alas, he soon found out that the Germans had another weapon, just as potent as their guns and their hate—starvation!

Not long after they had commandeered all the houses in the Triangle, they started driving through the villages and confiscating whatever food they could find—chickens, goats, sacks of grain and vegetables, and jars of olive oil. They did not care that they left nothing for the locals to eat. They paid for nothing, pointed to what they wanted, and barked out orders in German that had the peasants quaking in fear.

Whenever the Germans ran out of supplies, they'd go back to the villages again. They would stomp through the barns and the windmills where they knew they would find wheat flour. They threatened the peasants with death if they dared hide any of the thick, rich olive oil or corn or even the eggplants and beans they grew in their gardens. They didn't care they were condemning these families, who lived off the land, to a terrible fate of starvation. Instead, they drove back to the Triangle, insulated from all the suffering, and feasted on the delicious food they had stolen.

In town, the shelves in the grocery stores were quickly emptied, and the supply boats that used to arrive faithfully twice a week, laden with all the goods the islanders needed, stopped coming. The Greek drachma had collapsed when the government fell, and was worthless. Food became more valuable than gold.

The Erythans began to starve.

As harvest time approached that first year, the peasants would dash out into their fields at night, plucking what they could and hiding it wherever possible, hoping they'd never be discovered. Luckily, there were fig trees all over the island. Yanni and his friends took turns surreptitiously dashing into the orchards on the way home from school, so they could stuff their book bags full of the sweet, nutritious fruit. They knew where the apple and almond trees were, too, but even what they could take was not enough.

What saved Yanni and his family was the haberdashery.

Bartering became the only way most families survived. Anyone from the villages who could spare some of the crops hidden from the Germans, came to town and exchanged them for gold coins, jewelry, or clothing, shoes, medicine, even furniture. Fortunately, before the Germans came, Uncle George and Aunt Athena had stocked the store, their shelves full with yarn, clothing, and other household items. These goods became their passport to survival. The proceeds from a day's business were no longer drachmas but a few pounds of beans, chickpeas, lentils, occasionally corn, and, on a very fortuitous day, a bag of wheat.

Yanni missed his daily bread more than anything. What he wouldn't have given for a fresh pita or a thick slice from a long white loaf, hot from the oven and dipped in pungent green olive oil or slathered with Grandma's fig jam. Instead, Aunt Athena took charge of the food rationing; she was fair but unyielding. Everyone got the same amount even if they were exceptionally hungry. Every day they had their small portions of boiled beans or peas or lentils, a tiny sliver of bread—if flour had magically appeared at the store in exchange for shoelaces or towels—some olives, vegetables, and fruit. There was no cheese or milk or the yogurt Yanni used to eat for breakfast that kept him full until lunch. No meat. There was no sugar anywhere on the island, not even for the Germans. Those peasants who had well-established beehives, took great care to keep them hidden from the Germans, as honey became a rare and precious trading commodity.

Liquid gold, Aunt Athena called it.

Those meals were barely enough, but the thought that so many other families had even less or nothing helped keep them going. "Funny, isn't it," Aunt Athena told Yanni and Costas one day, "that Uncle George was forced to retire early, and we got the store when we did. Can you imagine how bad things would be without it?"

Yanni often visited Grandma, who was depressed and alone. Her house no longer had that familiar scent of Grandpa's cigarettes and her baking. Thanks to some of his colleagues in the Coast Guard, Uncle Dimitri, his wife, and sister-in-law had managed to sneak off the island in a well-tended boat, and arrived safely in Athens. They sent back a message that Aunt Angela was well, but Maria's condition was unchanged.

Yanni was glad to hear about his beloved Uncle Dimitri. He treasured the moments when they both got down on their knees and said the Prayer Toward the Unknown together. "O Lord, You who steadied the hand of Peter as he began to sink on the stormy sea, if you are with me, no one is against me," they would say. "Grant to me the shield of faith and the mighty armor of the Holy Spirit to protect me and guide me to do Your will. The future I put into Your hands, O Lord, and I follow You to a life in Christ. Amen."

That always made Yanni feel a bit better.

During these dark days of the German occupation, Yanni did not forget to stop in to see Grandma Barbara, too. "Did you bring me anything to eat?" she'd ask without even saying hello. The family helped both grandmothers as best they could, but Yanni's hands were always empty.

"I'm sorry, Grandma," he'd reply as she frowned. He didn't mention how the constant hunger was gnawing at his still-growing body, and that some nights he could barely sleep from the pain of his knotted stomach, begging for something to fill it.

One day dragged into the next, as the locals became even more jittery and uncertain. The only bright spot, it seemed, took place during the second summer of the German occupation. Uncle Dimitri, his wife, and Aunt Angela managed to return to Erytha in a small, wooden boat from Piraeus. They were going to attend a church memorial for Great-Uncle Elias, their mother's brother-in-law, who'd been married to Grandma's sister. They were planning to go to their remote, tiny village perched on top of a hill in the northwest corner of the island. Yanni eagerly asked to join them, desperate for a break from the fearful tedium of German rule.

Early one bright morning, they set out on foot, knowing they had to cover nearly forty kilometers, walking up and down ragged trails on barren mountains, to reach the village. It was a brutal trek that took them all day. Every muscle in Yanni's body ached as they mercifully arrived at the small home late at night. Great-Aunt Joy welcomed them with warmth and kindness. The house was sparsely furnished and the thin mattress Yanni slept on was lumpy, but none of that mattered. It was a house filled with hospitality and love, and for the first time since the Germans had arrived, everyone relaxed.

Many people arrived at the small, whitewashed local church for the service that Sunday morning. Uncle Elias had owned the village windmill, and the local farmers would bring their heavy sacks of freshly harvested wheat and corn to the mill where Uncle Elias would grind them to flour. It was this windmill that made Uncle Elias the most prosperous man in his village—and it was also this windmill that was responsible for his death.

The grindstones were powered by several open sails on long posts, attached to a central axle connected to the grindstones, rotating endlessly whenever a strong wind blew over the village. On that fateful day, the northerly wind coming over the mountains and through the ravines had been fitful; growing strong and steady before suddenly dying down only to start up again suddenly. Uncle Elias was used to the caprices of the wind, and he barely paid it much attention. He had several sacks of grain to grind. At one point, after the wind had completely died down, the sails had barely turned, even once round the mill before drooping idly in the heat. Uncle Elias checked outside, where the air was still. It was a safe moment, he decided, to lock some of the gears over the center of the grindstones, sitting still and heavy inside the open circular chamber of the mill. He often had to do this task to run the windmill efficiently, and he always took care to wrap the sails carefully before securing the gears inside. This time, though, he chose not to take down the sails. It was too hot, he was tired, and the wind had died down. Instead, he would just lock the gears with wooden keys.

Just as he secured the gears and reached for the controls inside the circular chamber, a sudden burst of strong northerly wind blew over the village. The sails started turning and the wooden keys locking the gears shattered. Uncle Elias, surprised by the unexpected wind, lost his balance as the grindstone started rotating. Unable to jump out, he was dragged around and around the turning grindstone. By the time passing villagers heard his screams, he was mortally maimed. Despite a frantic, painful transfer to the town's hospital several kilometers away, he could not be saved.

The day after the memorial, Yanni's uncle and aunts returned to town. Yanni was asked by Aunt Joy to stay with her and help with the farming for two weeks. His mother, Silvia, was her godchild, and she had always had a soft spot for Yanni. He, in turn, adored her. They'd chat over an early breakfast of soft bread, olives, and tea before leaving to do the chores in the fields or go tend the beehives Aunt Joy kept near the village. The fresh, clean mountain air was crisp and invigorating, and for the first time in as far back as he could remember, Yanni had enough to eat. There was fresh bread every day made with grain ground at the mill, and vegetables from the garden and wonderful goat cheese to snack on. Up in that tiny stone farmhouse, far from the rest of the world, it seemed to Yanni that the war was a distant memory and life was good again.

He was sad to leave, although his return trip was not as

tiring, thanks to an obliging little donkey accompanying villagers going to town, that they took turns riding.

⁓◈⁓

Soon school started again. The students were listless from hunger and the stress of the occupation. Their teacher, Mr. Elias, spent hours reading them poetry to lift their spirits. Among them was Victor Hugo's long poem, "The Child."

"It's about an orphan from the massacre on the island in 1822," he explained. "The Turks were ruling over Greece at the time, and the islanders who had enough of the Turkish tyranny, decided to declare independence in 1822. Erytha had always been known as an important trading island, and as such had been given some autonomy and privileges thanks to our unique mastic plant. The resin from this plant is very potent, and we Erythans have known since ancient times that it's a cure for many stomach ailments."

The class was very quiet as the teacher continued. "The Sultan was so angry by what he considered to be an act of betrayal and rebellion by those in Erytha, that he sent a fleet full of the wildest, most depraved barbarian fighters from the depths of Anatolia to the island. As soon as they set foot on the shore, out came their swords." He paused, and stared out the window toward the Triangle, wiping his glasses slowly with his necktie. "There were approximately 120,000 people living on the island at the time. Few of them managed to escape. Most were not so lucky. We don't know for certain, but at least 50,000 people—men, women, children—were slaughtered. Another 50,000 or so were taken as slaves. Women jumped off the cliffs into the sea, their babies in their arms, rather than be violated by the Turks. The savagery shocked the world."

He stared out the window again. Yanni knew what he was thinking. The Germans weren't much different than the Turks had been. Except they weren't using swords to kill the islanders. They were letting starvation do it for them.

"When news of this horrible massacre reached Europe, the outrage was universal," Mr. Elias went on. "The French painter Eugene Delacroix created what became a famous painting of the massacre. And this is what inspired Victor Hugo to write his poem. It is from a series of poems called 'Les Orientales,' based on the Greek War of Independence. It was published in 1829."

He picked up a thick volume and turned a few pages. "The Turks have been. Destruction is everywhere," he started. After finishing with the poem, he read them a few more poems by Lord Byron, who died from typhus when he went to join the Greek soldiers and fight for independence in Missolonghi. He was only thirty-six.

"Tyranny," Byron wrote, "is far the worst of treasons."

All the students knew why their teacher had chosen those poems, but it gave them no comfort. Especially when terrifying sights greeted them nearly every day as they slowly made their way home. Several emaciated locals, aimlessly walked down the streets, desperately searching for something to eat. Sometimes they'd be sitting, for hours, listless, on the stoop of a house, unable to walk any farther because they were so weak. On the worst of these afternoons, Yanni would see someone keel over, curled in the fetal position where they'd fallen in the street, dying from starvation. It was a horrible sight that lingered with him the rest of his life.

Every afternoon, it seemed, the church bells began to peal. Yanni grew to hate that mournful sound. It meant another funeral. The priest from the Church of the Annunciation grew thin and weary, walking down the street at night, whispering prayers and holding a covered chalice, an altar boy with a censer and a lantern, preceding him. Yet another of the local folk was dying and the priest had been called to administer the last rites.

When he had the energy, Yanni would bundle up in his coat and walk down to the library and lose himself in books for hours. The lighting was poor and he often had to squint to see the words. Often, he'd pull out a volume by one of his favorite writers, who had a deft way of romanticizing what life would have been like in the early nineteenth century along the Greek countryside. Yanni would put the book down when his eyes got tired, and dream of days like that, when the island belonged to its people, and the harvests were bountiful, and no one was starving.

Other times, he'd walk down to the seashore, away from the Triangle and the fear and suffering on the streets of his town. He'd stand on the shore, staring at the brilliant turquoise of the sea as small, short waves broke softly, lapping against the beach. Hunger gnawed at him. Across the narrow straits lay the silent, mysterious, distant Turkish coast, dark mountains looming behind it. He wondered what the Turkish villages looked like. If the inhabitants dressed like him and liked the same kind of things he did. And if they had enough to eat.

Sometimes, Yanni would stay at the beach until the sky started to darken, the lights of the villages across the narrow strait flickering on. Occasionally, the dark silhouette of a passing steamship would appear on the horizon. Yanni would imagine that he was the captain of the ship, standing at the bridge, enjoying the wide open sea, eating figs and a handful of Grandma's famous almond cookies. There were no German submarines lurking under the surface of the calm turquoise waters, he thought, waiting to blow his ship into oblivion.

And then as the evening star suddenly appeared high up in the night sky, Yanni would hurry home to be safe and warm before curfew, rushing into the house and pulling tight the shutters, trying to keep the darkness at bay.

CHAPTER 5

Doom and Delivery

ow could I ever have been excited by the idea of war? Yanni thought. *War is pain and suffering and fear and death.*

As the months dragged on, the locals felt more isolated than ever. Nearly all communication with the outside world had been cut off. Occasionally, letters from other Greek cities managed to arrive—already opened and poorly resealed, heavily censored by the Germans. The only news of the war came from clandestine radios that crackled with static and were rarely put into use for risk of exposure. Only once since the occupation started, had Yanni been given a message, filtered from the Swiss Red Cross. His parents had been asking about him. Yet it was hard for him to think of them as real. They were far away, in America. They weren't at war. They had plenty of food to eat. They were safe.

If they had sent for me before the war, I wouldn't be here,

Yanni couldn't help thinking, his stomach knotted in hunger.

And then a message arrived in a telegram that everyone wished had never been sent. His cousin Maria, still bedridden in the hospital outside of Athens, was getting worse. She had developed serious complications—something terrible called meningitis. Aunt Angela was with her, but the situation was dire.

Yanni had never seen his Aunt Athena—the dynamic, self-assured, take-charge woman—in such a state of desperate worry. There was no way for her to get to the mainland, and it was impossible for Uncle George, too. The fighting was so intense all over the Mediterranean that no ships could risk leaving the islands, not even with the partisans at the helm.

Yanni's family had never felt more isolated and alone and frightened. Even the telegrams stopped coming, and everyone prayed that it was a good sign that Maria was getting better.

One Saturday afternoon, Aunt Athena's cousin Michael—a bank officer who lived down the street with his wife Nelly, their baby daughter, and widowed mother—came to the house for a visit, as they often did. He and Aunt Athena had been close since childhood, and they relished each other's company. But not that day. Frantic with worry, Aunt Athena was pacing back and forth in the kitchen, unable to sit still. Yanni went into the backyard with Costas, trying to keep busy to take his mind off the gloom that had enveloped the household. Then they heard a sharp knock at the door, and before they went back into the house, they heard the sound of running followed by heart-rending shrieks.

A telegram had finally arrived, with the worst possible news.

Yanni and Costas hurried into the house, where they found Aunt Athena face-down on the bed, sobbing hysterically. "Oh God, help me! Let me cry for my daughter!" she kept crying, repeating herself over and over. *"Let me cry let me cry let me cry!"*

Yanni looked at Costas's ashen face. His cousin's baby sister was dead, and there was nothing Yanni could do about it. He couldn't help thinking of that strange afternoon with Maria, when her eyes had been alight and she'd pushed him down on the bed. She'd been so full of energy, so curious, so sweet. And now she would never know what it was like to love a man, to get married, to have children, to watch them grow from babies to teenagers, to sit in her garden and smell the mint, to splash in the sea and buy a new dress and curl her hair and roast a lamb so deliciously the way her mother did. How could she possibly be gone?

And they'd never had a chance to say goodbye.

Later that night, as Yanni couldn't sleep, thinking of his beautiful cousin, a strange memory popped into his mind. He recalled having heard of Aunt Athena's prayers many years before, forced to choose between her love for a sister, wronged by their mother's choices, and the love for her own children.

"Merciful Virgin Mary," Aunt Athena had said. "My sister only has one child. Please let her keep it. I have two. If one must go, take one of my own."

She'd said those words as Yanni had lay feverish with pneumonia, all those years ago. Her fateful prayers, he realized, had finally been answered, in the most tragic, heartbreaking way possible. Her nephew had survived but her daughter paid the price she had offered in her prayers. Tears trickled from Yanni's eyes, as he tossed and turned, ravaged by guilt. And, he realized, if he felt this terrible, how was his aunt feeling? She, too, must be tormented that one answered prayer had led to such an unthinkable loss.

Kyrie Eleison, Kyrie Eleison.

⊣⊨⊢

Not long after that, Yanni was told that Grandma Barbara, who had become even more of a recluse, had died. It seemed that nothing was alive anymore, only tragedy and death.

Yanni and Costas became closer than ever, although they rarely talked of Maria. It was simply too painful. Yanni remembered how he felt when Grandpa had died, but this was different. Grandpa was old. He had been in pain, and suffering with every tortured breath. He'd lived a good life, and died with those he loved surrounding him.

But Maria—she was close to Yanni's age, only two

years older. Poor sweet Maria, separated from her family by the wretched war, unable to come home. Lying in a bed, immobilized for months while battles raged around her. Greeks starved on the streets and no one was able to reassure her that the war would be over soon or that she'd finally get better and walk and run and sit without pain anymore. Forced to live there, in terrible isolation, knowing she'd never see her big brother or parents or cousin again.

Yanni tried to summon her face when he closed his eyes, remembering the way she tilted her head when she frowned and how the light glowed in her gorgeous big brown eyes when she laughed.

He knew why Aunt Athena was inconsolable.

Many afternoons, after school, Yanni continued to find solace by walking down to the library and burying himself in the books. He became an insatiable reader of poetry and contemporary short stories and even, occasionally, philosophy. He'd read pages from Goethe or the maddening pessimism of Schopenhauer and then shut the books in frustration, too despairing of the world and the war to want to think of hard truths. Sometimes, he put pen to paper and poured out his thoughts in the form of poems or short stories.

But gradually an overwhelming feeling of emptiness—the sense that he'd been brought into this world and seemingly abandoned by a mother he had never known or remembered—became stronger and stronger. Thinking of how Maria had never had the chance to really *live* fueled these thoughts. He wondered what life was like in America. Was it noisy and busy and large and overwhelming, or easy and small and safe, as Erytha had once been, before the war started? What did his father and his mother and his little sister look like after all these years? Did his mother bake almond cookies, crisp and sweet, like Grandma used to, when they had a kitchen full of delectable things to eat, before the Germans came and took everything they wanted? Did they think about him? Did they care about him? Did they even love him?

I want my own mother to take care of me, Yanni realized. Aunt Athena had always been affectionate and caring, but she was also brusque and strict. With Maria's death, she had withdrawn into herself, becoming distant, even cold. Yanni could hardly blame her. He understood. But she was now going through the motions, making dinner and eating in silence with the family and then going to her bedroom and shutting the door. Her thoughts were elsewhere. And Uncle George stayed in the store as long as he could. He, too, had become almost frighteningly detached and embittered.

A few weeks later, during the middle of a cold winter night, Yanni woke up to the strange sound of hushed voices. They were coming from the dining room, next to the small bedroom he was sharing with Costas. Someone was talking with Uncle George in broken Greek, and Yanni couldn't make out what was being said. He lay motionless, his heart thumping, terrified that Uncle

George was in trouble with the Germans. Yanni felt more vulnerable than ever. If anything happened to his uncle, the man providing for and protecting his family, what would become of them? The voices suddenly stopped and Yanni lay in the dark for a while, too scared to fall back to sleep.

At breakfast, where all Yanni was given was a cup of weak tea and a tiny slice of dry bread, Uncle George told him and Costas that a petty officer of the German army occupying the island had unexpectedly come to see him. But he was not a German. He was an Austrian named Wagner, one of the thousands of Austrians the Germans had conscripted into their army following their annexation of that country. He was a decent man, Uncle George said, with a kind heart, and he was deeply distressed by how cruelly the Germans were treating everyone in Erytha. He even claimed to be a distant relative to the famous Austrian composer, Richard Wagner.

"Why did he come here?" Costas asked.

"He met me through a friend working in the Triangle, who told him I used to be an officer in the army," Uncle George explained. "He wanted to find a way to desert. He knew that some people were able to sneak out, in boats at night, and find their way to Turkey. He asked for my help."

Yanni nodded. He'd heard stories about some of the islanders, desperate to get out, who paid enormous sums to be taken by boat across the straits where, hopefully, they'd land in a safe place. If they were intercepted by the Germans or by the Turkish police or soldiers, punishment would be swift and severe. It was a risk few were willing to take.

"Can you help him?" Yanni asked. Uncle George shook his head. "It's too dangerous," he said. "Meantime make sure you keep this very quiet. Don't tell anyone. If the Germans ever found out, this kind man would be summarily executed."

Yanni never heard of or saw that German officer again. No one found out if he had managed to escape and find his way to Turkey. But all thoughts of him soon disappeared as welcome news soon arrived.

The war was not going well for the Germans, and they installed several powerful sirens in the Triangle to warn the islanders of impending air raids. The Allies were coming. Maybe there was hope, after all.

At home, in the backyard, Uncle George supervised Costas and Yanni as they tried to build a bunker. They dug down a few feet, but Uncle George decided the yard was too small and exposed from above, and the cramped, dark basement under the house—really not much lower than ground level—would be a safer place.

The first time they heard the air-raid siren sound in the middle of the night, was the worst. They hurried down into the dark, huddled together, not knowing what to expect, wondering if bombs would actually rain down upon their heads. Nothing happened, though, and the all clear sounded an hour later. The family slowly went back upstairs, peering helplessly into the night sky and seeing nothing before falling back into a restless sleep.

Over time, the raids by Allied warplanes became more frequent. As soon as the ominous wailing of the sirens began, the family would drop everything and hurry downstairs. *It sounds like Judgment Day,* Yanni thought, shivering in the cold, *with the angels blowing their horns.* The horrible sound of the sirens, followed by a deadly silence, and then the distant humming of approaching airplanes. As soon as he heard the planes, Yanni would start a silent countdown, wondering if he would hear the terrible loud whistling, that meant bombs were coming down. If he did hear that frightening sound, could the bombs fall near the house and kill them all? He couldn't help asking himself that question every time. Thankfully, seconds later, the sound of explosions would fill his ears as he would shut his eyes and pray.

Strangely, the more the bombs fell, the less Yanni and Costas were afraid. They figured the Allies were targeting the Triangle, and the cousins were unworried that the bombers might miss and hit the rest of the town instead. They merely shrugged when, one morning after a particularly heavy bombardment, Uncle George pointed out a large gash at the side of the house. It was shrapnel damage from an explosion in a nearby open field. Yanni told himself that the Allies were on their side. They were trying to beat the Germans. And that made him feel safe, even when bombs were falling from British planes.

Because there were so many bombings, schools were closed, and the students quickly became bored and restless. Yanni and Costas often occupied their time with their own army of small lead figurines, toy soldiers they had been collecting for years. They spent many hours shaping their own miniature cannons, tanks, and airplanes from pieces of wood and thin scraps of metal. They acted out battles they'd studied in school or Uncle George had told them about.

But when the pent-up frustration and adolescent need for self-expression became overwhelming, the boys took their battles outside, and acted them out for real with their classmates and friends from nearby neighborhoods. Usually, all they did was run around with a lot of shouting and occasional stone-throwing, mostly at distances beyond harm's way. They made up their own regiments and plotted how to "invade" the enemy lines, laughing as they made their maneuvers while jostling for position in the fallow, open fields behind their neighborhood.

Yanni's make-believe regiment was named after their local church, the Evangelistria. As he organized the boys and was the second-oldest, after Costas, he was appointed General, thrillingly so. Each of his loyal foot soldiers took the name of a war hero from the Allied forces. Yanni also commandeered a makeshift shed in his backyard, hastily put together with scraps of old cartons and jagged pieces of wood, next to the back wall facing the open field. This became not only his little army's headquarters, but an ideal place to simply be with his friends, pretending that a real war wasn't raging in cities across Europe, or that those terrible battles hadn't led to all those bombs raining down on their island nearly every night.

All they needed, Yanni thought one afternoon as he waited for his friends to arrive, was a huge plate of Grandma's almond cookies to give them sustenance before their mock battles commenced. His mouth watered at the thought. He couldn't remember the last time he'd had a cookie, though, or anything sweet other than figs; or the occasional dab of honey Uncle George had managed to procure by a villager bartering for soap or shoelaces in the haberdashery.

He couldn't remember the last time he wasn't hungry, either.

One sultry day in July, as Yanni and his soldiers were engaged in fending off hostilities from his friend Mark's invading army, an incident that could have been disastrous took place. Mark's soldiers, imagining they were flying bombers over the enemy's headquarters, lit up some kindling and threw it over the wall to the rough shed in Yanni's backyard. They were hitting the enemy, they thought, with incendiary bombs! But the kindling was still aflame when it hit the roof of the shed, and the dusty, dried-up cartons instantly caught fire. Before the boys had a chance to realize what had happened, the entire shed went up in flames and quickly spread to a nearby pile of straw.

Flames shot up into the sky as the boys panicked, frantic that the fire might spread to the house itself. There was nothing they could do to stop it. Thankfully, the fire burned itself out as quickly as it had spread, consuming the cartons along with the rest of the shed and the family goat's winter rations. Yanni's army bade him a speedy farewell and took off as fast as they could, hoping to evade any punishment at home. Their leader, on the other hand, sat dejected and worried, waiting for the inevitable walloping Uncle George would administer that night when he saw the damage. A walloping Yanni knew, deep down, that he deserved.

Strangely, though, when Uncle George and Aunt Athena came in that evening, Yanni was shocked to see them smiling and to hear Uncle George whistling a happy tune. A rumor had spread like the fire on Yanni's shed, that the German resistance had managed to assassinate Hitler. Seemingly, the tide was turning. The Allies were advancing farther into enemy territory. It was the first truly bright spot of news they'd had in a long time, and Uncle George was in such a good mood that he said nothing at first. Then Yanni, his voice quivering with anxiety, confessed what had happened. A severe tongue-lashing ensued, but Yanni was spared the belt. He silently said a prayer of gratitude to those who'd risked their lives to bring Hitler down—not just for the good of the world but because it had saved him that night, too.

Although the assassination attempt turned out to

have been a failure, more rumors continued to fly and Uncle George remained positive even as the nightly bombing raids increased in intensity. At one point, however, safety became an issue. The family no longer felt immune from a stray bomb, as the Allies kept hammering the Germans almost every night. Eventually, they decided to temporarily move into a distant relative's house near the top of a small hill on the outskirts of town. It was safer there as the house was a few kilometers farther away from the dreaded Triangle, and it had a true basement that provided more shelter. There they'd sit, huddled and shivering in the dank cellar, as soon as they heard the sirens, counting softly to themselves between the dreadful whistling of the falling bombs and the sound of the explosions.

Yanni had no idea when they would return home, and he was glad when a temporary high school was set up at a nearby school building. Classes were infrequent as the teachers and students often couldn't manage to get to the makeshift schoolhouse, but at least they were trying to keep up with their studies. Everyone was so exhausted from famine and from endless broken nights, punctuated by the wail of the sirens, that they were barely functioning. Yanni was trying to stay busy and keep his mind occupied by reading and by writing short stories, essays, and an occasional poem.

There were even a few air raids during the day, which did scare Yanni a lot more. There was something quite terrifying about being able to see the bombers droning overhead. Then, looking up into the vast blue sky, he'd see what appeared to be gaping mouths on the underbellies of the planes, spewing out dark shapes that quickly dropped down, inexorably. During one of those raids, the Allies made a terrible mistake. A Red Cross vessel had been allowed in for a few days to unload food for the starving islanders. Misled by the English counterintelligence that the ship had been a clandestine weapons depot, the bombers during the next raid targeted the Red Cross vessel. Several civilians who happened to be in the area, as well as some crew members, were killed.

As time went on, though, something shifted and rumors began to fly. The bombings slowed considerably and Yanni's family thankfully moved back into their home in town, hoping for the best. The Allies were steadily advancing on German territory; the English and Americans from the west and the Russians from the east. From time to time, Uncle George shared information with Costas and Yanni, his voice low and cautious. His mood was improving with every passing day, and when a more powerful radio was smuggled into town, he was better able to keep track of the fighting. He was rarely home anymore—not even for dinner—meeting his friends at the store and keeping silent about what was discussed. Aunt Athena was still grieving, and she served the meals in silence before retreating to her room most nights.

As time went on, the German garrison was getting

more and more cautious. They would no longer roam around town as soon as darkness fell, carrying loaded weapons, enforcing curfew with fierce looks and shouts and the threat of their capricious anger. They stayed within the confines of their guarded Triangle at night and soon stopped walking around town during the day, too.

⚜

Freed from the risk of encountering German soldiers, clandestine members of the local Resistance decided to act. Knowing that the enemy was no longer interested in policing the island with their typical impunity, small squads of Resistance fighters began to hunt down and assassinate the cowardly locals who'd collaborated during the occupation. As word of these daring exploits began to circulate, the townsfolk became even more nervous. What if they were falsely accused?

"That's nonsense," Uncle George said one night. "Everyone knows who was collaborating. They're the scum who thought they'd get rich exploiting and betraying their fellow countrymen. Anyone who joins up with the enemy *is* the enemy as well."

One dark night, the stillness was broken not by Allied bombers but by loud bursts of rapid gunfire coming from the northern section of Erytha's harbor. There were several deafening explosions, followed by crossfire and shouting. The shooting continued for several minutes, and then there was deadly silence.

Yanni was so worn out by tension and hunger that he slept soundly through the battle, and Costas eagerly shared all the details the next morning. The Resistance fighters had snuck up on the harbor from the mountains and attacked the Triangle before slipping back into the mountains they knew so well. They wouldn't have dared such a raid even a few months before, for fear of swift retaliation. It was clear that the end of the German occupation was approaching.

About a week later, during a bright and cloudless Sunday morning in September, Yanni was roused from his exhausted slumber by the sound of shouting in the streets. He rubbed the sleep from his eyes and peered out. Several of his friends were jumping up and down in excitement. Costas was already up and getting dressed.

"Yanni! Yanni! Come outside!" they called up to him. "*Christos anesti! Christos anesti!* Christ is risen. Christ is risen!" they shouted over and over again.

"The Germans are gone! All of them!" Costas said. "The Triangle is empty. No one's there anymore. They all left in the middle of the night!"

"All of them?" Yanni asked in disbelief.

"That's what I was told—all of them!" Costas replied. "Hurry up and get dressed. There may be some food there for everyone and we're going to go look for it."

Yanni threw on his clothes and raced out the door with Costas. They joined their friends, elated and disbelieving.

It had been three years, four months, and six days

of hell on earth!

Christos anesti! Christ is risen indeed! Liberation! The island was finally free.

The townsfolk poured out into the streets, their gaunt cheeks suddenly rosy with excitement. Euphoria filled the air, and that morning, a Sunday, the church was packed with parishioners saying prayers of thanksgiving. Everyone was in shock at the suddenness of the German departure.

"And they're never coming back." Uncle George said. He was soon called into active duty, as the Greek government was trying to bring some semblance of order and normalcy back to the country. Before he left, Uncle George somberly told Yanni and Costas that he'd been in the Resistance, and the shop had given him a perfect cover for meeting with the Greek fighters. Along with his trusted friends, he was able to constantly pass along information to the partisans, hiding up in the mountain villages, about the German movements in town.

Costas practically glowed. "I had a feeling, Papa," he said. "I just knew. But I wasn't going to ask. And of course I understand why you didn't tell us."

Other Resistance members came down from the mountains and cleaned up the Triangle. The home owners who'd been so cruelly displaced, were finally able to return to their homes. Within days, English cargo ships sailed into port loaded with crates of food and other desperately needed supplies. Practically the entire town gathered at the quay to feast their eyes on the marvelous sight of the Union Jack flying high over the vessels, the sailors shouting out friendly greetings with wide smiles while unloading their goods. Even Aunt Athena was happy that day, beaming at Yanni and Costas at the sight of cartons of dry goods and large sacks of wheat at the docks. An elderly priest passed by at that moment, softly singing a beloved hymn of the Resurrection:

Thy Resurrection/O Christ Savior/
The angels hymn in the heavens/
Vouchsafe us on earth/
With pure heart to glorify Thee.

Aunt Athena crossed herself and smiled as she loudly said, "Amen."

Vouchsafe us on earth, Yanni thought, still unused to the idea that his little island home was itself again, freed from tyranny. School would be opening soon, he heard, and he'd see all his friends, especially Dimitris. The Boy Scouts of Greece—not its fascist cousin, but the real, loving Scouts—would be starting up again too. Yanni closed his eyes to dream of the fun he would have, watching Costas create a Cub Scout pack for the little ones, taking long hikes and helping plant more forests. Packing up rucksacks for overnight trips to the northern shores of the island with the Boy Scouts. They would sit around campfires and tell tales and breathe in the crisp fresh mountain air and know that no one was out there, lurking, waiting to steal their food and kill their souls.

They'd have good things to eat again, too, as more and more supply ships would arrive and the grocery store shelves would no longer be empty. The thought of fresh, warm pita bread dipped in honey and yogurt for breakfast, made Yanni's mouth water. Maybe there'd be a lamb to roast, or fresh fish to grill with lemon and onions.

He'd also sit in the kitchen with Grandma, watching in sheer bliss as she whipped up a batch of her famous almond cookies, inhaling the delectable scent, and then slipping them, warm and fresh and sweet, into his pockets, not caring if they crumbled.

CHAPTER 6

Exciting Times in Athens

"You know what I really want to do, don't you?" Costas asked Yanni one afternoon as they sat down by the harbor, watching the small boats putter in and out. They were enjoying the normal bustle of island life they had been deprived of for more than three nightmarish years. Schools had reopened and the shelves in the stores were once again laden with goods. Yanni would look at them almost in disbelief, thinking that they could just as easily disappear again and the gnawing feeling of hunger would return.

"Be like your dad, of course," Yanni replied. He knew that as a recent high school graduate, Costas wanted, more than anything, to have a career in the military. To follow in his father's footsteps and attend the officers' academy in Athens. To someday command his own battalion. Yanni did wonder, sometimes, however, if it was the best career choice, because Costas, who was brave and strong, was also sensitive and shy. He had never once found the courage to stand up to his parents when they were nagging about something innocuous—or even when they were totally in the wrong. He didn't have Yanni's drive and resourcefulness; he simply did as he was told. Yanni's rebellious streak deeply frustrated Uncle George and Aunt Athena even as they secretly liked the strength of his convictions. Once, after an argument about a task Uncle George accused him of shirking, Yanni caught Aunt Athena in a little secret smile to herself. He thought he saw a quick nod as if to acknowledge that her nephew was far more able to speak his mind when her own son could not. He knew they were silently comparing the cousins, and Costas was often found wanting next to Yanni's sense of independence and fluent, critical thinking. As much as it pleased Yanni to know that his aunt and uncle secretly liked his character, it pained him that they thought so little of their own son.

Yanni was also gratified that they liked his restless creativity as he continued to write articles, commentaries, short stories, and even poems—for his own satisfaction and for the school's magazine, *The Student's Echo,* and for the Boy Scouts' monthly, *Clover.* It gave them pleasure to see him hunched over the kitchen table, chewing on a pencil as he stared out the window, deeply lost in thought, before returning to his paper and quickly jotting down his musings.

Costas smiled. "The big talk is coming tonight," he

said. "Papa and Mama and I are going to discuss my plans. I hope I can start my training soon."

"Me, too," Yanni said, "but you know I'll miss you."

"I'll come back for visits, don't worry," Costas replied, his eyes alight. "And you can come visit me in Athens." He looked at his watch. "I better not be late, not tonight, for sure. They want me to meet them at Miski's at seven."

"Well, it must be a celebration," Yanni said with a smile. Miski's was the local pastry shop famous for its sumptuous assortment of sweets Yanni loved. "Bring me back some *bougatsa*."

"Get it yourself," Costas teased as he stood up and smoothed his trousers. "This is a private, grown-up's conversation. You're not invited." He winked. "Besides, you'd eat everything in Miski's if they let you."

"Of course I would," Yanni said with a laugh as he watched his cousin saunter off. He couldn't remember the last time he had seen Costas in such a good mood. He sat for a while longer, enjoying the balmy breezes and the sight of the fishermen coming back into the harbor, their small boats sputtering. Soon, he started to head home to enjoy the quiet in the house. Back in his room, he thought about the conversation Costas would be having over a cup of thick sweet Greek coffee and a plate of sesame cookies.

Running footsteps broke Yanni out of his reverie as Costas flung the door open and stormed to the room, slamming the door so hard that one of Aunt Athena's favorite icons fell off the wall. Costas laid facedown on his bed, his shoulders heaving.

"What happened?" Yanni asked. "What did they say?"

"Papa said the army ruined his life and he wasn't going to let it ruin mine."

"But that's not fair," Yanni replied. "You're not your dad. Besides, things are different now."

"I know!" Costas said angrily. He sat up on his bed. "I told him just because he was bitter and angry about getting forced to retire, he shouldn't take it out on me." He looked at Yanni and almost smiled. "I thought he was going to slap me when I said that. He got all red in the face and glared at me like he was ready to hit me, for a moment. But he realized he was out in public so he stopped. A moment later he said there was no way he was going to expose his son to the sufferings and humiliations he went through as a military officer.

"So I asked him, 'What am I supposed to do? What am I going to do with my life?'

'You should have *ambitions*,' he told me. 'Always look up, high!'

'My ambition is to be an officer in the army!' I said.

'That's not an ambition. That's a ridiculous dream,' he replied as he slurped down his coffee. Then he announced: 'You're going to be a doctor!'

"I was so shocked I couldn't even say a word," Costas went on. "The last thing I want to be is a doctor. I don't want to go to the university and study medicine. I'm not even all that good in science." He flung himself back on the bed. "This is the worst thing I've ever heard. It's the worst day of my life." Then he sighed deeply. "Well, the second worst. The worst was when my sister died. But this is close. Because he's killing me."

"What did your mother say?" Yanni asked.

"Not a word. She just sat there. His word is the law. It always has been and always will be," Costas said bitterly. "You know that, don't you? He tells me what to do and I don't have any choice."

"Of course," Yanni said. He knew. "I'm really sorry," he added.

"This is terrible," Costas said as his eyes filled with tears again and his shoulders drooped. The light had gone out of him, Yanni realized with a sharp sting. The Costas who'd been so giddy with excitement such a short time ago had disappeared, along with his dreams.

Yanni couldn't stop thinking about the stricken look on his cousin's face as he tried to sleep later that night. His aunt and uncle had come into the house late, and were very quiet as they shut off the lights and went to bed. They didn't try to talk to Costas. The decision was made. And it was irrevocable.

But from that day on, Yanni looked at Uncle George in a new light. Yanni knew the rules; he had been raised with them. But Costas's heart was broken. Surely that counted for something.

The farewells were brief. Costas gave his mother a quick hug and avoided his father before hurrying onto the ship, large enough only for a few small passenger cabins, that would take him to Athens, and the university. He was lucky to have gotten a passage. Transportation linking Erytha to the rest of Greece was still spotty. The sun and clouds made dazzling patterns on the sparkling water. Yanni, shielding his eyes from the glare, waved from the dock until the ship was out of sight.

⊣☗☖⊢

When his high school classes started, Yanni contently fell back into the familiar routine he'd been deprived of for more than three long years. He was a top student and had many friends, and he studied hard. Often, when he got home from an afternoon spent in his beloved library, there was a letter waiting on the table for him. A letter with the brightly colored American stamps.

Yanni's parents wanted him in New York as quickly as possible.

At first, he was consumed with ambivalence. Then, the realization sank in that he might actually be leaving everything and everyone he had ever known. He'd be leaving his friends, his classmates, his gruff aunt and uncle, his beloved grandma who seemed more and more shriveled with each passing day. He will be leaving the intoxicating scent of the almond trees in blossom behind his house, the rich tangy sweetness of fresh figs just plucked, the clear azure sky, the ever-changing swells of the sea surrounding him. Gone would be the comfort of life in a small town where he felt safe and loved. Suddenly, he felt very lonely. His usual sense of self-assurance was giving way to a worrisome feeling of insecurity about the unknown.

As it did, his anxieties bloomed like the geraniums on Grandma's windowsill. He veered from the thrill of the anticipation to impatience that he couldn't somehow magically be transported across the Atlantic that very second. The fear of the unknown instilled by the German occupation, shifted into the fear of what might happen to him once he left Erytha. Sometimes, the idea of leaving was inconceivable, and then a package from his parents would arrive, shifting his feelings to potent longing. Aunt Athena would sit with Yanni in the kitchen as he carefully cut the string and the sturdy brown wrapping paper covering the package, leaning forward eagerly to see what was inside: A pair of button-down oxford shirts, crisply folded; a soft black shaving kit; even a pair of stylish leather brogues so highly polished Yanni could practically use them as a mirror.

Yanni would take the beautiful new items to his room and place them carefully on a shelf that contained everything American. He'd stare at them, gently running his fingers over their newness, inhaling their unusual scents. And then he would close his eyes and imagine life in the New World; a life of comfort, affluence, and glamour, engulfed in a magic embrace of unrestrained affection from his adoring parents and little sister. These dreams filled him with such elation that he'd grab a pen and paper and spill out his feelings in letters to his mother, letters filled with a driving, impatient desire to join them without delay.

He was done with Greece, he kept saying to himself. He was trapped on this tiny island, with nowhere to go. He wanted to leave. He wanted his parents to speed up the process, to find some way to cut the spool of red tape interfering with his wishes. His feelings of elation would transform into an impatient anger and disappointment, even at times, tinged with a hard edge of bitterness. He began to suspect this was all a ruse to placate him for the lifetime of abandonment he'd already endured. Nothing would ever change. They didn't really love him.

When these thoughts jumbled around wildly in Yanni's head, he became distant and moody, even to his friends. He spent more time alone than usual, moping and morose.

One day, as he was sitting in the backyard, idly kicking at pebbles and wondering why life was so unfair, Aunt Athena appeared on the small upstairs balcony, waving a letter.

"Yanni, look," she said, "You thought you'd never be going to America. Well, here's a letter from the American embassy in Athens."

There was a touch of sadness, regret even, in his aunt's voice. Despite her hard sternness, he realized, she loved him deeply, and that he felt like a son to her; even more so after the death of her daughter. She didn't want him to go away, leaving the house quiet and empty. She was already missing Costas more than she cared to admit.

Yanni ran into the house and tore open the envelope. It was a message from the State Department, informing him that his parents had petitioned for an American passport so he could be allowed into the United States. He needed to report to the embassy in Athens for the paperwork, before he could apply for the passport and arrange for transport on a ship to New York.

That night, Yanni and his aunt and uncle talked over what to do. He had to get to Athens without delay, they decided, where he would stay with Aunt Angela and the husband she had finally married; Uncle Stavros, a well-established lawyer and a first cousin, she had fallen in love with, several years ago. Yanni would finish out the last year of high school there.

"But then I won't be able to graduate with my class," Yanni said, suddenly realizing the importance of the decision. He was still a junior and had been looking forward to his senior year, sitting in the classroom with his friends, with the familiar teachers who relished his contributions and nimble mind.

Uncle George looked at him sternly. "You have to go now, Yanni. There isn't any other way." Aunt Athena nodded in agreement. "If the Americans say do this now, you have to do it. You're seventeen years old. You have a whole life ahead of you. They won't give you another chance."

Yanni sighed. Deep down, he knew he was ready to go.

In the days that followed, while plans for his departure were made, he was astonished to notice his aunt's sudden change in character; especially when she announced that they had to have a farewell party, complete with ice cream, a rare treat on the island. Gone was the unbending, stern aloofness. Now, there was an affectionate, even teary sweetness that reminded Yanni of Grandma's all-encompassing love.

On the day of the party, Aunt Athena borrowed a hand-cranked ice-cream maker and Yanni ran off to get the ice. After his school and family friends arrived, each took a turn at the hand crank, laughing while they churned the ice cream. Dimitris took his turn, too, but he was very quiet. He was bereft at the impending loss of his best and most trusted friend. An articulate top student in school, Dimitris was blessed with an esoteric, analytical mind, a velvety voice, and deeply religious beliefs. He shared many of Yanni's values and interests. More than anyone, Yanni would miss him as well.

When the party wound down and the guests were leaving, Dimitris stayed behind, helping Yanni clean up, before embracing him in a bear hug. The two friends swore to remain close for the rest of their lives, no matter where the future took them. They stayed true to their promise to the end.

After Yanni watched Dimitris hurry off into the warm stillness of the night, the excitement and impatience about his new life in America receded and the enormity of what awaited him became more tangible. He really was leaving Erytha, he realized while he slowly packed his belongings into two small, battered suitcases. He couldn't help shedding a few tears of sadness and nervousness. He found one of his small leather diaries and started writing down his thoughts, hoping that the forming of the words would somehow relieve him from his anxieties.

The next day, when Yanni stepped onto the passenger ship—the same one that had taken Costas off to Athens and the university—he felt a certain sense of maturity, of becoming a different person. Aunt Athena, eager to see her son and sister, decided to accompany him. He gently helped her into their tiny cabin, then went out to the railing as the ship slowly pulled away from the dock. He stood, watching, while his beloved Erytha gradually disappeared into the haze, the tang of the sea salt on his skin and the wind whipping his hair. His feelings of sadness and anxiety soon disappeared in the thrill of the voyage. How he loved the sea! He never became seasick, unlike Aunt Athena, who spent the entire voyage moaning in their cabin with bouts of nausea roiling her with each passing wave. Yanni did his best to make her less uncomfortable.

⊰⊱

Aunt Angela and Uncle Stavros lived in a small apartment on a twisting, narrow street off one of the main avenues, near the embassy. She was delighted to host her favorite nephew, and they spent the first evening sharing stories. The next morning, Yanni eagerly got up early and headed for the embassy. Long lines of applicants were already waiting, and he was stunned to realize that he was not the only person in need of assistance. Impatient and worried, he stood for hours in the hot sunshine, wondering if everyone ahead of him wanted passports, too. What if he got his passport and the Americans then told him he had to wait and couldn't leave? What if the paperwork sent by his parents wasn't good enough and there wasn't anything he could do about it? What if this was all a terrible mistake?

The line slowly snaked forward until Yanni stood at the window of a bored clerk, who looked over his papers and then told him he would have to return in a month's time. "Washington needs to review this," he said, his accent flat. "It's not a quick process. I'm just telling you so you don't waste your time and mine coming back every day to check. You just have to wait. Washington calls the shots. They take their time. Do you understand?"

Yanni nodded miserably, trying to mask his disappointment as the clerk waved him away. He thought he'd just be able to walk in, sign some papers, and walk out with the coveted passport. He took his time getting back to the apartment, sometimes stepping over rubble still uncleared from the bombings during the war; a heartbreaking reminder of the damage done to this city, and to Yanni's dreams.

As the days slowly ticked by, Yanni grew depressed and morose. Coming to Athens was a mistake. It was hot and dirty and noisy, and he missed the sweetness of the island's salt air. He missed the quiet and the calm and the island life. He missed sharing jokes with Dimitris and teasing the girls. He missed knowing his way around every narrow passageway as he ran home from school. He even missed Uncle George's frowns and Aunt Athena's nagging as he lay in bed at Aunt Angela's, listening to the unfamiliar sounds of a large city. He convinced himself that he'd never get the coveted passport. Everything was going wrong.

To cheer him out of his funk, Aunt Stella came to the rescue. She was his father's sister, and she lived with her husband, Uncle Nikos, and her children in a nice, private home in Clearview, an Athens suburb.

"It's just what the boy needs," Aunt Stella announced to Aunt Angela when she came to see her nephew a week later. She was stout and self-assured and reminded Yanni of Uncle George, who brooked no dissent once he'd made up his mind. "Let him come just for a few days. To relax. He can go back to the embassy when he has to."

Yanni looked at Aunt Angela, who smiled and shrugged. "Why not?" she said. "A little bit of new scenery will do you good."

⊰⧉⊱

Yanni had no idea that once he settled into his own room at Aunt Stella's, he'd be calling this pleasant space his own for the rest of his stay in Athens. As he unpacked, his cousin Christopher, who was Yanni's age, eagerly chatted and told him about the school and the neighborhood. He was thrilled to have Yanni there, as he missed his two older brothers. The eldest was at a military camp in Egypt. The second, Typhon, who was clever and adventurous, had wangled his way onto a small boat during the German occupation, sailed to Turkey, made his way to a larger ship, and ended up in New York City. He was staying with Yanni's parents, and his fearlessness was the talk of the family.

Yanni heard the door open, and went into the living room to see who had come in. Throwing down her schoolbooks and carefully fluffing her lustrous dark hair, stood his cousin Isabelle. She was fourteen. She was tall and slim, and her young breasts were protruding perfectly. How gorgeous she was.

She took Yanni's breath away.

Yanni stood transfixed. *This is a thunderbolt,* he told himself. He'd read about them in the pulpy novels Aunt Athena especially liked. The tattered paperbacks he'd skim through when she was out of the house, laughing at the florid descriptions of true love and hot-blooded passion. But he never thought he'd be struck by the real thing.

Yanni hadn't seen Isabelle since she was a baby, playing with him on Erytha before her family moved to the mainland. She always wanted to tag along on Yanni's adventures, toddling after him and crying in frustration when she couldn't keep up. Now, she looked up at him shyly, her long lashes sweeping her eyes, as she said hello.

Yanni just stared for another moment, intoxicated by her beauty. As he did, she stared back, and a growing light began to shine in her eyes. *I wish I could kiss her,* Yanni thought wildly. *That is a terrible idea. It's sinful. She's my cousin. But I really really want to hold her in my arms and kiss her and fondle her and caress her until she begs me to stop.*

"Hello, Isabelle," he forced himself to say instead. "It's wonderful to see you again. You're all grown up."

"You, too, Yanni," she replied. "I'm glad you're staying with us."

"So am I," he said, all thoughts of anxious frustration flying instantly out of his head. Life was suddenly very sweet again, laden with dizzying possibilities at the sight of his beautiful cousin.

How could he ever have wanted to go back to Erytha? That thought crossed Yanni's mind every time he took the train back into Athens and stood in the heat in the line outside the embassy. No matter how early he arrived, others had gotten in place before him, their faces creased with worry. Every time, the message was the same from the same indifferent clerk. "No news. Come back in a month," he would tell Yanni in the same bored, flat tone. "Move along. *Next.*"

No one had anticipated such a long wait, so Yanni decided to enroll in the local high school as a senior and graduate. The first day, he was a bundle of nerves, looking at the faces of his new classmates who all knew one another and chattered eagerly going into their familiar classrooms. He kept to himself and studied hard at home to keep up with his new assignments. It wasn't long, though, before his natural gregariousness took over and he made new friends. They relished the weekends they could spend showing off their knowledge of Athens, sitting with him in their favorite coffee shops or bakeries. They explained how the trolleys worked, and proudly showed him the famous ruins of the ancients. They teased him by poking fun at his island ways and lack of big-city sophistication they were certain they possessed. He teased them right back that they'd never learned how to milk a goat or pluck the eggs from beneath a squawking chicken.

Their friendship turned to admiration when Yanni turned in his first essay assignment in his Greek literature class. "Who is Yanni Sitakos?" the teacher called out as they slid into their seats. Shyly, Yanni raised his hand. All eyes turned toward him. "This is an excellent essay," he said, making color quickly seep into Yanni's cheeks. The assignment had been to discuss deprivation and longing. Yanni had poured out his heart, illuminating the frustrations and fears at the upheavals and challenges in his life in succinct yet descriptive prose.

"It's so good that I want to share several passages with the class," the teacher added, peering over his spectacles at the students. "I hope this might make you accomplished writers also."

In the days that followed, Yanni's classmates clamored to study with him and work on their writing skills together. He no longer minded living on the mainland, or not being in New York yet. His schoolmates were delightful and his classwork stimulating.

And so was Isabelle. *Isabelle.* Even the mere sound of her voice filled him with desire. What a miracle to live in the same house, his room just down the hall from hers.

Just the sight of her inflamed his senses. He was exhilarated, enchanted, intoxicated by the daily glimpses of his cousin, and the realization that she liked him, too. That she reciprocated his shy, discreet advances.

There was Isabelle in the morning, slowly eating her yogurt and honey, licking her lips when she smiled at him. There was Isabelle in the evening, talking about the day's news with her parents and Christopher and Yanni at the dinner table.

Most of all, there was Isabelle in the afternoon, when they could be alone, together, lost in longing for each other in the shared bliss and urgency of teenage romance. Needing to help her with homework was their perfect cover. They would hurry to her bedroom, lock the door, and throw down their book bags. Hands intertwining, the first of a thousand endless kisses. On perfect days she would bare the beauty of her firm young breasts, and Yanni would bury his face in them while she writhed and moaned. Or she would slide her bare feet up Yanni's legs till he thought he would go mad with desire.

But then they had to stop. To actually make love was unthinkable, impossible. She was his cousin. He was living in her house as a guest. He had been raised with military precision to know the difference between right and wrong. All his years of praying in church and the Sunday school classes and thought of the punishment for sinners, brought him to a halt before they crossed that invisible line from which they could never return. Yanni would ache all over in longing by the time they quietly tugged at their disheveled clothing and unlocked the door, throwing each other guilty looks and knowing smiles. It was a pain he was more than willing to endure for the gentle touch of Isabelle's soft fingers, her long waves of hair brushing against his, for the taste of her sweet mouth and milky-white breasts, for the thrilling feel of stretching out next to her and imagining she was lying naked in his arms.

Some afternoons, when the sun shone brightly and the autumn air held a tang of cooler nights to come, they'd walk down the street, hand in hand, to sit by the edge of the nearby brook and talk sweet nothings for endless blissful hours until it was time to go home for dinner. Sometimes, when Isabelle stayed late in school, Yanni would go down to the brook by himself, diary in hand, and let his imagination fly away into the unknown, letting the pen take his thoughts where they led him. Writing about the soothing sound of the rushing water, the clouds skittering above him, the feel of Isabelle's fingers as they slowly pulled his head down for another kiss. Isabelle herself often surprised him, on especially magical afternoons, with a laugh and a swift hug as she greeted him by that brook, demanding to read whatever notes of love Yanni had just written.

Life could not be happier.

Until the inevitable guilt took further root, plaguing Yanni's sleep. Every few weeks, he'd attend classes at the Christian Students Association in Athens, discussing who they were and who they hoped to be. The students would banter back and forth about religion and metaphysics and how to live a Christian life in a world filled with sin. Afterward, Yanni would return to the house of his aunt and uncle, searching for Isabelle even as he knew he shouldn't be, longing for even a momentary glimpse of her as she set the table for dinner.

On weekends, Yanni often visited Aunt Angela in Athens or went on local jaunts with Isabelle and her friends. One of them was Helen. She had rosy plump cheeks, cascades of long curly hair, and a bright, enticing smile for Yanni, every time she saw him. She'd brush up against him, not accidentally he soon realized. She would ask him endless questions so she could sidle even closer, bending her head down before looking shyly up at him, her lips quivering.

Yanni was flattered by the attention, and he flirted back when Isabelle was out of earshot. Helen was personable and fun and he liked her. He was deeply relieved to find himself fantasizing about Helen instead of Isabelle, comparing her to the beauteous Helen of

Troy, a platonic ideal. She was chaste, he knew. She was not the kind of girl who would lock herself in a room with her cousin, her hands roaming all over his body as she pulled him into a tight embrace. She was the kind of girl you would marry. That you would ask to be patient, as Yanni wrote down in a poem, while you sailed off to see the world, and to wait for you until your unknown return. Helen, he decided, would endure the wait.

The days grew shorter, and Yanni spent more afternoons with Isabelle and Helen and their friends than he did at the brook. After school, they'd walk up the boulevard to a broad, shaded square and buy a small bottle of lemonade, Yanni proudly spending the pocket money his mother sent him in the letters from New York. He sipped slowly as they sat and talked about nothing and everything until the skies darkened and it was time to head home.

Life was even happier.

⧗

One early afternoon, Yanni came home from school to find Aunt Stella plucking a freshly slaughtered chicken. She kept several chickens and roosters in a coop positioned at the side of the front yard, next to a flower bed. She tended them carefully, and the family relished the taste of the fresh eggs she collected and scrambled with chives she snipped from her garden.

"Did you just kill this chicken?" he asked.

"Yes, and I'm going to butcher another one," she replied matter-of-factly. "One is not enough for dinner. Will you help me catch it?"

Yanni hesitated for a moment before replying. His cheeks instantly flushed, and there was a sharp pain in his groin. His heart started to beat with that same, familiar feeling of strange, unusual excitement. Aunt Stella threw him an indifferent glance and continued plucking the chicken.

"Yes," he said reluctantly. He went into the living room, pretending he was concentrating on his homework. The thought of chickens about to be slaughtered always triggered this bizarre reaction. He didn't know why. It had always been there, he realized, ever since he was a little child. Images of Aunt Stella in the backyard in Erytha suddenly flooded his memories. He closed his eyes and could see her so clearly, ignoring him and his noisy playmates darting in and out of the dusty yard, concentrating on the dreadful task of methodically slaughtering one chicken after another.

When Isabelle came home a few minutes later, Aunt Stella was still in the kitchen, gutting the chicken. Realizing her nephew's reluctance, she called out to her daughter to catch the second condemned bird from the coop. Isabelle quickly complied, if only to be able to tease her cousin who stayed out of sight in the living room. His heart was still pounding and his cheeks still flaming. Isabelle playfully ran into the room, clucking chicken in hand, laughing as she pushed the hapless bird in front of Yanni's mortified face, then taking it outside to the waiting knife in her mother's hand. Yanni heard a short, loud squawk, and then all was quiet. He hurried into his room and shut the door, lying down on the bed until the frightful thumping of his heart slowed down to normal.

Several weeks later, when Aunt Stella decided it was time for the largest strutting rooster, the top cock of the coop, to be sacrificed for Sunday's dinner, Isabelle insisted on doing the deed herself, even though she had never killed a chicken before. Yanni knew she wanted to do it to tease him. Her mother reluctantly agreed.

To hide the cheeks he knew would be afire, Yanni announced that he wanted to take photos of the brave Isabelle, lying that he wanted them to show to his parents some day. He held the camera carefully as he steeled his nerves and followed Isabelle to the yard, holding the camera up even as his heart skittered painfully in his chest. Isabelle grabbed the rooster, held it up for Yanni as he snapped a photo, then held it down under her bare feet as she'd watched her mother do hundreds of times before. Then swiftly cut its throat. When the rooster was dead, Isabelle carried it into the kitchen. Yanni stayed in the yard, breathing deep to clear his thoughts as he waited for the pain in his groin to go away.

"What is it about the chickens?" Isabelle asked him later. They were lying intertwined on the floor, the door locked as they pretended to do their homework. "You get the funniest look on your face when they're about to meet their maker."

Yanni didn't want to discuss it. "It's because I've decided to become a vegetarian," he fibbed.

Isabelle threw her head back and laughed. Yanni kissed the base of her throat where he could see her pulse racing. The exact spot where the knife had plunged its way into the squirming rooster. "You're such a liar," she said. "You might not like it when the chickens die, but you sure like to eat them later."

She pulled him closer, and all thoughts of chickens disappeared in the sweetness of her touch.

⚬⚬⚬

Slowly, winter melted into spring, and the news from the embassy was surprisingly encouraging. Yanni would be cleared to join the next group of expatriates returning to the United States. Suddenly, there was so much to do before he left. He decided he had to see his friends and family on Erytha before his journey. Especially Grandma. How long would it be before he'd be with them again? He wrote Aunt Athena to ask for her permission—ever the obedient nephew, he still felt the need to ask. She was overjoyed with the idea.

Yanni's ship arrived at the familiar docks of Erytha early one morning, and he was thrilled to see Costas, back home from the university on his Easter break, along with Uncle George and Aunt Athena, both of them beaming with pride trying to hide their tears.

The next two weeks passed in a blissful haze of happiness. Yanni saw his friends and neighbors and spent happy hours with Dimitris, sitting by the harbor and talking like they'd never been apart. He visited Grandma every day, helping her with her chores and talking about the trips they had taken with Grandpa and smiling sadly at the memories. He was particularly relieved when Costas told him that he actually liked his classes, and that maybe being a doctor wasn't such a bad idea after all.

"As long as you never treat me," Yanni teased, thrilled to see the light back in his cousin's eyes. "Am I supposed to *trust* you?"

He even asked for permission to attend a class in his old high school, sitting together with his former classmates. Funny how the gruff, remote principal he had feared for so many years, was now so much friendlier and approachable, lecturing Yanni about his responsibilities as an ambassador from the island of Erytha to those fortunate enough to dwell in the land of the rich and the powerful. They posed for photos along with all of Yanni's former classmates in the courtyard of the school. It was the yard where Yanni had spent so many happy hours running around at recess, screaming at the top of his lungs as he played volleyball with his friends, insisting on being the server and the captain of his team.

At the end of his stay, Yanni stepped on board the ship with Aunt Athena and Costas, who were coming along to spend more time with him in Athens. He stood on deck, watching Uncle George wave sadly from the dock. Gone was the trepidation about what lay ahead. He felt so much older and wiser, a confident city boy now, no longer the shy youngster from a small island. He was soon to sail on a much bigger voyage to a new land; to finally be with the parents he had no recollection of and the sister he had never met.

His dreams shone as brightly as the sun dappling the waves.

Back in Athens, Yanni was so busy cramming for his final exams and spending as much time with his family as he could, that the days passed by in a blur. Visits to the embassy became more frequent. The paperwork was seemingly endless while Yanni anxiously awaited the issuance of the precious American passport. The day it arrived after all the long months of worrying and waiting, he stared at it in disbelief, running his fingers over the official document as if it were a magic talisman. He was instructed to hurry to the American Express agency, that would provide the ticket for the next available navy ship taking American citizens to New York. Yanni laughed in sheer delight when he heard that the ship was named *Marine Shark*.

A few days before his departure, Grandma came to Athens with Uncle George to say her final farewells. Yanni hugged her tight as he wiped away her tears, listening to her loving prayers for his good health and happiness. *I don't want this to be the last time I ever see her,* he thought, realizing that it likely was. And he hugged her a little tighter.

The last few days were like a fleeting dream. Yanni said good-bye to his friends and classmates, and to his teachers and the principal who gave him his graduation diploma.

"Keep writing," said his Greek literature teacher, and Yanni promised that he would.

He said good-bye to Helen, who tearfully said she would never forget him as he kissed her and said the same. "I'll write you all the time," he said, his heart swelling at the sight of the hopeful longing filling her eyes.

On Yanni's last day in Greece, a sweltering hot day at the end of June, he woke up just before dawn, too excited to stay in bed a minute longer. A somber Isabelle came with him on the trolley into Athens for last-minute errands. He bought her a beautiful necklace with a small silver cross as a good-bye present, and she began to cry when he fastened it around her neck and kissed her cheeks.

"Why do you have to go?" she wailed. "It's not fair! I want to go with you!"

"I wish you could come, too," Yanni told her, kissing her again. But even as he said that, knowing how much he would miss her, he was also relieved that this forbidden relationship would progress no further.

Once they returned to the house and packed up his luggage, everyone was very quiet and somber. They arrived at the Custom House in the early afternoon, and his entire family assembled at the entrance to see him off. He never thought this day would come. Yanni looked at all of them—his adoring Grandma, his aunt and uncles and cousins—and smiled through his tears.

How lucky he was to have so many people who loved him so much.

How lucky to have survived the horrors of the war, when so many others had suffered even worse deprivations and perished with such cruelty.

How lucky to be sailing off into a new world, a new life, a new adventure and a hopeful future.

How lucky to be reunited with the parents and sister he'd never known.

How lucky indeed.

PART III

THE NEW WORLD

On the trip you are taken
By the horseman of the night
Anything that he offers you
You must refuse outright.
—From "On the Trip You Are Taken"
by Kostis Palamas

The sun was shining brightly again and the heat was intensifying. The old man got up and went into the kitchen, where he poured himself a cool glass of orange juice squeezed from the plump, sweet, local oranges. The sounds of the little children playing by the swimming pool drew him back to the veranda.

My wife must be enjoying herself, he thought, as she'd been gone for over an hour. He sat back heavily on the chaise and sighed deeply, inhaling the fresh clean air sweetened by the sea breezes. A tanker eased into view and he watched it until it disappeared over the horizon.

And then he remembered the time a different tanker disappeared, this one forever, as it sank in a terrible storm, not long after he became a partner in his law firm. He was sent to talk to the families of the crewmembers that had been lost, to discuss their future, and the compensation they deserved. Some of the wives refused to believe their husbands were really gone. There were no bodies. There was no closure.

"He will come home," one widow stoutly declared. "I saw the village psychic. She is never wrong. She told me he was ensnared by Sirens onto a deserted island, and having the time of his life, and when he is ready, he will come back to me."

The old man remembered his feelings of despair at hearing that. *Sometimes,* he wanted to say, *you have to find a way to push past the loss. You must deal with the present, in whichever way it comes to you and however much it hurts you, and face your future with a hopeful heart.*

But he didn't have the words.

CHAPTER 7

A Painful Appointment with Tomorrow

From the harbor, a small tender puttered Yanni and dozens of fellow travelers to the enormous-looking American navy ship anchored off the port of Piraeus. A long, sturdy ladder was hanging by the ship's side and, slowly, one by one, the passengers climbed up to the deck.

Yanni moved toward the bow of the open deck, not wanting to speak to anyone quite yet. He glanced around while the other passengers jabbered in excited anticipation. It still didn't seem real, this voyage, so long awaited that it had seemed no more tangible than one of the daydreams he used to have in school, staring out the window and losing himself in fantasies. Yet there he was, leaning on the railing, watching the smaller ships pull in and out of the harbor, other travelers busy with their own voyages and their own dreams. His was about to come true.

The ship was due to set sail in the morning and Yanni went below to see where he'd be sleeping. There were no cabins for passengers; only a large open area filled with rows of plain metal bunk beds. He had never slept in such an unenclosed space before, but once he chose a top bunk and placed his small pack atop the scratchy, olive drab army blanket, he realized he didn't mind. That was before he went into the large, communal bathroom, where the showers were completely exposed. Yanni was embarrassed. He couldn't imagine being bold enough to bare his nakedness to complete strangers on a ship.

Ah, well, that's what soldiers did during the war, he told himself, *and they never knew if they'd live to take another shower. Might as well begin to get used to it.*

There were so many things, he realized, that he'd be getting used to in his new life.

After a while, he decided to go topside to gaze at the lights of Piraeus twinkling brightly in the gloaming. Passengers milled about, some talking animatedly; others stood as Yanni did, in silence, absorbed in their thoughts, looking on their homeland and, perhaps, wondering, as Yanni was, when they would see it again.

In the morning, Yanni woke early and hurried up to watch the ship hoist the anchor. The day was already hot and bright, the sky a vivid, cloudless azure. He jumped when the enormous horn suddenly sounded, and the great ship began to shudder as it slowly pulled away from the shore, away from Yanni's childhood. He moved to the stern so he could fix his eyes on the shore passing from view. For the briefest of seconds, Yanni saw episodes of his young life flash through his mind's eye, speeding faster than the ship as it plowed through the placid bay. He closed his eyes, and the images disappeared. When he opened them again, all he saw was sea and sky and a few seagulls, chirping mournfully while they flapped their wings in search of food.

Yanni's stomach began to rumble, and he made his way below to the mess hall, where he followed the line of passengers waiting patiently to pass through the self-service buffet. Yanni had never seen so much food laid out, all at once, and he helped himself to scrambled eggs and toast. He was surprised to hear his name being called. He turned, and was thrilled to see two friends from Erytha, Nikos and Danny, who were also sailing to join family in America. A wave of relief swept over him like water hitting the bow. The journey wouldn't be twelve days of strangers and pains of lonely homesickness anymore.

"Hey, Yanni," Nikos said that afternoon as they played cards at an empty table in the ship's salon. "Let me give you something for good luck." He reached into his wallet and pulled out nine American dollar bills. "Here. Three for each of us." He handed the bills to Yanni and

Danny, then winked. "Don't spend it all at once!"

Yanni examined the bills carefully. He had never handled real American currency before, and it looked strange, in an odd shade of green, with an unfamiliar face of a man in a white wig on the front and strange symbols on the back.

"Thanks, Nikos, that's really nice," Danny said, while Yanni nodded in agreement. "And I know what I'm going to do with mine. Well, just part of one. Come on, Yanni. You're going to want to do this, too."

Yanni followed Danny until he stopped in front of the counter in the mess hall where drinks were sold. He asked for a Coke and Yanni did the same. Yanni held his frosty glass up to his lips. What an amazing treat—his first glass of Coca-Cola. How American! Tiny bubbles popped under his nose the instant he took his first sip. It was absolutely delicious.

Yanni spent another one of the precious dollars on several glasses of Coke over the next few days. He couldn't help himself. He sipped the drink slowly, savoring every drop as he sat with passengers who had gathered around some Greek musicians, playing the accordion and guitar in a makeshift band. They all joined in singing folk songs. A few couples got up and danced, to much laughter.

As the days passed slowly by, with the endless expanse of ocean blurring into the horizon, Yanni often sat in the ship's small library and wrote what he'd later dub "all sorts of nothing" stories. He often read and reread the ship-to-shore cable he had received from his parents, wishing him a bon voyage and saying how excited they were about his impending arrival. During the long, lonely, sleepless nights, he'd listen to the uneven rhythm of snoring from the passengers surrounding him, and feel his anxieties come flooding back. He had spent practically his entire lifetime daydreaming and fantasizing about his parents, about New York, about a new life. It was all about to become very real. What were his parents really like, or the eight-year-old sister he had seen only in small photographs? What kind of house did they have? How would he get around? Who would be his friends? Did they speak Greek? Would they understand his halting English? Would he ever fit in?

And then he thought about Isabelle, and wondered what she was doing, and if she missed him as much as he missed her, or if she had found another cousin to pull into her bedroom under the pretext of doing homework. What if she forgot about him? What if this trip away from everything he'd ever known was all going to be a terrible mistake?

The passengers became more excited when the trip neared its end. The great ship approached New York harbor on a sultry July evening, and Yanni stood with them at the railings, marveling at the sight of the Statue of Liberty, her arm holding its iconic lamp high in silent welcome. The crowd fell silent at the immensity of the skyscrapers lit up against the deepening night sky. Yanni stayed at the railing for a long time, lost in thought.

Finally, the ship docked and the luggage was taken off to be laid out in the huge customs hangar at the pier. They would disembark in the morning, and his parents and sister would be there, waiting for him.

⚎

Early in the morning, after breakfast, Yanni paced back and forth while he waited for his name to be called over the loudspeakers in the ship's salon. When he heard it, he said good-bye to his friends, and walked down the plank to a large waiting area. He realized he was stepping onto a new continent. America! He found his luggage, and was wondering what to do next, when a well-dressed gentleman approached him, introduced himself, and gave him a short note. Yanni instantly recognized his mother's handwriting and his heart started pounding as he read: "We are waiting outside customs." A tidal wave of towering emotions rushed through his chest and he thought for a moment that he might faint. There they were, not far away, standing among the milling crowds, waiting for him. In the flesh, not in photographs. His beautiful, elegant mother. His warm and caring father. His sweet and adorable little sister. Waiting outside, just for him. To take him into the fold. To see him. To touch him, to embrace, kiss each other for the first time in nearly his entire lifetime. He wanted to cry, but there were no tears.

Yanni thanked the kind gentleman and quickly

followed him out of the customs area and into complete pandemonium. Hundreds of people were running about in all directions, searching for their loved ones.

And then he saw his mother, Silvia, waving frantically as she shouted something he couldn't hear in the din of the crowd. She looked just like Aunt Athena. He ran toward her and they fell into a long, endless, wordless embrace and both burst into tears. They kept kissing each other's cheeks over and over again until their lips were nearly raw.

Georgia, Yanni's little sister, started tugging at their mother's skirt. "What about me?" she asked. Yanni picked her up and twirled her around, laughing in pure joy. "Look, Yanni, here's Pop!"

Yanni put her down carefully to hug his father, Andreas, who tried to hide his tears as he held him so tight, his shoulders shaking, that he could scarcely breathe.

"Last night, I had to get up every ten minutes to pee. I was so excited!" Georgia blurted out, and they all laughed.

It was a wonderful welcome.

During the long ride in a taxi to their home, Yanni kept staring up at the passing skyscrapers. They were so big, and he felt so small as the driver hurried across Manhattan and over the East River to Astoria, in the heart of Queens. The family's apartment was located in a nondescript, walk-up brick building. There were "welcome home" signs in front of the building, and in front of other buildings on the streets. "They're for the veterans," his father explained. "And for you, too, of course! Welcome home, my son."

While Yanni was helping his father lug the suitcases up the staircase, his heart fell a little. The building was plain brick and the apartment was cramped, with only four small rooms whose windows faced an inside courtyard. Yanni's bed was the sofa in the living room. He hadn't known what to expect—his father worked in a restaurant and his mother in the garment district. He knew how tight their finances were but this didn't look like the home in his fantasies. It wasn't bright and sunny like Aunt Stella's large suburban home. But it would have to do.

Georgia sat on the sofa, chattering away, as Yanni unpacked his brown footlocker with beige straps and shiny metal hinges, crammed full of gifts. She reminded him of his cousin Christopher, when he had moved into Aunt Stella's house.

That had been a big adjustment, too, Yanni remembered. But then Isabelle had walked into the house and made it all better.

"Wow, you sure have a lot of books!" Georgia exclaimed as Yanni opened his smaller suitcases, made of cheap hard plastic that soon fell apart, spilling out dozens of volumes. "Do you like to read?"

"I do," Yanni replied. "Especially these authors." He picked up a collection of short stories by Alexandros Papadiamantis and showed it to her. "This is my favorite writer. And I also love what the poets Kostis Palamas and Lambros Porfyras wrote. Maybe you'll like them too, when you're older."

Georgia shrugged and Yanni laughed at the look on her face. "Do you like school?" he asked, remembering how he used to lie about his homework.

"Oh, it's okay," she said. "I like being with my friends. I don't like my homework, especially math. But I get to miss it a lot because I have to go to the doctor so much."

"I see," Yanni said. He knew from what his mother had written over the years, that Georgia had a very serious blood disorder. The family curse, his mother said. The same disease that took the life of his eldest brother and other relatives mentioned in hushed whispers during family conversations over the years. Because the disease was incurable, Georgia needed regular blood transfusions. Without them, she would die. Yanni pushed the thoughts out of his mind. His sweet little sister was only eight. She had to get better. Surely, someone would find a cure, and soon.

That weekend, the family took the train to the Rockaways, for a picnic on the beach. There, they would meet several family friends, all from Erytha. Yanni leaned into the wall of the station as the train thundered in, wheels shrieking, and Georgia laughed at the shocked look on his face. He stared in amazement out the window as the neighborhoods changed. He simply couldn't yet wrap his mind around the immensity of the city, how densely jammed it was. At the beach, he relished the feel of the sand under his feet when he waded into the sea. How different the ocean seemed from here! It wasn't the same dazzling azure. The clouds skittering across the sky and the endless calls of the gulls, made him think poignantly of home.

Ah, but that isn't home anymore, he thought to himself. *This is my home now, here, with these people who love me but don't know anything about me yet.*

Georgia ran off happily with several of her friends to splash in the sea while Yanni's parents set up the picnic blankets with the other girls' parents. They were all down-to-earth, hardworking people like his own parents. Some of them had children close to Yanni's age who taught him some slang when they sat to eat their mother's delicious *spanakopita* under the hot sun. They were nice enough, but they were American-born, and spoke broken Greek with a strange accent. He had little in common with them; Yanni realized with a sinking heart. They weren't like Dimitris or his cousin Costas.

⚜

I can't be this homesick already, Yanni said to himself once the week went by and other family friends came to meet him and have dinner with his family. But he was. He settled into a routine as his parents left early for work, reading his beloved books and writing endless letters to his friends and relatives back in Greece. The apartment was very quiet. His sister spent most of the time with her friends, playing with them or fussing about in her tiny bedroom. Yanni didn't mind her happy chatter, but there was such an age difference that her excitement at his arrival soon faded, and they spent little time together.

His mother was worried, he could tell. There wasn't enough she could do for him, to try to make up for the long years of separation. Even though she had a long day ahead of her, she got up early to make him delicious lunches before leaving for work. Once she got home, she'd hurry into the kitchen to make a hot dinner, talking to Yanni as she stirred one of her fragrant dishes. She described what it was like to live in the city, how to shop and navigate his way around, what to wear and what to eat, how the New Yorkers differed from the Greeks. Yanni listened in silence, and was almost annoyed by her anxious, fluttering words.

"Why are you staying cooped up in this apartment all day?" his father would say every night when he came home and asked his son about his day.

"I didn't feel like going out," Yanni would reply. He had absolutely no interest in exploring the neighborhood. He wanted to stay home, to be alone. He knew he was depressed, but he couldn't bring himself to admit it. Somehow, in his endless daydreams back in Erytha, he had thought he would be magically awaken and be speaking fluent English, or even more magically, that everyone in America would speak Greek, too. He didn't know how to express himself in this strange place.

He couldn't understand what was being said all around him. Better to stay in the house and study his English verb tenses and read the poetry that wasn't soothing him as it once had. Adjusting to this strange new country was just too complicated.

Soon, Yanni's father found him a job in a Greek importing house in Lower Manhattan, typing business letters in Greek. There wasn't enough work to keep him busy all day, but he had to stay in the office. He hated taking the long commute on the elevated train every morning, eventually making its way down into the city where it was sweltering and noisy and scary. Where in the train the other riders pushed themselves into crowded cars without caring whose toes they stepped on.

A few weeks later, his mother found him a better-paying job as a machine operator in a tool factory run by a Greek friend. There was another long, tiresome commute. He had to punch in on time or have his pay docked. In the afternoon, he'd punch out, exhausted and grimy, and face the subway again for the wearisome ride home. He'd stand in the shower at home for a long time, trying to get the oil out of his fingernails, then collapse on his sofa bed, even more depressed. Why had he left Greece to come here and stand in front of a machine every day? What was the point?

Despite his exhaustion, he found sleep elusive. His years of dreaming about the life that awaited him in New York were just disillusioned fantasies. The American wealth and comforts, the beautiful, sophisticated parents who owned a big car and a big house with a yard and had interesting jobs and sophisticated friends, were illusions that came crashing down. All in a lamentable pile of broken dreams.

One Saturday morning, a bright blue fall day, he woke up with his heart pounding so quickly he thought he was going to die. He started reciting the Lord's Prayer so loudly that his mother came running into the living room. She started yelling when she saw his pale face and heaving chest, close to fainting. She quickly woke his father and the two ran out to find a doctor, but there was no one nearby. After a while, his frantic parents returned and by then, Yanni was feeling a little better. He decided to go out with his father, walking slowly around the neighborhood, looking for a doctor's office as well. They also had no luck. His mother had frantically called everyone she knew, and finally a doctor was on the way. Yanni lay down on the sofa, his eyes shut tight as he tried to calm his ragged breathing. He could hear his mother and sister softly crying in the kitchen. His father paced back and forth, laying cool napkins on Yanni's forehead, silently praying for help.

Eventually, the doctor arrived, and examined Yanni carefully. He asked him several pointed questions about his routine and his life, and made his diagnosis. Stress. A panic attack. That was all. It was understandable, the doctor explained, as he took off his stethoscope and packed up his bag. He, too, had come from the old country, and knew all about the pressures, the anxieties, the difficulties of adjustment to a strange new world and an unknown language.

"It catches up to you," the kindly doctor told Yanni. "Give yourself time. You'll be fine."

Yanni tried to nod as the doctor bid good-bye. He didn't think he would ever be fine. When he went to work that week, he found his resentment growing. He didn't like his parents. They were peasants. He hated the small apartment that always seemed to smell of the previous night's cooking. It felt like the prison of Bastille to him. He hated the flowery, plastic curtains in the kitchen window. He hated his mother's fussing and placating. He hated his father for being simple and passive. He hated not being able to see the sun and the sky.

One night as he sat, exhausted and miserable after dinner, Yanni had a nasty argument with his father and stopped talking to him. His mother, in a tizzy of desperation to make Yanni feel closer to the family, told him to sleep on his father's side of their bed at night. Andreas was banished to the sofa. Yanni simply shrugged angrily; he couldn't believe his father was such a pushover that he'd agree to such a thing.

Several days of silence later, his father tiptoed into the bedroom early in the morning while Yanni was huddled under the blankets, trying to shake the sleep from his eyes. His father sat down gingerly on the bed.

"I am sorry, my dearest boy, my flesh and blood," he said, plucking at the sheet nervously. "Talk to me. Talk to your father. I seeded you, I don't want to be apart from you."

"Do you take back all you said to me?" Yanni asked coldly, even though he knew, deep down, he was to blame for the argument.

"Everything, everything, my son."

Yanni nodded in acknowledgment. His father's expression brightened and he hurried off to work.

But that was a small, useless victory for Yanni as he sank deeper into depression. His happy, zestful confidence and boundless drive had disappeared. His distraught mother, concerned that he might have another panic attack, decided to take him to Dr. Elias, a Greek psychiatrist. Weekly sessions with the doctor, trying to talk about his crushed self-esteem, did not seem to ease Yanni's distress. Everything about his new life was a huge, disappointing experience. Dr. Elias tried to see him twice a week, but again, there was no improvement.

"Yanni must be admitted to the psychiatric ward of the Bronx hospital," Dr. Elias told his parents after one of their sessions.

When he heard the news, Yanni was so shut down and lost in his despair, that he just shrugged. The pained, desperate expressions on his parents' weary faces when they dropped him off at the hospital, made no impression. Yet, deep inside, he was terrified. Vulnerable, alone, abandoned by his parents again. Well, at least he would be freed from the stifling surroundings in the apartment, he told himself. However, a few moments later, the loneliness and enormity of the situation hit home. He quickly realized how homey the tiny apartment was, compared to the antiseptic reality of hospital life. He was forced to endure daily therapy sessions in rapid English he barely understood, punctuated by check-ins with the dour nurses who handed him the medications that made him dull and sleepy, watching with a frown until he swallowed them.

A few days later, his parents and sister came to see him on a lovely Sunday afternoon.

"Why did you come?" he said, still seething with hurt and resentment. "You should have gone to the beach." Georgia began to sob and buried her head in her mother's lap. Silvia hung her head and tried to hold back her tears. He hadn't meant to offend them so badly, he thought. But he also had a hard time trying to control his despair.

Yanni was just getting used to daily life on the ward when he noticed some patients on the floor disappearing for a long time, only to be wheeled back on hospital beds, their faces grey and their lips slack. They were getting electric shock treatments, he was told.

A sense of fear overwhelmed him. He did not want to be like them, a helpless patient lying dazed and drugged in the bilious green halls of the psychiatric ward. He had to get over whatever was bothering him so badly. He realized he was living through an enormous upheaval. *It's excruciating for me not to be the best, not to be able to express myself properly with words in English, to be so humiliated everyday,* Yanni admitted to himself, *but I have to face it.* He was a survivor. He had survived without his parents and he had survived the iron discipline in his aunt and uncle's house and he had survived the Germans and the famine. He had survived the deaths of his beloved Grandpa and cousin Maria. He was going to be all right. He had to make it through, to deal with his disappointments, to get used to a world he had never imagined. The choice was his: to move forward or to stay trapped in the shell of his own frustrations.

Dr. Elias noticed the subtle improvement in Yanni's state of mind, and he was released a few days later. His mother picked him up, and they went home in silence. She was too scared to say anything that might upset him. Still too drained and dispirited to do much of anything, he went to the weekly sessions with Dr. Elias in his nearby office. The rest of the time he stayed shut in the apartment, trying to sort things out. The days were growing shorter and the nights became cool and pleasant. *If I were still in Athens, I would be going to the university with Dimitris,* he told himself.

Unexpectedly, at church a few Sundays later, Yanni recognized John, a happy-go-lucky bon vivant classmate from Clearview High School. What a wonderful surprise to see his friend in New York. John felt the same way.

"Gosh, Yanni, you look awful," John said. "Is something wrong?

Yanni didn't want to tell him. "Oh, I've been sick a lot since I got here," he said quickly. "Must be all these stupid American germs."

John laughed. "I don't believe you. It must be the American *girls*," he teased.

"What brings you here?" Yanni asked.

"I got a student visa to study in the United States. But right now I'm taking special English language classes at Queens College. They're especially for foreign students who need more English before enrolling at the university. Why don't you join me?"

Yanni was elated. He felt some of the crushing burden of depression lifted off his chest.

"That is a great idea," he said. "Let me talk to my parents." Deep inside he knew they would be ecstatic with the idea. They wanted him to go to college, get a good education, and be somebody in the world. They wanted him to succeed where they had not.

⤙ ⤚

Yanni threw himself into his studies with surprising energy. He loved being back in a classroom, surrounded by other hard-working, mature students from various parts of the world. They were trying to learn English so they could study at universities far from their homelands. He had so much in common with them, he realized.

They shared their plans and dreams at lunchtime, carefully unwrapping lunches lovingly prepared by mothers who lived in apartments like Yanni's. It was the best possible therapy.

It was just what he needed.

Best of all, the professors were wonderful people. They were committed to helping these foreign youngsters learn and speak the language correctly; they were so understanding and accommodating. They took their students in small groups to their homes and showed them how Americans lived and how they entertained their guests. Yanni was delighted by his first American cocktail party, held at the house of Professor McGuire, a former Army officer who'd served overseas during the war. Once in a while, Professor McGuire would take the class to educational movies, so they could watch the body language and hear the slang and see how casually adults and children spoke to each other.

It wasn't just English that Yanni needed to learn, these wise teachers knew. It was all the subtle social cues that were so different from how he was raised and how the Greeks normally interacted with one another. He had already realized that Greeks spoke volumes with their hands and gestures in a way that Americans found off-putting, rude even; especially when the Greeks yelled and insulted each other—and forgave all trespasses a few minutes later. The Americans, Yanni noticed, were often loud, but had a less expressive temperament, and spoke with their voices, not their hands. They were more measured in what they said. An American wouldn't want to cause a scene in public that a Greek would barely notice as out of the ordinary.

Unlike those dreadful steamy summer days when Yanni had trudged to the menial jobs he hated, he now looked forward to his subway and bus rides every morning, meeting his friends on the open campus green and walking to class together. They all looked forward to field-trip days, when their professors would take them to museums, to Central Park, to the Statue of Liberty. There was so much to see, and so much to do—and all in English. Yanni studied for hours every night, often asking Georgia, whose English was flawless, for help on words or pronunciation that particularly stumped him. She beamed with pride when he did. She wanted her big brother to look up to her as she looked up to him.

On Sundays, Yanni taught Sunday school at the Greek Cathedral in Manhattan, and also sang with the choir. The soaring sound of the blended voices calmed his nerves and soothed his senses. He relished the time he could spend with the dean and, particularly, his assistant. He also became friends with several of the choir members. But there was still a reserve holding him back; he felt hampered by his nascent English. He couldn't yet follow the jokes and rapid teasing, and it still hurt his pride that he could not communicate with his new friends as he did so freely back in Greece.

But things were getting better. Every day, he added

more words to his blossoming vocabulary. Every day his confidence was getting just a little bit stronger.

"One step at a time, Yanni," Dr. Elias kept telling him, trying to encourage him. "And baby steps at that. Baby steps are good. When babies are learning to walk, they fall and fall, and they just pick themselves up again and keep at it till they can walk straight. Same for you. When you fall down, you must pick yourself up. You're doing a good job at it. I'm proud of you." Yanni's heart swelled as he thought of those kind, wise words.

Christmas was approaching—his first Christmas in America!—and his mood improved with the sprit of the holiday. Georgia ran around the house in a frenzy of excitement as their mother baked huge pans of Greek delicacies for the party they were throwing. A party to celebrate the birth of Christ and Yanni's arrival.

It was a wonderful evening. Family friends from all over the area came in, stomping the snow off their boots and laughing in pure merriment at the sight of the groaning table and the heaps of presents under the fragrant tree. The drinks were flowing and Yanni went with his friends into the building's courtyard, their breath steamy and their voices exhilarated, eating and drinking and telling stories. They were happy just to be together.

A week later, Yanni braved the enormous throng in Times Square, gathered for New Year's Eve, with John and several friends from college. He had never seen so many people crowded in one place at the same time, and the sheer noise and mayhem was infectious. As the clock neared midnight and the countdown began, Yanni joined the huge crowd, shouting out loud with his friends, in between gales of laughter. At the stroke of midnight, the crowd screamed and yelled in blissful pandemonium.

"It's going to be a great year!" John yelled above the noise, jumping up and down. "Look out, world! Nineteen forty-seven, here we come!"

Yanni threw back his head and laughed uproariously. He couldn't remember the last time he had been so happy. But that didn't matter. That was the past. This was a brand new year.

And a brand new future.

CHAPTER 8

Building for the Future

College life suited Yanni. He loved the challenges of his class work, the daily routine, learning the intricacies of English, the kind and encouraging professors, the hours spent with his friends—all so very different yet striving for the same goals. Silvia was thrilled by his growing confidence, and they spent many weekend afternoons discussing his dreams and fears and ambitions. She wanted the best for her son. She expected great things from him. Funny enough, Yanni didn't mind her constant conversation about college and his future. It reminded him of the long hours he had to spend enduring the lectures of her sisters, Aunt Athena and Aunt Angela.

He knew they did this out of love.

As Silvia talked, Yanni's father sat quietly in the corner, reading the Greek papers or simply listening. Andreas was reserved and timid by nature, the polar opposite of the stern and dynamic Uncle George. Yanni often wondered what the attraction had been between his parents, as they were so different. Like her sisters, Silvia was vocal about Yanni's future, his ambition to be successful, to be somebody. She beamed with pride as Yanni carefully filled out applications to colleges his English professors had suggested, and then tried not to worry about his admission possibilities.

One bright and chilly day, he took the subway to the Battery and got on the ferry to Staten Island. He had applied to Statenville, a small Lutheran college, as his first choice, and he wanted to see the campus. As the ferry's horn blew and the boat pulled away from the dock, Yanni's heart soared. An island, what an amazing omen! His cheeks turned ruddy when he leaned into the breeze for the short ride, admiring the Statue of Liberty as they slowly chugged by, enjoying the chop of the waves and grinning at the lonely sound of the gulls hoping for a stale hot dog bun thrown overboard by the tourists.

A bus brought him to the foot of a hill and he walked up a long, steep, narrow street, breathing hard as he climbed up a set of steps that took him to the campus. A surging feeling of excitement filled him at the vista unfolded before his eyes: The impressive Gothic building housing the classrooms; and the spire of a large church at the center of a green lawn, with pathways radiating from it. He could see the rooftops of the nearby neighborhoods and, far in the distance, the impassive enormity of the Lower Manhattan skyline. Yanni sighed happily, already feeling at home in this beautiful spot, hoping that he would get in. He knew that the commute would be long, and freezing cold on the winter weekends when he would return to Astoria for home-cooked meals and church on Sunday. But it would be worth it, taking the ferry and relishing the sea spray and the always-mesmerizing return towards Manhattan as the skyscrapers drew into view.

Only a few weeks later, the letters began to arrive. Several rejections, and a couple of admissions, including one from the coveted Statenville College. Silvia's eyes welled up as Yanni read her the acceptance letter, over and over. Her son, so newly in America, going to an American college! What blissful relief.

As his classes at Queens College drew to a close, Yanni said good-bye to his friends, who were all leaving for different schools around the country. Concerns about his readiness for college began to creep in, and he spent most of his summer days studying hard, trying to improve his English even more.

⊰≒ ≒⊱

Although more than a year had gone by since he had joined his family, Yanni still did not have the spontaneous kind of love for his parents, the love he had for the family who'd raised him in Greece. The longer he spent in New York, the more a sense of detachment took root and grew deeper. He couldn't help it, particularly when his parents would say something that made no sense to him. He continued talking to Dr. Elias about his troubled feelings, and he often tried to convince himself that his mother and father really did love him.

Silvia's motherly instinct picked up on her son's moody indifference, and she sighed loudly in guilty regret about her decision to leave her baby behind.

One quiet, muggy afternoon, when Yanni thought his head was going to explode from the humidity and the sheer boredom of being stuck in that tiny apartment, he went into the kitchen for a glass of cool water. His mother was making dinner, and he sat at the table, idly watching her chop tomatoes. It was too hot to move, or to think.

"I never expected to stay in America forever," Silvia blurted out suddenly, her back to him. "I was just going to come here to work and be with your father for a few years, save enough money and return to Erytha and my little boy." Her knife hit the cutting board with increasing rapidity. "I know you are angry with me," she went on as she held the knife in midair and turned to him, tears streaming down her flushed cheeks. "My heart was bleeding when it was time to go," she said, "bleeding as red as these tomatoes. I remember it as clear as day. Like it just happened yesterday."

Silvia put the knife down, wiped her hands, and sat down heavily by the table. "The ship to Piraeus was leaving in the evening," she said. "My baby, my sweet little Yanni, was always a nice, quiet baby. You never fussed. But not that day. You were crying and crying all day. You must have felt I was going to leave you, because I was so upset." She began to sob. "I loved my beautiful little baby so much. Did you know—I breastfed you well past your twelfth month." She stopped crying and actually laughed. "Once, your Aunt Athena yelled at me. 'Stop breastfeeding right now or he'll squeeze you dry!' she shouted."

For a moment, Yanni smiled, picturing his aunt letting her younger sister have it.

"'He wants my milk,' I yelled back. 'Not the milk from the rotten goat.' I could see you enjoyed my milk. And I just loved feeding you. You'd look up at me with those beautiful big brown eyes and those chubby cheeks, and your little fingers would grab on to my breast." Silvia started to sob again. "In the harbor, by the quay, I bid good-bye to your grandparents and my sweet little baby and walked up the plank to the ship with tears in my eyes. I cried for the rest of the trip, until there were just no more tears." She sighed heavily, then got up and went back to the stove. "But then the Great Depression hit, and we lost our jobs. We tried and tried to get work, and when I was lucky I would find some horrible job, sewing shirts all day. The bosses were so rotten, you have no idea. Heartless. They'd keep us in the room and pay us starvation wages. They knew our English wasn't good and we had nowhere to go to complain. 'If you don't like it here,' they would say, 'go sell apples.'

"We were barely making ends meet. I can't tell you," she went on, sweeping the tomatoes and some onions to a large skillet. "Every month, we had to send all the money we could spare to Grandma and Grandpa. They needed the help so much. I felt so guilty they had to pay for everything raising you, that I always tried to send a little bit more. It just killed me whenever I realized it wasn't enough. Or when they asked for just a dollar more so they could buy some yogurt or a leg of lamb once in a while. So they could give my growing little boy some extra meat. They didn't know how hard it was to spare even that dollar. At one time, we almost had to go on welfare when your father suddenly lost his job. No notice or anything. He was just let go."

"What did you do?" Yanni asked.

"I worked more hours and your father went all over town looking for any kind of work. There was no way we were going to take a handout. Not us," she said fiercely, her Greek pride welling up. "So we scrimped and saved every penny and economized to the bone. I wore the same cheap dress over and over again." She shuddered. "I hated that ugly thing. Even if I didn't have the money for a new one, I was so glad when it finally fell apart."

Yanni didn't know what to say, so he remained silent as Silvia continued to make dinner, avoiding his glance as she sniffled, trying to hold back her tears. Yet, hearing his mother pouring out her heart, did not make him get up and throw his arms around her to ease her pain and guilt, and tell her he loved her. He wasn't as disillusioned as he had been, when he'd first arrived and had such a culture shock; instead, he thought about how wonderful his childhood had been, even with all the hardships they'd endured, because he was surrounded by love. And, he suddenly realized, it was so much easier to be poor and go without on Erytha, than it was in America. Everything was so much more plentiful here. It was all so much bigger. But that didn't make it better.

"I'm sorry you're so unhappy, Mom," he said eventually. "I realize you didn't mean any harm. It wasn't your fault."

Silvia was not convinced. "I know you will never forgive me," she replied. "You will never love me like a son loves his mother, the way Georgia loves me. It serves me right. This is my punishment for not taking you with me!"

Yanni had heard enough. He got up and kissed his mother on the cheek and went into the living room to lie down. It was still sweltering, and when Georgia came in a few minutes later her cheeks were red and her hair was plastered to her head with sweat. She plopped down on the couch next to Yanni and leaned against him.

"I really don't feel so good," she said.

Yanni felt a sharp twinge of guilt. Georgia was a sweet, loving, and intelligent little girl with a bubbly personality. She had a lot of friends and did well at school. And she was brave; she never complained about her condition, even though she needed blood transfusions every two weeks to keep her alive. Yanni knew how hard it was for their parents to take off from work to stay with Georgia in the hospital on transfusion days, and what the emotional toll was on everyone.

"Do you want some cold water?" Yanni asked as he stroked her lovely, thick curls. She shook her head no. "I just want to sit here for a few minutes. I'll be okay."

Yanni got an even deeper sense of guilt. Georgia was so beautiful, so stoic, so brave! He wished their bond was stronger, like the one he felt for Costas and even Maria. They had always been his family, from his earliest memories. They'd lived together for years. They were part of who he was. Sadly, Georgia, his own sister, was still a stranger to him. There were ten years between them and they had little in common. They had no intimate bonds of childhood.

❧❧

The rest of the summer passed in a hazy, hot blur. Yanni felt completely at ease on city streets now, and he enjoyed walking around his neighborhood, window shopping. Sometimes he'd stand with a small crowd to watch something on one of the small black-and-white television sets displayed in the windows of appliance stores. No one he knew could afford their own set. Often, he took his diary and sat on a bench in the park near the East River, hoping for a breeze as he wrote down his thoughts. And he was thrilled when his parents surprised him and Georgia, with a week's vacation at a motel run by some friends up in the Catskills. They took a boat up the Hudson River, and, as ever, Yanni's heart was full of contentment when the ship pulled away from the dock and headed north. Nothing was better than being on the water, as the river gradually narrowed and the city disappeared. The hills lining the river grew taller, dense with deeply green forest, and Yanni marveled at the enormity of the sight. It was so lush, so verdant, so vast, suggesting even larger spaciousness beyond. The sight was utterly different from the sparse vegetation of the Erytha mountains. The crisp mountain air was positively invigorating, and the week passed all too quickly. Yanni, nonetheless, was glad to get back home and prepare for college.

A few days before the semester was due to start, Yanni went to the bank with his mother to arrange for his tuition payment. The bill for tuition, room, and board was four hundred dollars for a year. He watched Silvia's face blanch as she wrote out the withdrawal slip. "Our bank account is getting a pretty good beating," she said before throwing Yanni a worried glance for fear he would get upset. Yanni realized this was an enormous sum for his family and he felt guilty he hadn't been contributing more to their finances. Strangely, for the first time, he felt a sense of gratitude for the painful sacrifices his parents had made.

On the weekend, Yanni took the ferry with his parents and sister to the campus. As they stepped off the bus and walked slowly up the hill, he was struck again by the beauty of the surroundings and his parents' happy murmurs of pleasure that their son was now a college student. They helped him unpack in his room in the Quonset huts that served as makeshift dormitories. It was too soon after the war to find supplies to build permanent dormitories. Yanni thought of the rubble covering so much of Athens when he had moved there, and tried to shake the memories away.

After tearful good-byes, Yanni heaved an anxious sigh as he rearranged his books for the third time on the shelves over his desk in the small room. What if his classes were too hard? What if they made fun of his foreign accent? What if no one liked him? His worries deepened when his roommate, Hank, arrived. He was blond and blue-eyed, a German-American veteran. Although he was only three years older than Yanni, he seemed almost of another generation. He silently sized Yanni up and clearly found him wanting. He unpacked in aloof silence and quickly left the room.

Yanni felt a lot better when he went to orientation later in the day and saw how many other students looked as nervous as he was. They looked just as scared the next day, when classes started. French and English classes would be difficult, and chemistry was going to be an even tougher slog, he realized, listening to the heavy accent of his Russian émigré professor. He loved history, though, and the history class was going to be a wonderful challenge.

As the semester went on, Yanni spent most of his time studying, and he slowly made some friends. They took him to pep rallies held on Friday nights, before Saturday's football games, and it was easy to get caught up in the school spirit, sitting in the stands of the large stadium, cheering for the team. It was a sport that took a while to understand; the rules of soccer that Yanni had grown up with, were so much easier to follow! The home games played on Saturday afternoons reminded Yanni of New Year's Eve in Times Square, with crowds cheering in breathless excitement, free to shout and scream and jump up and down when a touchdown was scored. It was a thrilling way to blow off steam and frustrations, and it bonded the students in a way Yanni had never seen before. It also made him feel much more a part of the student body.

On the Saturdays when the team was playing away, Yanni went home for the weekend. His parents were ecstatic to see him, his mother cooking his favorite dishes and doing his laundry, and his father asking questions about schoolwork and friends. Being able to talk about anything and everything made him so happy and relaxed. No one judged his English skills or his accent when he was back home. They loved him just the way he was. And Yanni was beginning to realize how important their emotional support was, after all.

Just before Christmas, Yanni crammed hard for his final exams, and did well in all of his classes except for chemistry, which he barely passed. He was happy to be home, where the family celebrated the holiday as they had the year before, inviting all of their friends to their annual party. Silvia cooked for days with her childhood friend, Helen, shooing Yanni and Georgia out of the kitchen as they snuck in for nibbles. Several of Yanni's college friends came for the party, and they spent the evening dancing and singing and eating and thoroughly enjoying the holiday spirit. During the evening, it started to snow and they ran down to the courtyard, throwing snowballs at each other and collapsing in laughter. What a difference a year makes, Yanni thought.

When classes started again, Yanni was relieved to see that Hank was gone, and his new roommate, Johnny, was an altogether different kind of person—much friendlier and more talkative. He was fascinated by Yanni's stories of island life and wartime hardships, and introduced him to his circle of friends. They went to basketball games on weekends or downtown to the movies. One of Johnny's friends, a striking sophomore named Sally, flirted with Yanni, and he reciprocated. On a Saturday afternoon, the two of them took the ferry and went to a show at Radio City Music Hall. Not unexpectedly, as the show went on, they found themselves more interested in kissing and touching than watching the Rockettes. It was Yanni's first American date. He had barely thought about girls and flirting and the marvels of intimate embraces since his arrival in New York. He still fantasized about Isabelle, writing her long letters and pouring out his heart. But it had been nearly two years since he had seen her, and the memories of her soft fingers and luscious probing lips were starting to fade. How lovely it was to put his arm around Sally's shoulders, and being able to pull her close.

⌁

A few weeks later, Yanni went home for the weekend and was surprised to hear his father talk about a listing he'd seen in the local Greek paper. A coffee shop in a small Pennsylvania town called Roxy, was up for sale. Andreas was a kind and simple man, passive and indecisive, with limited education and even less daring ambition. Much to Silvia's dismay, he was content to lead a quiet life. She often complained to Yanni that their financial problems were due to his father's lack of initiative. Andreas had often talked about owning a restaurant and being his own boss, but his fear of failure held him back.

"Well, Pop, this sounds like a great idea," Yanni said, glancing at his mother, who was nodding vigorously. "I think we should go take a look at it right away."

Andreas beamed at his son's praise, but then his face fell. "Thank you, my boy," he said. "But I don't know how we can afford it. It's five thousand dollars. We don't have that kind of money."

"It doesn't cost anything to take a look at the place," Yanni replied. "Let's see if we like it first."

The following Saturday, Yanni, his father, and the

broker took the train to Philadelphia and then switched to a commuter train for Roxy. The stocky Greek owner and his American wife were waiting, friendly and chatty, as they showed them around the dining area and the kitchen. It was small and homey, and had a devoted clientele. They discussed the finances and the broker was encouraging, telling Andreas that he'd help them get the loan they needed, and manage the paperwork. They discussed the pros and cons all the way home. If they bought this place, Andreas and Silvia would finally be their own bosses. The fresh air would be good for Georgia. Yanni would have to transfer colleges, but he didn't mind. He loved his school, but he had no fear of change any more, and he was confident he'd get in somewhere near Roxy. Andreas looked at him and smiled broadly. What a man his son was becoming—so confident, so smart, so ambitious! What a change from the fearful and resentful Yanni who'd been cold and harsh and distant. Maybe owning this restaurant wasn't such a bad idea, after all.

In early spring, the family moved to Roxy, renting a small apartment on the second floor of a two-family house half a block away from the restaurant. Yanni stayed at Statenville to finish the semester.

Georgia was the only one who was not happy. She didn't like leaving her friends or the only neighborhood she'd ever known. She didn't want to start in a new school. She didn't want to live in a small town. Yanni was glad to be at school during the worst of the arguments, where he could avoid hearing her tearful pleas to go back home.

He was even happier when he heard from two colleges in Philadelphia; both had accepted him for the fall semester. He chose Lexerd, located near the main railroad station so he'd have an easy commute. His parents were proud. Not only was their son thriving in college, but he was just like his American-born peers. They always knew he was smart. And here he was, proving it every day.

As the second semester drew to a close at Statenville, Yanni said a fond farewell to Johnny and Sally and his other friends and joined his family in Roxy. The restaurant was open six days a week, from daybreak until late at night, and Yanni spent most of the summer helping out. It was exhausting, with his parents alternating duties between morning and late afternoon. Yanni did what he could, even as he started to worry that this move might have been a mistake. He hated seeing his parents so worn out.

Every Sunday, the family attended services at the local Orthodox Church of St. George, where they were quickly welcomed into the community. Several Greek-American families also hailed from Erytha, and they became their new friends. Georgia was thrilled to find girls her age, and she finally stopped moping as she ran off every morning to be with her new playmates. Yanni met several American-born boys and girls close to his age, and they soon bonded over their shared experiences. Church became their second home, and Yanni gladly agreed to teach Sunday school in the fall. Maybe, he thought as he pushed his anxieties away, moving to Pennsylvania was all for the best.

As summer drew to a close, Yanni started his classes at Lexerd. Unlike Statenville, this campus was located in the heart of Philadelphia, and noisy traffic whooshed by the classrooms all day. But Yanni was always buried in a textbook as he commuted to school every morning, and on the way back home. Most of the male students were hardened veterans returning from fighting abroad, taking advantage of the G.I. Bill that allowed them to attend college for free. They were older, and as uninterested in students like Yanni as Hank, his first roommate, had been. Yanni joined the Glee Club and started writing features for the college newspaper.

Yet he never felt wholly at home. Deep inside, daunting feelings of inferiority and inadequacy continued to plague him. He called Dr. Elias for advice, and saw the student health psychologist, trying to get his bearings. He was worried all the time. Worried about fitting in and staying on par with his peers. They spoke English with such perfect fluency and had no qualms about their place in the world. He was worried about money, even though he was as frugal as he could with his three-dollar-a-week allowance. He kept fretting about how hard his parents worked to earn a living and pay off their loan. And, more than anything, he was worried about his little sister.

Georgia's doctors didn't want her to be treated at a different hospital, so she took the train with her mother every two weeks for the trip to New York and her blood transfusions. In the winter, the cold made her much more susceptible to infections, and she needed even more frequent transfusions. She got so bad that year that her spleen had to be removed at the hospital that had always treated her in New York.

When spring finally arrived, everyone's spirits improved with the weather. Georgia was finally feeling better, and Yanni decided he liked Lexerd after all, especially the business courses. The placement office helped him get a well-paying summer job at the local auto plant, a short bus ride away from home.

Yanni had never seen such a large factory before. After he punched in the first day, he was shown to his place on the assembly line and given instructions about his designated task. Stationed between other workers on the slow-moving, enormously long belt carrying skeletons of sedans, he had twenty-five seconds to slide and fit two small panels next to the front seat on the passenger's side. The belt never stopped moving, and Yanni quickly mastered his task. Within the first hour, however, he felt completely stifled, as if the world had ceased to exist outside the slow, endless expanse of the assembly line; the cars coming and coming and coming. *I'm turning into a robot,* Yanni told himself as he tried to think of ways to keep alert during the stupifyingly boring hours at work. He realized that if he had to work in a factory like this for the rest of his life, he would lose his mind. He was again grateful for his family's encouragement to go to college and get a good education.

The only thing that kept Yanni persevering for the next two months was the paycheck he received every week. By the time school was about to start and he mercifully punched out for the last time, he had earned enough to pay for half his tuition, all his textbooks and supplies, and a small typewriter he had always wanted to buy. What blissful relief it was to know he would not be coming back there, ever again.

"Look, Georgia," he said happily to his sister as he poked at the keys. "This is an Olympus typewriter. It's a good omen, don't you think?"

She laughed. "Sure. And you're Zeus, too. Right?"

"Of course," he replied with a grin. "Who else would I be?"

"Hades is more like it."

Yanni fake-swatted her and she scampered off.

As Yanni's second year at Lexerd began, he easily fell into the routine of the commute and classwork and seeing his friends. He became even busier when the youngsters he taught in Sunday school, asked him to help choose and stage a Greek play. He picked a comedy called *Troubled Waters*, which he knew would elicit a lot of laughter. The budding actors and actresses looked to Yanni to help them with their halting Greek, and they spent much of the rehearsal time laughing at their mispronunciations that Yanni gently corrected.

They all clamored for his expertise and guidance, and Yanni's chronic sense of inferiority about his English skills started to melt away.

When the play premiered at the Greek church hall, the audience roared with laughter. Yanni even caught some of the parents wiping tears from their eyes as they heard their American-born children speaking only in Greek, up on a stage. The play was such a hit that it was presented again two weeks later, in the much larger Orthodox Cathedral in Philadelphia.

Even better, through one of his friends in Philadelphia, Yanni met the owner of a store selling Greek favors and gifts for parties, weddings, and baptisms, who also had a radio program Sunday afternoons. In a stroke of good fortune, Yanni was hired to be his radio announcer, discussing the latest news and playing Greek music. The show became popular in their close-knit community, and Yanni's parents were his greatest fans and critics. They even joined him in Philadelphia, when Greek recording artists came on his radio program during their tours in the Greek-American community. They were so happy to meet the stars their son confidently interviewed live, before asking them to sing their most well-known hits.

With every passing day, Yanni's energy and confidence increased, and he couldn't believe he was once uncomfortable at Lexerd. He cherished his routine, enjoying the short commute, where he prepared himself for the day or just daydreamed as he stared out the window at the passing small towns. Hanging out with his friends and relishing the camaraderie with fellow students, he felt a burst of pride when he saw them reading his features in the college weekly. Singing in the Glee Club, attending meetings of the business management club, joining the chess team and competing against other schools, gave him a sense of belonging. *Can you believe it?* He asked himself one day. *You're no longer the outsider.*

At the restaurant, he worked behind the counter after finishing his course work, and sometimes helped his mother in the kitchen. His English had so vastly improved that he easily conversed with the customers, talking about the events of the day and even joking about sports and politics. Whenever he mispronounced a word, he'd appreciate the correction, and would even laugh about it. *That's the best way to learn,* he realized. And no one was judging his mistakes. The customers often made them, too.

One of the highlights of that year was the thrilling moment when the parish priest asked Yanni to give a short sermon during a Sunday service. It was a special honor for him. The first time he was asked, Yanni had a momentary flashback to his younger self, stamping his feet and crying to Grandma and Grandpa that he wanted to be an altar boy, and he wasn't going to wait!

How proud his grandparents would have been if they could have seen their beloved Yanni, standing on the podium, confidently sharing his words of wisdom as all the eyes of the congregation were on him. His lovely little sister, her eyes round at the sight of her big brother, his voice echoing in the chapel. The beaming faces of his parents, practically bursting with joy.

⊰ ⊱

When Yanni began his senior year at Lexerd, he spent many pleasantly intense hours with his classmates to discuss their hopes and dreams and plans for the future. He knew that as much as he'd grown to enjoy this college, as well as Philadelphia, and Roxy, they were not what he wanted to do in the future. He had never stopped thinking about New York. Although he had spent only two years in the big city, he often daydreamed about being back, steeping himself in its frantic pace and its twenty-four hour opportunities. Yanni smiled to himself at the thought. How small Erytha seemed in comparison; how quiet and quaint. Leaving it was actually the best thing he could have done!

Georgia, too, was desperately ready to go back. Although she had made some friends, she missed the girls she'd grown up with, and her school. The biweekly train rides to the hospital for her transfusions exhausted her. She was a big-city girl as her older brother had become a big-city boy.

And so were their parents, as much as they hated to admit it. The restaurant turned a small profit, but the work was a relentless, exhausting grind, and the pleasures of small-town life paled beside the opportunities of New

York and the comfort of their familiar neighborhood. It was time for a change.

As Yanni kept turning over ideas about his future, he suddenly realized that his childhood infatuation with becoming a ship's captain, was no more tangible than waves breaking on the shore. He always thrilled to the shudder of a ship when it was about to set sail, and he still relished the salty tang of the sea air. But he knew he was destined to work on land. Perhaps a shipping office might offer him a job that would engage all his senses, and challenge his keen mind, he thought; but what kind of opportunities would such a career provide for an ambitious young man like him?

Just as he was laboring with these questions and ideas in his mind, the words "law school" popped into his consciousness, seemingly appearing from nowhere. Yanni shivered keenly. Yes, that was it. He would go to law school, and when he was done he could still be close to the sea by concentrating in maritime law. He could apply to law schools that offered night classes, so he could work during the day, to ease the financial burden on his parents and also get some business experience. It didn't matter how long it would take to earn his degree. Four years, instead of three. What did that matter? He would learn about the business world as he worked. Yanni sighed in pure pleasure, knowing that he'd chosen the right path toward his ultimate destiny.

And when the letter of acceptance from his first choice came from a fine law school in New York, Yanni floated through the rest of his last semester in a haze of delighted anticipation. When the day of graduation came, he thought his face would burst from smiling at the sheer intoxication of the graduation day pageantry. The first in his family to earn an American college degree! And go on to law school! Yanni's mother was sobbing in joy with such fervor that Georgia had to shake her to make her stop. It was all worth it. All the sacrifices. All the hardship. All the worrying about where her next meal or next job would come from. All the lost years far from her son. There he was, cap squarely on his head and gown swirling in the breeze, as he firmly shook the hand of the college president and took his coveted sheepskin.

Yanni was ready to take on the world.

CHAPTER 9

Initiation and a Mother's Confession

Yanni threw his head back and laughed at his friend Paul's silly joke. Paul was a good friend from way back in Erytha, and they enjoyed each other's company. What a joy it was to just be sitting, relaxing at their favorite Italian restaurant in Philadelphia. To think of nothing more complicated than whether to have an espresso or another glass of Chianti after the remnants of their spaghetti puttanesca were cleared away.

It was an early summer evening, and Yanni was taking advantage of a brief lull in his overbooked schedule to spend the weekend with Paul, who'd moved to Philadelphia from Erytha a few years before. Yanni hadn't had many weekends like this for the last year, and it was just the kind of refreshing break he needed to clear his head for the work he knew awaited him back in New York.

He thought back for a minute to everything that had happened since he graduated from Lexerd. The euphoria of the ceremony had soon dissipated, blurred by the summer heat shimmering up from the Manhattan sidewalks as he walked dispiritedly from one job interview to another. There were no bidders yet for his parents' restaurant, so they stayed in Roxy that summer while Georgia fretted and moped in bored frustration. Yanni rented a small room at a family friend's home in the Brightside area of Queens and continued looking for a job. Finally, he landed a good position as a cargo claims adjuster for a shipping company that had a liner service with South American ports. His salary of two hundred fifty dollars a month would be enough to pay for his room, board, daily expenses, and tuition for law school.

Silvia cried tears of relief when Yanni shared his good news during his next visit home. Her son, the college graduate, with such a good job, and law school classes about to start! Who could ask for a better child?

Yanni quickly fell into the routine at work, but his classes in law school were much harder than he expected. There were three courses, four nights a week, totaling ten hours. The law professors sternly warned all students that they would need two hours of study for every hour of class. After a long day at the office and the intensity of his classes, Yanni had to try hard to stay awake in the subway so he wouldn't miss his stop on the way home. He worked on his assignments in the early hours in the subway to work, and from work to school, and then again all day Saturdays and Sundays. He was too busy to feel the twangs of loneliness, being separated from his family. And he was so determined not to fail that he got up every day and faced the grueling routine, counting off the weeks till his classes would be over. That entire first year of law school passed by in a haze of fatigue and stress, he had never expected.

After what seemed like an interminable wait, his parents found a buyer for the restaurant, and Yanni convinced them to take a look at a small, two-family house for sale in Timberside, a small neighborhood, close to their friends in Queens. They had never owned a home in America, and Andreas blanched at the thought. His passive nature conflicted with his son's methodical thinking: The money from the sale of the restaurant could easily provide for the down payment. The rent from the tenant would pay for the mortgage. Ultimately, Andreas was convinced. His son was right. Besides, Yanni had learned so much about money and business from his classes and all his jobs. His confidence was encouraging.

⊰ ⊱

The summer passed by in an easy and happy blur. Yanni helped his family with the move to Timberside, and worked overtime at the office to earn some extra money. How nice it was to go to a job he liked during the day, with no exhausting classes at night! How splendid it was, too, to spend two weeks with his parents and sister, vacationing at a family friend's house in a small hamlet on Long Island Sound. To sleep in and do nothing more strenuous than walk to the nearby beach in the late morning, rest on the soft sand, shaded by a large umbrella, and listen to the radio before diving into the cool water for a quick swim. It was nirvana!

In the fall, when his classes started again, Yanni was surprised to see that several of his classmates had disappeared, unable to keep up with the demanding pace and the pressure. The sight of empty seats in the classrooms made him even more determined not to join them. Also, with one year behind him, he realized that his daytime job was getting easier to handle, and his law studies were not as hard and frightening as they seemed in his first year. He was even able to steal away once in a while on Saturdays, to go see his friend Paul, back in Philly.

During one of those visits, after dinner at their customary Italian restaurant, they ambled up the street towards Paul's car. Two women passed by, talking animatedly in Greek. Paul called out a greeting in Greek and the women turned, surprised to hear their native tongue. Introductions quickly followed. Both women appeared to be in their early twenties. Sonia was tall and slim, a little older, and had been in America for several years. Her friend, Callista, had a beautiful smile and dark blonde curls that caught Yanni's eye. She had arrived only a few weeks back, a refugee from the civil war that had raged in northern Greece.

"As if the Germans weren't bad enough," Callista said, her large brown eyes flashing. "Why do we have to fight each other?"

The vibrant energy she exuded reminded Yanni of Isabelle. The foursome continued talking, wandering around the neighborhood until they came to a small, deserted park. Callista and Yanni sat on a damp bench. She was living in a small apartment with her aunt, she told him, waiting for her boyfriend to come from Greece. She had no idea when he'd be able to get a visa and come over. As she chatted, her fingers crept toward his, and she flashed him a knowing look. Paul noticed it, and he took Sonia's hand and winked at Yanni, before heading off to a dark corner of the park. As soon as Paul and Sonia disappeared, Callista stood, then pulled Yanni up as he thrilled to the feel of her nimble fingers intertwining tightly with his. Before long, in a darker area, dense with bushes, Callista pulled him down, her lips searching for his. There, on the soft, spongy ground damp with the burgeoning springtime—the most inauspicious place possible—Yanni tasted, for the first time in his young life, the pleasures of unencumbered, fully uninhibited lovemaking. It felt so natural, so perfect, and even more blissful for being so unexpected.

An hour later, the couples reunited at Paul's car, throwing each other coy smiles and embracing in unabashed and surprised delight. They spent another hour driving around mindlessly, joking and talking and exchanging lingering kisses, before Paul dropped the girls off at Sonia's apartment building. They waved goodbye and Paul drove Yanni to the station for the late bus back to New York.

Yanni ran his fingers over the phone number Callista had written down on a scrap of paper, then over his bruised and tender lips, wondering what had just happened. He was no longer a virgin. Had it been a dream? Was he wrong to have made love to a woman he'd just met? In a public park, under a bush? What if she wasn't who she said she was? What if he'd put himself at risk? What if she got pregnant?

Yanni's thoughts flickered from guilt to elation and back again in the span of mere minutes. How could something that had felt so good be bad? It had been something Callista clearly wanted, the sound of her soft moans still echoing in his ears. And that he wanted, too. But had he done wrong to someone who was far from her home, feeling lonely and needy, and missing her boyfriend—a victim of circumstances? Was he now obligated, as a matter of honor, to ask her to marry him, even though she already had a boyfriend?

Yanni couldn't help brooding about it, and he started having trouble concentrating on his studies. His mother sensed that something was wrong. He hesitated, then told her only that he had met someone nice, a Greek woman newly arrived, who had a boyfriend in Greece. Silvia's eyes grew wide and Yanni almost laughed at the look on her face. He knew what she was thinking. This was a situation out of her control. Would worries—or, worse, lustful thoughts—stop Yanni from working so hard on his studies? Would they send him spiraling into depression again? Oh, dear God, what if this harlot was pregnant?

"Do you want me to go talk to her?" Silvia offered. "I can tell her that you offered to marry her."

"Thank you, Mom," Yanni said, panicking at the thought of his mother grilling Callista about their unexpectedly thrilling encounter under thick bushes in a public park. "But I can handle it. I'll talk to her myself."

Over the next few weeks, Yanni would tell his parents he was heading off to the law library as he always did early on Saturday mornings. Instead, he would hop on a bus to Philadelphia, call Callista, then meet her at a nearby motel and fall into bed. She was an uninhibited, delightful partner, and Yanni was intoxicated by her body, her touch, the feel of her writhing underneath him. They wrote each other letters, and spoke on the phone. Yanni couldn't stop daydreaming about the gorgeousness of her youthful nakedness, her firm bare breasts, there for the taking.

As his midterm grades started to slip, Silvia's worries and lectures intensified. Her son's entire future, all his plans, the bright career awaiting him, could not possibly be undone by a barely educated greenhorn from a small Greek village, who just happened to give him his first taste of bliss. It wasn't true love. It was merely lust. Understandable, but lust just the same.

Deep down, Yanni knew his mother was right. Callista was sweet and kind, and a willing, voracious lover in bed, but as he got to know her better, he realized they had little in common and few interests to share. It was getting harder to keep on seeing her almost every weekend, because of Yanni's pressure-cooker daily life distractions. One weekend went by without seeing her, and then another. Soon they drifted apart, much to Silvia's relief. Yanni threw himself back into his studies. She had initiated him into the previously unknown, blissful, sexual realm, asking nothing of him except for his body, and he had eagerly complied.

❧❦

An unexpected fifty-dollar raise to his monthly salary was a welcome surprise. Yanni used it to get a loan for a brand-new, shiny, blue-and-white Oldsmobile sedan. Nothing made him happier than studying all day Saturday and half the day on Sundays, then taking his sister and parents, who'd never had a car, for long rides. They explored the towns and villages along the shores of Long Island, walking along deserted beaches and gazing at the waves, sometimes gentle and rolling, sometimes angry and grey. *As moody as I am,* Yanni told himself with a laugh.

One day, as he came home from work, Silvia waved

a letter at him, her face alight. "Your cousin Isabelle is coming for a visit," she announced. "She'll be here in a few weeks to visit her brother."

Yanni sat down and smiled at her eager happiness as she read the letter, his mind transporting him back to the pink bedroom in Aunt Stella's house. There, in the privacy of the locked room, he and Isabelle would practically trip over their book bags

in their eagerness to embrace one another on the floor, covering each other's mouths in fits of giggles and tender kisses.

Isabelle's family had moved to North Carolina a few years before, where her eldest brother, John, had established what became a thriving furniture business. What Silvia did not know was that late one night, Yanni had overheard her speaking to Andreas about the real reason for their journey to the United States. Aunt Stella had written her brother in despair that Isabelle had gotten involved with one of her classmates, and they were discovered having sex in the boy's bedroom by his mother. She nearly fainted! So they quickly worked out their visa requirements and came to America to remove Isabelle from the temptations of the Greek boys who could lead her further astray. Once they settled in their new house in the small town of Monroeville, deep in the Smoky Mountains, they sent Isabelle to a boarding school an hour's drive away. Her parents, meanwhile, put out feelers that their beautiful daughter, while young, was looking for a nice Greek-American boy to marry and start a family with. They believed that settling down would put a halt to more embarrassments.

What Silvia also didn't know was that Isabelle had been secretly writing to Yanni at his office, as soon as she'd gotten settled in her boarding school. Tucking small photographs in the letters, she described how boring her life was, and how adept she was at sneaking out at night. Over time, the letters diminished in frequency as the name Markos started to appear. Then, one day, Andreas got a call from his sister saying that not only had Isabelle gotten married, but that she was soon to be a mother. Her new husband, Markos, was a nice, successful Greek-American boy from South Carolina.

Two years and another child later, the marriage ended in divorce, and Isabelle began sending letters to Yanni's office again, sharing her stories and asking what he thought she should do. He always thrilled to the sight of her handwriting, and was flattered that she looked up to him for advice.

Yanni had only seen her once since he'd left Greece, when she came with her family for the wedding of her eldest brother to a girl from Astoria. As soon as he laid eyes on her, he wished he could pull her out and ravish her from head to toe, so beautiful and alluring was she, with her dark hair still cascading in curls around her shoulders, and her eyes flashing with hints of naughtiness and adoration. But she was on the arm of her husband, and Yanni kept his distance.

Now, Silvia was telling him that Isabelle was divorced

and arriving soon in New York to see her younger brother. "We'll have to have a nice dinner for her," she said.

"That's a great idea, Mom," Yanni said, teasingly. "I wonder if she's coming up with fiancé number two."

"Oh my God, I hope not," she replied, looking shocked.

Yanni grinned. "I was joking. I'm sure she's not. At least I hope she's not." He meant that wholeheartedly, as he was longing to see her alone. "If she was involved with another man again, she would have said something about it in her letter, right?"

Silvia nodded vigorously, relieved.

Yanni counted the days till Isabelle's arrival. She had written him that she'd be staying in a hotel near Times Square before going to her brother's. Her children were staying with their father. Could he take her somewhere nice for dinner?

Isabelle was waiting for Yanni in the hotel lobby, and her eyes lit up when she saw him. He hugged her, and as soon as her arms were around him, his knees nearly buckled. He was intoxicated by the familiar, maddening scent of her hair and the firmness of her breasts and the warm curves of her body.

"Let me look at you," she said as she gazed at him with a coy smile. "You look just the same as in Clearview."

"So do you," he said as he took her arm and led her out into the bustling crowds strolling through the area, admiring the flashing lights of the theaters and the noise and the general merriment. They strolled aimlessly, too happy with each other's presence to say much, stopping only to kiss gently at street corners while waiting for the lights to change. Before they knew it, they were standing in front of Yanni's shiny car in the garage. Up the West Side Highway he drove, straight to the George Washington Bridge, crossing over into New Jersey and stopping at the first motel off the road. No sooner had they entered their room than their hands roamed frantically over each other. They tore at their clothes and tossed them in a heap on the floor and then they were, at last, naked together on a bed, pulling each other even tighter on the scratchy sheets. Finally, after all those years of yearning and waiting with an unbridled desire for each other, they could see and touch each other as they wished, uninterrupted.

What a heavenly time they had, their breathing ragged and their hearts pounding hard making love, murmuring words of endearment, wishing the rest of the world could disappear and leave only the two of them, in bed, alone with each other, forever.

But they knew it was not possible. Only an hour or so later, they checked out and Yanni drove her back to the hotel. They remained silent, because they knew there was nothing to say. That they could never be together. That she had children she loved. That they had parents who would have collapsed in horrified shock if they knew the truth.

That this one perfect evening would have to satisfy them both for a lifetime.

Yanni drove slowly home and spent most of the night awake, reliving what had just happened. Early in the morning, he hurried out of the house and went to the library. Not to study, because his thoughts were so jumbled and his body was aching, but to avoid being questioned by his mother, who would surely see his lips swollen from kisses and his eyes glazed with satiation.

A few days later, when Yanni saw Isabelle again at his house for dinner, he knew he could remain calm in her presence. He gave no hint of what happened to anyone in their family. No one ever suspected. They were simply two cousins who cherished each other.

After Isabelle left, Yanni was glad when his third year of night classes started. It kept him too busy to think of what he was missing. Even more classmates had dropped out, but Yanni knew he could manage. His classes were easier to deal with and more interesting. He had the time not only to visit Paul in Philadelphia on occasional weekends, but to join, at his father's behest, the Erytha Benevolent Society, organized years ago for Erythans to stay in touch with each other and share friendship and advice. Spending time with fellow Erythans kept Yanni happily occupied, and his third year in law school passed without as much pain and hard work as it felt the previous two years.

When summer set in, there was another piece of good news. Through his Erythan friends, he was offered a more lucrative and important position. Claims and insurance manager for a larger Greek shipping firm in downtown Manhattan. At first, Yanni wondered if he had made a mistake taking on this new job with more responsibilities he was not familiar with. Fortunately, his supportive colleagues helped him cope, and with hard work and persistence, he managed his new tasks well.

Before he knew it, another summer had passed. Fall arrived and with it, the beginning of his fourth and final year in law school. Life was smiling at Yanni again. A few more months and he would finally be a lawyer.

⇥ ⇤

Fate could not be so kind for Yanni. Instead of clear, sunny skies ahead, an unexpected incident stirred up a devastating emotional hurricane. On a Saturday afternoon when he was alone at home, he noticed something wrapped in toilet paper, lying on the bathroom floor. Puzzled, he unwrapped it, only to find a used, dried-out condom.

Yanni sat down hard on the toilet seat, blood rushing into his head, giving him a pounding headache. How *could* they, his parents? How disgusting to soil their bedroom at their age! Wasn't his mother fifty-one and his father sixty-two? When was it going to stop? Painful feelings of anger, betrayal, and disappointment swept over him, even as a small little voice nagged at him, *your parents are married adults, and their private life is none of your business.*

Yanni pushed that small little annoying voice away,

and never said a word to his father. Instead, he lit into his mother, accusing her of being a tramp. Cruelly, he told her to stop sleeping with Andreas, and that he was going to share their bed instead. She was so taken aback at her son's fury that, fearful he would have another breakdown, she reluctantly complied, embarrassed and apologetic. Andreas, concerned about Yanni's rage and hoping that his acquiescence would improve his son's mood, quietly agreed

I'm going to quit school, Yanni told himself as he took the subway to work that Monday. *That'll show them. That'll be the perfect revenge.* But something inside him told him otherwise. He knew he had to look after himself. He wanted to be a lawyer. He was so close to being done. He had worked so hard and sacrificed so much for so long. He didn't want to punish himself—only his parents.

Later that week, he scheduled an emergency session with Dr. Elias, and confessed his anger and contempt. Dr. Elias looked at him soberly. Yanni suspected that the doctor did not agree with him and was doing his utmost to mask disappointment at Yanni's strange rage. After a long silence, Dr. Elias spoke. "What your parents do in the privacy of their bedroom is *not* your concern. It is not your business," he said. "Children have *no* right to demand that their married parents who love each other, must stop engaging in behavior that gives them pleasure." He sighed, and wiped his glasses. "I'm the same age as your mother, Yanni," he went on. "Believe me, it's really not that *old.*" He smiled. "I always think it's wonderful when two people who love each other find ways to show it, in the bedroom and out of it. Do you understand what I'm saying?"

Yanni nodded, deeply humiliated. Yes, of course he understood. But what he didn't understand was the depth of his rage, and the anger towards his mother. He continued to see Dr. Elias, but the sessions didn't help. For weeks, Yanni was a seething mess of confusion. Georgia stayed out of sight as their bewildered parents tried their best to placate their son.

⊰ ⊱

One night, after yet another accusatory confrontation, Silvia was lying on her side of the bed, staring up at the ceiling. Yanni lay on his side, away from her, his eyes shut tight.

"I know you're awake," she said as she started to talk. Haltingly, then with growing force, she began her confession. She told him about her childhood in Erytha, how innocent and happy and carefree she had been. By the time she was fifteen, she and her seventeen-year-old sister Athena were the talk of town. They both had stunningly beautiful faces and bodies so shapely, that the local boys would literally pray that they'd walk by so they could feast their eyes on the lovely curves of their calves. Silvia was a bright student and loved to read. She knew she was pretty, and she spent a lot of time fussing with her hair, staring into the mirror and dreaming about marrying a young, handsome, successful boy from the island she had fallen in love with.

She was jolted out of one of her daily reveries when Barbara, the widow who lived across the street, came for a visit with her mother and great aunt Sophie, her parents' widowed sister-in-law. Would her mother agree, Barbara inquired, to one of her lovely daughters going with her to America, to marry her son who lived there? Barbara was about to go for a long visit, and she wanted to take her future daughter-in-law with her. After all, she went on, going to America and marrying a successful man from Erytha, was a stroke of good luck.

Yanni sat up in bed and looked at his mother. "Several days later, I overheard my mother talking to aunt Sophie," Silvia continued, still lying in bed and staring up at the ceiling, her eyes filling with tears.

"'If Barbara wants Athena, I would say no—but if she wants Silvia, I would agree.' I almost fainted when I heard that—I was so hurt. My own mother saying that she didn't want me any more. To her, to my father, I was clearly not as good or as important as my sister, Athena."

Tears kept rolling slowly down Silvia's cheeks, unaware, as she was wrapped in her painful memories. Yanni sat silently listening. "I was not even sixteen. I didn't want to leave my home, my siblings, my friends, and go into the unknown, to marry someone I had never met or known or even seen walking down the street. But my pride was so deeply wounded that I didn't want to stay in that house with my mother any more. I made up my mind. I was going to leave. They'd be sorry when they missed me, but I was not coming back.

"Oh, how I cried," she continued, sitting up and wiping her eyes. *She was just getting warmed up,* Yanni realized. "I cried for days, cried so much that my sister Athena begged me to stop and not leave her. Our sister Angela was too little to understand. But nothing was going to change my mind or wipe out my bitterness. How could my mother agree to let her innocent little girl—who was just about to turn sixteen—sail across the ocean, into the unknown, to marry a man she had never met? How could she do that? Unless she just didn't care for me. But she let me go. I took that ship with Barbara and I lied about my age at Ellis Island, so Immigration would let me in. For a moment I thought I should tell the truth, so they would send me back. But then I thought again of what my own mother had said. I never wanted to go back."

Silvia sighed deeply and paused for a moment. The tears started falling again. "I loved my parents, Yanni. You know that," she said. "For years I struggled and worked hard to send them all the money I could spare and help them in their old age, and to take care of you. But to this day, I still feel bitterness in my heart. I will never overcome the hurt my mother inflicted on that day.

"I met my future husband, your father, in Norfolk, Virginia," she went on. "I cried and cried all that day. Fortunately, he was a kind, compassionate man, eager to make me happy. He was very handsome. And he was so grateful I had come all that way to marry him. He did not have much education, but he was sensitive and had a kind heart.

"'Don't cry, my little girl,' he told me. 'You are too young, and weeping could make you ill. If you are unhappy, don't worry. I will pay for your ticket to go back home.'

"I looked at him, when he said that, and saw nothing but tenderness in his eyes. The tenderness I should have seen from my mother. And I never forgot these words from your father. How kind he was. How unhappy about my distress. I didn't tell him I never wanted to go back. I felt it would be disgraceful for me, too embarrassing. Besides, I had already made up my mind, my mother did not want me."

She wiped her eyes again and blew her nose, then lay back down on the bed. "So I married your father, but was ignorant about the facts of life. Unbelievable as it sounds, I did not know anything about sex. Marriage, I thought, was about two people just being together. Our first night, after your father fell asleep, I got up; went to the hotel balcony; and, for a moment, thought about jumping over, committing suicide," she said, her voice flat. She sighed deeply. "But I did not. As bad as I felt, I didn't want to hurt my new husband. Or my siblings and my parents."

"As I got to know him better, I could see how your father was a very considerate man, with such a gentle heart. He always tried to please me. He never refused anything I ever asked. He didn't have much education, but he was honest and a hard worker, laboring in the steel mills, and hat and shoe stores in Clarksburg, West Virginia, or working in different restaurants at all hours. He worked hard all his life. But he was indecisive and passive, always too unsure of himself. Never had much of a backbone. I had to be the man of the house and make the hard decisions. Even when I was still so young and inexperienced.

"Your father was always very nice to me, but I was still miserable during our first years of marriage. Your grandmother and Aunt Stella were in charge of running our house. I was there simply as a maid. A year and a half after we were married, your brother, Nick, was born. It was a difficult pregnancy and after Nick was born, I didn't feel any better. I had no appetite and had lost a lot of weight. I was crying all the time, more than the baby. I didn't know it yet, but I was in the early stages of tuberculosis. I got sicker and sicker, and your father was alarmed. He suggested I go back to my parents with our baby so I could recover in the fresh air of Erytha, and have my family look after me. I agreed. I knew I had to go, or I would have died otherwise."

Silvia sat back up, still not looking at Yanni. "When I went back to Erytha and my father saw me, he just walked out of the room. He was very angry. His beautiful little girl was a shadow of herself, thin as a wraith and white as a sheet. I'd never seen him in such a rage. He yelled at my mother and his sister-in-law.

"'What the hell did you do to our Silvia?' he screamed. My mother felt terrible, I could tell. Very unhappy and ashamed, but I didn't care. She tried her hardest to make up for what she had done. To make me happy and comfortable. Doctors came all the time, the best doctors on the island, and I started to feel better. The TB was caught early. But just when I was feeling better, my little baby—your brother—got sick. He cried and cried all day, and nobody could figure out what was wrong with him. He stopped eating. He was inconsolable. I was frantic."

She stopped, and her voice became flat again, then trailed off. "He died when he was only nineteen months old. I am sure he had what your sister has. The blood disease that runs in our family. But nobody knew it then. Nobody knew what to say when they put his tiny white coffin in the ground. I didn't want to live anymore. When your little brother died, I felt a piece of myself being torn out.

"And then, to make things worse, your father stopped sending me money. I didn't know it at the time, but he was getting disparaging letters from his mother and sister. They were telling him stories that I would recover, divorce him, and marry some wealthy man from Erytha. They didn't care that my parents were trying to make me happy so I could feel better and recover from the loss of my little boy. They were jealous. And my mother was absolutely tortured with guilt. She did everything she could to have my old friends come over, to take me out for picnics to the mountains. Anything to try to help me recover from the loss of my little baby. My sweet little Nicky."

Tears had started to fall again. Yanni thought for a minute about Aunt Stella, how she had welcomed him into her home and taken such good care of him in Clearview. He had a hard time believing she had once been so mean and awful to his mother.

"Your father, though, he loved me. He was madly in love with me, and very upset that our baby had died," Silvia went on after a few long minutes. "One day, there was a knock on my parents' door. They opened it and there stood your father. He came back to Erytha unannounced. He was so contrite, so humiliated. I accepted him, forgave him. When he found out what his mother had done, it was the first time I ever heard him raise his voice and lose his temper." She managed a wan smile "'I hope your soul is dragged out of your body and you die a miserable death, the way you embarrassed me to my in-laws and made me ashamed to face them now,' he had screamed at his mother."

Well, that explains it, Yanni said to himself when he heard that. *It explains why Grandma Barbara was always so cold to and uninterested in me. That makes sense.*

"Not long after, I learned why my mother-in-law was so much in a hurry to find a bride for her son. She had learned that the daughter of her son's boss in America had fallen in love with your father and took him to her apartment and slept with him for several weeks. My mother-in-law became scared she was going to lose her son to an American girl. That's when she came to my mother." She sighed again, even more deeply. "I have to admit, I did get some satisfaction from seeing how upset my mother was when she heard that. Devastated, even. She'd fallen for her neighbor's story, and she'd sent off her innocent little not-quite-sixteen-year-old girl to marry a man who'd been carrying on with the boss's daughter! Sending her little girl to marry a man who could have been carrying syphilis or some other disease!

"I am sure she meant well and did not intend to hurt me, but she did," Silvia added. "The damage was done, forever. How in the world do you send your little child off, to marry a man neither of us had ever met or heard of? I tried to forgive her, and I did. But to this day, Yanni, I am still bitter about what she did to me.

"You were born a couple of years later, in Erytha. Your father tried to make a living trading goods from other islands. It didn't work out. He decided to come back to America to build a new future, starting from scratch. He left for New York shortly after you were baptized. Worked in the big city and sent me money and letters regularly. Then, one day he wrote saying he was bedridden, sick in New York, all alone. He asked me to join him, help him recover. We didn't have any money. I decided to go to my husband, and leave you with my parents. I felt it was my duty to help your father get well. Our plan was to work hard for a few years, earn some money, and then return to Erytha for good.

"Immigrants like us, from all over the world, lived with the same dreams for many years. Dreams destined to crash, unfulfilled, victims of unexpected events, destroying peoples' lives," her voice tinged with resignation. "The Great Depression set in, made our lives miserable. Your father recovered, got well after I joined him, but there were no jobs. People did not have money to even buy food. Your father and I had to scrape up a few extra dollars every month, to send back to my parents to take care of you. Then, when you were ten, your sister, Georgia, was born. She cried and cried, just like my little Nicky, and the doctors found she was sick with thalassemia. Cooley's anemia, they called it. I had to endure seeing my baby being pierced with needles in the hospital, to get blood transfusions every two weeks so she could stay alive. It was so painful for both of us, Yanni. My heart was sick. Every morning I had to get up early, fix up my little baby, take her to a kind lady across the street who babysat her during the day, so I could go and earn a few dollars working in the garment factories. This was my life," she said, "struggling, agonizing about my little girl, worrying sick about my boy I left behind in Greece, trying to make ends meet here, together with a husband who was kind and caring, but timid and unable to make the hard decisions.

"I have no complaints about your father," she hastened to say again, as if she was talking to herself. "He tried as best he could, loved me very much, worked hard. But as much as he tried, he couldn't do any better and get ahead. He was not the kind of husband I was dreaming about as a little girl. Honestly, I cannot say I ever fell in love with your father. Not like he fell in love with me. I never learned how it feels being in love, thanks to my own mother, who sent me off to marry a strange man."

Silvia got up and peered out the window for a moment, then lay back on the bed, her back to Yanni. "But I respect him, he is the father of my children," she said. "He is a good man. He is an affectionate, caring man, and he loves me."

"Then why are you still having sex with him?" Yanni said pointedly.

Deep down, the small little annoying voice scolded that he shouldn't have said those words. That his mother was pouring out her heart to him, that she had an unhappy, difficult life, that he should not be so selfish and unable to control his strange anger.

"Sex is dirty, disgusting," she replied. "It is for animals if there is no purpose. Your father missed it, though. He was begging me. I felt sorry for him."

Yanni frowned. The sex he'd had wasn't dirty and disgusting. Callista had been a joyful, eager lover, as willing to give him waves of pleasure as he gave them to her. And Isabelle? Wasn't their time spent in that motel in New Jersey together, dirty or disgusting?

He paused and thought again about his mother. To her terrible, tragic, heartbreaking story. He realized that his long years of separation had left their relationship completely upended. He didn't see her only as his mother, because he had no memories of her taking care of him as a child; of being his mother. He saw her as an attractive woman. *Dr. Elias will be proud of my analysis,* he thought. *It's so very Oedipal.*

"I feel unhappy when I see you with other men in social events, dancing and laughing and having a good time. That's terrible," he blurted.

Silvia nodded. "It's a sin," she replied, "but I have the same reaction when I see you with other women."

Now it was Yanni's turn to sigh deeply. Was she telling the truth? Or, he wondered, was she merely trying to help her son push past his Oedipus complex? Was she asking herself why he had been so unfeeling when she'd shared such a desperately sad story with him? Had treated him as an adult with the truth that she had never shared with anyone else in such painful detail?

He just didn't want to discuss it, Yanni realized. He thanked his mother for confiding in him, and threw himself into his work and his last semester of studies. His daily challenges provided a strong counterweight against the unhappiness at home. Soon, he was able to sleep without knowing that his mother was nearby, as Grandma and Grandpa once had done, making him feel enclosed and protected and safe. Eventually, he asked his mother to share her bed with his father. After what had taken place, he did not think his parents would have any more sex.

But then, he realized as he was falling asleep one

night, it didn't matter to him anymore.

⸙

Later that night, Yanni had a dream. He was standing at the bow of an enormous ship, crossing the Atlantic, a wind steady in his face as the waves endlessly rose and fell. By his side stood Isabelle, her hair streaming behind her as she leaned in to Yanni for a kiss.

"Why did you abandon me?" she asked, the wind whipping her words away as she turned back to the waves.

"I didn't!" Yanni protested, placing his hand gently on her shoulders to turn her face to him. "You know I love you." As she turned, Yanni saw his mother's face instead.

"Why did you abandon me?" she asked. "Why did you let me go?"

"What are you talking about?" Yanni shouted. "*You* are the one who abandoned *me!*"

"But *she* abandoned *me*," Silvia said, her eyes focusing on some indeterminate point on the horizon. "My own mother!"

"That's no excuse for what you did to me," Yanni said.

"It's the bad blood," she said. "Bad blood, bad blood. We are cursed. Cursed and abandoned."

"No, we're not," Yanni said. "We *aren't*. We are a family. We belong together. We're here, now."

"I never learned how it feels being in love," Silvia said sadly. "Never."

She'd said those very same words when she had confessed her story to him, Yanni realized.

"I love you, Mom," Yanni murmured before he had a chance to realize what he'd said. He closed his eyes, in his dream, and reached out for his mother, but when he opened them there was no one there. Only the sea and the sky, merging into each other, midnight blue as the ship sailed on.

Yanni woke suddenly, glad it was only a dream. It took him a few minutes to calm his pounding heart. But he was filled with a sense of peace he hadn't felt in a long time.

And that small little annoying voice that had been telling him he was wrong about his mother, finally went away.

CHAPTER 10

A Death in the Family

I know they're doing a lot of research," Georgia said to Yanni a few weeks later as she lay on the sofa in the living room, too weak to move. "I'm sure they'll find a cure some day, but it'll be too late for me."

She sighed with such forlorn resignation that Yanni's heart felt a sharp twinge of alarm. She wanted to *live*, so badly. Georgia had taken a turn for the worse. She'd been so excited about her upcoming high school graduation, and the nursing program she had gotten into at Queens College. She seemed to be feeling better for a while, but as the days grew warmer she was slowly wilting like a bouquet of flowers deprived of water.

"Can I get you anything?" Yanni asked. He adored his beautiful little sister, who was just as smart as he was, but their long separation meant they would never be as close as he was with his cousins in Erytha. She was pensive and thoughtful, emotional in a quiet way, but kept most of her feelings to herself. And she was always busy with friends her age, and these girls were as sweet and lovely as she was.

She shook her head. "A cure. That's the only thing I want," she said as tears filled her eyes. "Oh, and for Mom to stop nagging me."

Yanni laughed as he sat down next to her. "Believe me, if I could stop her nagging, I'd win the Nobel Peace Prize."

Georgia managed a grin. "She's just out of control, Yanni," she said. "I mean, I'm about to graduate and I'm starting college in the fall. Why won't she let me go out on dates?" Tears sprang back into her eyes. "It's a shame, because I'm not going to be around for much longer."

"Don't say that!" Yanni exclaimed. "You're going to get better. Really."

"Oh, come off it," Georgia yelled, exasperated. "I'm not stupid. You aren't either. I know how long kids with my problem live, and don't you pretend you don't know either. The only one who doesn't seem to care is our mother."

"She does care," Yanni said. "Only she shows it in the most peculiar ways, doesn't she?"

"That's for sure." Georgia wiped the tears away. "I mean, it's not the Middle Ages. We're not in Greece. I'm not about to run off and marry the first guy I kiss. I can't even run anywhere. I can barely walk out of this room as it is." She exhaled, another heartbreaking sigh.

"How long am I supposed to take it? I wish she'd just leave me alone and let me have some fun before it's too late."

Yanni didn't know what to say. He knew his mother was so terrified of Georgia's condition that she was in deep denial, pretending it wasn't serious. Treating Georgia as if she were healthy, like all the other Greek daughters she knew, was the only way she could cope.

"Do you want me to speak to her?" Yanni asked after a few minutes. "Not that she listens to me, but I can try."

Georgia shrugged. "You could get down on your knees and beg, but do you think it'll make a difference?"

Yanni grinned. At least his sister hadn't lost her sense of humor, he thought. "Not in the slightest. She's been in such a state lately, I'm trying to stay away as much as possible."

Georgia rolled her eyes. Silvia was not well, moody and snappish, verging on paranoid. Her poignant confession had not improved her relationship with Yanni; if anything, it was becoming even more fraught. Every day, it seemed, she was twisting the most benign comments he made, accusing him of not caring, of being indifferent to all her problems and ungrateful for everything she did for him. It wasn't just worries about Georgia, Yanni realized. The more successful he was becoming, the more insecure she felt, fearing her son would break away and leave her behind. For good.

"You're lucky," Georgia said. "You have a car. You have a job. You have a future. I have nothing."

Yanni got up and kissed his sister on the forehead. "I have to go to Bible study now, but I'll see what I can do," he said.

"It doesn't matter," she said softly, almost to herself, "it really doesn't. It's just too late for anything to matter."

Yanni thought about her terrible predicament as he took the subway into Manhattan, then pushed the thoughts away. His weekly Bible class was something he always looked forward to. It was a welcome distraction from the troubles at home, and he enjoyed the company of his fellow students. Matteos, a dentist from Athens, in particular, had become a good friend. They had met when Yanni was at Lexerd and Matteos was doing post-graduate studies at Penn. They had lost touch after graduation, but reconnected at one of the Erytha Society's meetings, and became close, sharing their hopes and dreams. When Matteos invited Yanni to Bible study at the home of his wealthy friend and distant relative, Nicholas, Yanni eagerly accepted.

Yanni's jaw dropped the first time he and Matteos walked into Nicholas's sumptuous Fifth Avenue apartment. He was the son of a successful ship owner, and had married Aspasia, an elegant and graceful beauty who was the even-wealthier daughter of another ship owner. The high-ceilinged rooms were enormous, with floor-to-ceiling windows overlooking Central Park, and the kitchen was nearly as large as the apartment where Yanni had lived with his family when he first came to New York.

But what made the apartment even more hospitable was the time the small group spent discussing and interpreting various passages from their beloved Bible. There was an air of thoughtful reflection, so different from many of the spirited exchanges Yanni had grown accustomed to in law school. Yanni always left the study group feeling serene and soothed, deeply gratified by the conversation, which was so intellectually engaging.

As final exams approached, Yanni was no longer worried. He easily aced them and found it hard to believe that four long years of grinding hard work had gone by, and he was now going to be a lawyer—a real, New York attorney!

Graduation itself seemed anticlimactic, and Yanni decided to skip the commencement exercises, preferring instead to pick up his law degree from the registrar's office. Georgia was too weak to attend, and the tense relations with his mother weren't helping. Better to say goodbye to his classmates and professors and move on.

It helped that Yanni was thriving in his office, becoming more comfortable each day with the demands and complexities of maritime insurance and claims. He worked hard during the day, but was happy. At night, he studied for the bar exams, taking a prep course with hundreds of other recent graduates, hunched over long tables in the cavernous ballroom of a midtown hotel. The sessions were intense, but Yanni felt right at home, as if he were still in night school, trying to unravel the intricacies of opinions in case books. The exams were difficult, lasting two days, and he could not tell whether or not he had passed them.

One evening, several weeks later, when Georgia had stabilized somewhat and Yanni was busy with work he had brought home from the office, his mother handed him a newspaper. "Congratulations," she said, her voice dripping not with praise but with sarcasm. Yanni looked inside and saw his name on a long list of law school graduates who had passed the bar exams. He'd passed them on his first try. He just had to complete the paperwork needed and pass muster before the character committee. After taking the official oath, he would finally be a bona fide lawyer, able to try his own cases. He had done it!

Yanni put the paper down and leaned back on the sofa. Yes, he'd really done it. It had taken him nine long years—years of disappointment and disillusionment, of conflicts, of dashed dreams about his family, of upheavals and turmoil, of wounded pride and insecurities, of his cheerful disposition disappearing into a haze of depression, of deepest misery and deepest joy, also—to arrive at this very moment, sitting in the living room and marveling at what his hard work and sacrifices had brought him. Wondering what path he would carve out that would serve him for the rest of his life.

※

Yanni didn't want to share his accomplishments

with his family and friends in New York. He had to go *home*, he realized. He wanted to be in Erytha, to see those who had loved him since childhood, to inhale the fresh sea air and walk through the town he could travel blindfolded without missing a step. He needed to see cousin Costas and beloved friend Dimitris; just be himself, as he'd once been. After all those years of pain, of extreme suffering, he had earned this visit. His boss, pleased as ever with Yanni's honesty and dedication—to say nothing of his new status as a lawyer admitted to the bar—gave Yanni his permission. He could take the entire month of August. How perfect!

On the eleven-day ocean liner voyage, Yanni slept in his own cozy, comfortable cabin, much nicer than the troop ship that had brought him to America. After dinner every night, a band played in the ballroom. Yanni had no shortage of delightful partners to dance with and flirt with and later talk to, when they strolled around the decks in the balmy evenings.

On a clear, sunny morning, when the ship dropped anchor and docked at the bustling port of Piraeus, Yanni was standing on deck, his heart beating so fast he thought it was going to jump out of his chest. He moved inside to the salon to wait for his name to be called for disembarkation. Suddenly, he saw his favorite uncle, Dimitri, walk into the huge room, clad in the crisp white uniform of a Coast Guard officer. Yanni shouted out to him, got up, and they grabbed each other in an endless, tearful bear hug.

"My God, Yanni, you'll crush my ribs!" Uncle Dimitri teased as he led Yanni aft, toward the gangplank.

Finally, after eleven long years, he was walking down the gangplank, back to the blessed soil of his motherland! They were all there, waiting. His cousin Costas, his aunts and uncles. Tears of happiness flowed freely, as his family clamored in excitement around him, oblivious to the noisy throng milling around. Yanni heard none of it. He was flying high on a cloud of pure happiness.

During the next few days, Costas took Yanni all over Athens. There was almost nothing to remind him of the city he had left behind over a decade ago. He marveled at the sight of the now-bustling city, shelves well stocked and stylish men and women ambling about on their way to their favorite coffeehouses. All the wartime rubble was long gone.

"I know it's not New York," Costas said, "but it'll do, right?"

"Absolutely! I'm here to get *away* from New York!" Yanni replied.

The next evening, they took the overnight boat to Erytha, eating dinner on board before retiring to their private cabins. Yanni barely slept, excited and pensive about his homecoming. As dawn began to break, he hurried up to the main deck to see the familiar silhouette of Erytha's southern mountains looming on the horizon. Home. No matter that he was a big-city American lawyer now—Erytha would always be *home*.

The ship slowly sailed along the coastline toward the main harbor, passing by tranquil shores and beaches, hamlets and villages, perched on hillsides, the occasional shepherd waving to them, watching carefully over his flock. Soon, the red-roofed houses, the church cupolas, the narrow streets, the coffeehouses by the quay he knew so well, became more distinct. It was as if a living, long-awaited, soulful dream was passing in front of Yanni's eyes.

The ship finally dropped anchor at the dock where throngs of waving Erythans were clustered. "There they are!" Costas shouted as he spied his parents, other cousins, and Yanni's dearest friend, Dimitris. The only person missing was his beloved Grandma, who had died more than a year earlier, leaving Yanni heartbroken at the news. Her loss was so painful that Yanni still had trouble believing she was gone, and he found it unbearable to mention it, pushing the grief and despair away. She had raised him, been his surrogate mother. She had loved him unconditionally. She'd understood him better than his own mother ever would. He'd always had a feeling that their lingering embrace at the dock in Piraeus eleven years ago would be their last.

After more tearful hugs, Yanni followed Aunt Athena and Uncle George to their house. Nothing seemed to have changed. He unpacked in the same tiny bedroom that he would be sharing now with Costas as they had once done; so many years, back when the Germans left the people terrified and starving. How much the world had changed, and how much had, blessedly, stayed the same!

Yanni's two weeks on the island flew by, visiting former classmates and relatives, and attending religious feasts in nearby villages. No longer was he just another boy that all the girls had grown up with. Now he was an independent, self-assured young lawyer in his late twenties, an eligible, handsome bachelor who had come from America to visit his childhood family. Subtle and not-so-subtle invitations arrived daily from eager mothers of local girls, making Aunt Athena proud about her nephew becoming such an eligible bachelor. But she was under strict instructions from her sister to keep Yanni out of their clutches and—horrors!—the clutches of Erytha's marriage brokers. Yanni himself was oblivious, too busy enjoying himself with Costas and Dimitris to think about romance.

On his last afternoon in Erytha, Yanni sat with Dimitris on a hill overlooking the harbor. Time seemed to melt away as they talked and talked, knowing each other so well that it seemed as if Yanni had only left the day before.

"Remember when we used to sit here after school, wishing we were somewhere else?" Yanni said. "You were always a better student than me in school. The number one in the class."

Dimitris grinned. "And you were always getting into more trouble."

Yanni grinned back. "I wish you could come live in

New York," his voice suddenly serious. "Nothing would make me happier."

"I wish I could, too, but I can't," Dimitris replied soberly. "My life is here. My family is here. I don't have the courage you had to change my world so completely."

"Courage? Are you kidding?"

Dimitris shook his head. "Of course not, but you don't realize how hard it is to do what you've done. I can't imagine."

"It was excruciating," Yanni admitted. "Much harder than I ever dreamed. It was sheer agony for me trying to adjust to so many painful realities. Different language, strange country, parents I had never really known before. But now, I guess I can't imagine staying here, either."

"You're a New Yorker now. You walk differently. And you're *louder*."

Yanni laughed. "You have to be, to make yourself heard," he said.

"You will always make yourself heard."

Yanni's heart filled to the brim at those words, touched, ineffably, at his very core.

"And you will always be my truest and best friend, Dimitris," he said, his voice choking. "My soulmate. We will always stay together, no matter where we are."

"Absolutely. You know I feel exactly the same way, Yanni."

They hugged briefly, then sat back in silence as the sun set and the lights came on in the streets. In a way, they were speaking to each other with the golden voice of silence.

Yanni and Costas sailed back to Athens the next morning, and took the train up to Salonika, to visit the city's annual fair. Next, they took a bus and went further east on a two-day pilgrimage to the monasteries at Mount Athos, called the "holy mountain." Its twenty monasteries are filled with priceless religious icons, relics, and manuscripts, banned to all women. Yanni's priest at his church in New York, had spent his early years in this marvelous place, and the abbot of the monastery where the priest had served, received them cordially. After taking them to the chapel to venerate the icons, he showed them to a simple, small cabin where they would sleep. It was furnished only with two cots, a dresser, and an icon of Jesus Christ. Worship in the monastery followed the old Byzantine timetable, starting at four o'clock in the morning and again in the early afternoon. The beginning of each service at the chapel was announced not by a bell, but by a monk striking a mallet on a wooden plank.

Time seemed to have stopped on this mountain. Everything was still. The surroundings were serene, and still; it was almost eerily tranquil, except for the rustling of the tall mulberry trees in the valley when an occasional gentle breeze blew in from the sea. Yanni and Costas joined the monks in prayer, and hiked to another nearby monastery, where they were again greeted warmly, this time with cognac, a glass of crystal-clear spring water, and some sweets.

It was the perfect way for Yanni to end his homecoming. Bathed in peacefulness and calm, surrounded by monks who devoted their lives to silence and worship, benevolence and reflection. The power of stillness and silence would linger in Yanni's memory for years.

When it was time for farewells back in Athens, Yanni was relaxed and happy. He knew he wouldn't have to wait another eleven years for the next reunion. His heart and mind had been soothed by the love and kindness he had exchanged so easily over the last month. All the strife with his mother and the worries about his sister had left him during this trip.

And he realized that Erytha would always be his home; yet he was convinced New York was now the place where he belonged.

Sailing back to America on the same liner that had brought him to Greece, Yanni fell easily into the daily rhythm of the ship. He was happy to see that a casual acquaintance from New York, a personable Greek-American girl named Maria, was also sailing back from her summer vacation. They weren't sexually attracted to each other, but Yanni found her so engaging as a friend that they spent many hours together, strolling around the decks or just talking.

Soon after passing Gibraltar, though, the weather quickly deteriorated as an enormous storm rolled in from the west. The ship pitched and rolled, first gently, then violently as it labored on. Yanni never became seasick, and he was one of the few on board who relished the ceaseless roller-coaster motion of the ship. Two nights after the storm started, it seemed to weaken a bit, and the passengers nervously tried to relax in the ballroom. Suddenly, an enormous, unexpected wave hit the big liner from the starboard side and the ship sharply listed to port. Shelf after shelf of glassware and plates fell onto the bar, shattering into thousands of pieces. Passengers were screaming and slipping, trying to find their balance. Yanni tried to grab Maria's hand and to help her sit on a bench. Instead, she lost her balance and fell awkwardly, hitting her back on the edge of a seat. Yanni helped her up as she cried out in pain. He supported her slowly limp to her cabin, and the next day, when the storm had subsided, Yanni took her for X-rays at the ship's sick bay. Maria had a small fracture to one of her lower vertebrae. They were both grateful it wasn't worse.

"I'll take care of all the paperwork for you," Yanni said, knowing exactly how to process her claim for personal injury once they were back home. An amicable settlement was reached, not long after their arrival in New York, and Maria gratefully paid Yanni one-third of her settlement money. It was more than enough to cover all of Yanni's expenses during his vacation, which was an unexpected bonus.

＋∃ ⫩＋

Back at home in New York, tanned and relaxed
and full of stories to eagerly share about the relatives
in Greece, the sour look on Silvia's face made Yanni's
happy memories vanish. Nothing seemed to please
her, and her nagging and complaining started in the
morning and resumed as soon as Yanni returned,
exhausted, from a long day at work. It didn't help that
Georgia was too weak to go to her classes, and kept the
door firmly shut, letting her mother in only to serve
meals she barely ate.

Late one afternoon, after an especially nasty
argument, something inside Yanni snapped. He quickly
threw some clothes into a small suitcase and took the
subway into Manhattan, to a midtown YMCA. The small,
spartan room he rented in a nondescript hall was a very
lonely place. Yanni, though, had made up his mind;
he would never return until his mother was willing to
change and called begging for him to come back home.
Even his sister's precarious health couldn't tempt him
back. With so much time on his hands, he threw himself
with extra vigor into long hours at the office. Once a
week, he'd call his father at work to make sure Georgia
was okay. He ate dinner alone at a nearby coffee shop
with only the newspaper for company. Then he went
back to an empty room to read or write long letters to
loved ones back in Erytha; or to stare at the ceiling, lost

in thought, with the alarm clock slowly ticking off the minutes. He was miserable.

This lonely monotony was suddenly broken when his father called, his voice shaking. Georgia's condition had become grave and had taken her to the hospital.

After work, Yanni hurried to visit his sister. There in the hospital room, were his parents, both relieved to see him again. His mother was sitting on a chair in the corner of Georgia's room, speechless, racked with worry about her daughter. Her petty grievances with her son were now meaningless. Georgia's eyes lit up when Yanni bent down to kiss her forehead.

"Don't worry. I feel much better now," she whispered to him, and Yanni felt a sharp spasm of guilt when she added, "I love you so much, it hurts."

Yanni smiled and whispered, "I love you, too." He shouldn't have left her at home, as sick as she was, to cope with Silvia's moodiness, and he was deeply relieved when his mother timidly asked if he might consider moving back. Yanni readily agreed. Even the daily harangues by his mother would be better than the painful loneliness of his solitary room.

When Dr. Carl Roberts, a prominent research scientist and an authority on thalassemia, came into the room to examine Georgia, Yanni could tell he was very worried. He followed the doctor into the hall and spoke to him in confidence. Dr. Roberts gave him the bad news. "Your sister is a very sick girl," he said soberly. "There must be a pound of iron around her heart. Her survival is hanging by a thread, and surgery, I'm sorry to say, is out of the question."

Georgia was dying. She was not even twenty years old. She had her whole life ahead of her. She had to live. She *had* to.

"Please, Dr. Roberts, you have to find something. You do have to do something, anything," Yanni pleaded.

But the doctor only shook his head. Nothing could be done.

On his daily visits to Georgia's room, Yanni tried to put on a brave, cheerful face. His sister was listless and pale and so weak, such a painful contrast to her desperate desire to stay alive. They all felt helpless, hoping for a miracle while knowing, deep down, that none was in sight. At one point, when Yanni's parents were out of the room, she turned and repeated the words she had said to him months before: "I'm sure they'll find a cure some day, but it'll be too late for me."

A solitary tear trickled down her cheek, and Yanni wiped it away. "You're going to get better," he said, hoping his lie would make her feel better. "I'm afraid of what it'll do to Mom if you don't get back in the house really soon."

Georgia mustered a wan smile at his teasing and fell into a fitful sleep.

A few days later, on a chilly, damp Saturday evening in early April, Yanni sat with his parents in Georgia's room. His mother turned to him and said, "You must go, Yanni. For the sake of the family. Don't worry. We'll be fine. Just go for an hour or so, please."

That night was the annual dance held by the Erytha Society in a large Manhattan hotel. It was the social event of the year, with the family discussing what to wear and who they'd go with, weeks ahead of time. They would spend a joyful evening with friends at the event, dancing to the tunes of a loud Greek band, talking, singing, drinking, and laughing until the wee hours. It was a night where all differences were forgotten, and friends and family came together solely to enjoy each other's company.

This year, everything was different. Silvia and Andreas were in no mood for merriment, and Georgia was far too weak to even contemplate getting out of her hospital bed.

"Your mother's right," Andreas said, with Silvia nodding in agreement. "Someone should represent our family there. Go, for a short time."

"I don't want to leave Georgia," Yanni protested. "We'll all go next year."

"Please go," Georgia said faintly. "Do it for me."

"Are you sure?" Yanni asked.

She nodded. "Come back and tell us how it was at the dance."

Yanni smiled. He knew what she meant. She wanted to know who was dancing with whom and who looked lovely and who looked silly, and who was getting too loudly drunk and who was caught sneaking a cigarette in the ladies' room.

"Okay," he said finally, sighing loudly. "But only because Georgia wants me to. I'll be back soon."

At the party, the festive atmosphere and crowds of people dancing and singing were as Yanni expected; but this year he felt different. He was so worried about his sister that he could barely drink, and only after he saw some old classmates from Erytha, who had just arrived in New York, did he start to warm up. Not long after, though, out of the corner of his eye, Yanni thought he saw people furtively looking at him sadly and then walking away. Nervously, he tried to convince himself they simply felt bad that Georgia was so ill. Shortly after, however, two friends quietly took him aside and told him it might be best if he went back to the hospital because his sister had taken a turn for the worse.

Yanni sped all the way and rushed up the stairs to his sister's room. He stopped short when he saw that her bed was empty. A nurse came in and took him to a small lounge where his parents were sitting, looking utterly devastated. He had never seen such terrible expressions on their faces, and he knew what that meant as he sat down beside them.

"She is gone," his father managed to whisper as his mother started to cry.

Yanni couldn't believe it. He knew Georgia's prognosis was dire, but how could she be dead, this night, when he had just left her? How could she be gone? She was not even twenty years old. Her birthday was coming up, in only a few weeks. It couldn't be true.

Yanni was in complete denial.

Rage took a hold of Yanni for a moment. He stood up, lashing out at whatever was nearby as he picked up a chair and threw it against the wall. A nurse ran in, looked at the family, shook her head scornfully, and hurried away.

He sat back down, not knowing what to do. A few minutes later, Dr. Roberts came into the lounge and ruefully expressed his condolences. He had tried his best to postpone the inevitable, but the disease betrayed him.

Yanni could tell the doctor was deeply upset, but his mother looked at him angrily. "Why didn't you tell us all these years that Georgia would not live long? Why did you hide it from us?" she wailed. "We should have known so that we would have treated her differently!"

Dr. Roberts sighed heavily. He knew that Silvia was so distressed that she wasn't rational. Over the years, he had many conversations with her about Georgia's condition. She'd already lost her first child to the horrible disease when he wasn't even two years old. She knew what was going to happen. But she just didn't want to believe it.

"I am truly sorry," he said. "You took the best possible care of her. We all did. And Georgia lived longer than most children suffering from the same condition. We're doing our best to try to find a cure, to save children like Georgia, if not to cure them then to prolong their lives even longer." He looked pleadingly at Yanni. "I know this is a terrible time and a terrible question, but I'm hoping you would consider allowing us to do an autopsy. It might help more—"

Before he could finish, Silvia stood up. "We will have none of that," she shouted before sitting back down and bursting into heartrending sobs. "Georgia suffered enough. I don't want you to torture her any more!"

"She will not feel anything." Dr. Roberts said gently. "If she could talk to you about this, I know she would ask you to agree."

"If you touch her, I will go to a lawyer," Andreas said indignantly.

The good doctor sighed again as he got up. He felt hurt and offended. "I am very sorry to hear you say that. Georgia has been my patient and I cared very much about her. I gave her twenty years of life trying the impossible, and now you talk to me about going to a lawyer!"

Andreas looked away, ashamed but unrepentant. No one was going to cut into his beloved daughter.

With one last plaintive glance toward Yanni, who knew he could not interfere with his parents' decision, Dr. Roberts left the room. Soon, friends and relatives who were at the dance came to offer their support and condolences. Yanni's parents went to see Georgia one last time before leaving the hospital, and a friend from Erytha drove Yanni home, knowing he was too shaken to take the wheel. It was one of the worst nights of Yanni's life, as friends came in and out and his parents eventually arrived home, grey and shattered. The Greek undertakers were called and the funeral arrangements were made in the middle of the night.

The two days before the funeral were miserable. Yanni was too numb to think of anything except his beautiful little sister, lying still and silent in her coffin, gone forever. He was in a trance, barely in touch with reality, with what was going on around him, lethargic with shock, staring off into space. He felt completely disembodied, as if looking at the other mourners through a thick, cloudy glass.

It just couldn't be true. At any minute, Georgia would come running through the door again, laughing and happy and healthy, throwing down her schoolbooks and grabbing the phone to chat with her friends, punctuated by fits of giggles.

But that didn't happen.

Throngs of visitors, including many of Georgia's classmates from high school, came to the funeral parlor for the wake. There were so many wreaths and flowers wilting under the lights, that Yanni developed an excruciating headache from the strong scent. Everyone who came to say good-bye to Georgia was distraught, expressing their sympathy to a forlorn Silvia, who sat, all in black, inconsolable, near her daughter, with her quietly weeping husband at her side.

Yanni thought about Grandpa's dying, and how peaceful it had been. He thought about Maria, dying in Athens during the war, without her mother by her side. He thought about his sister and the conversations they'd had when she was wondering if she would ever go on dates with boys that she so desperately wanted. If she would ever be kissed, or if she dreamt of true love, or marriage, or children. If she had known she would die on that day, and had sent her brother away so he wouldn't see her passing from this life to the next. The weight of the guilt he felt—that he had never tried to get to know her better; that he had moved out of the house when she was close to dying, depriving her of his comfort and company when she must have needed it— nearly crushed him.

On the morning of the funeral, an endless line of cars, headlights on, followed the main hearse and two open limousines, overflowing with rose-bedecked wreaths and crosses. The procession snaked from Astoria to Timberside and past the family home, where a hatless undertaker stood at attention at the front door. Neighbors watched from their homes, sadly crossing themselves. A huge crowd was waiting at the church, as the grieving family came in, walking behind the coffin with the priests and the cantors chanting in low voices. Yanni was still in a daze, the prayers and the blessings seeming to come from far away, no more tangible than a distant dream. He vaguely heard the sobbing of his mother and of Georgia's distraught classmates. The outpouring of grief was palpable. Finally, he approached the coffin one last time after the service, to kiss his sister's pale, cold cheeks in the most final of farewells.

"Until we meet again, until we meet again," he heard himself saying, weeping silently. Strange how death upended his feelings about his sister. Their lack of closeness over the years melted into a mountainous sea of love, affection, and desperate loss.

⚜

A week later, life resumed its daily grind as Yanni and his father went back to work. He was grateful for the busy distractions of the office. Silvia, though, was still so distraught that she was barely able to function. She ate almost nothing, and spent most of the day visiting Georgia's grave at the cemetery or sitting on her daughter's bed, staring into space as friends tried to comfort her. Alarmed and worried that she was headed for a breakdown, Yanni took her to Dr. Elias, who prescribed shock treatments. They seemed to help somewhat, and Silvia very slowly became more active. But something inside her had broken, irrevocably. Once, when her husband gently suggested that she should try to turn the bitter into sweet, to honor Georgia's memory, Silvia turned on him.

"The bitterness will never leave me," she said, her eyes flashing. *"Never."*

A few months later, Yanni was invited by Jack, the company's insurance broker, to join him for a trip to London, where they'd meet with the company's underwriters and brokers to discuss pending ship casualty claims, and perhaps get advance payments against those claims. They would also travel to Brussels to visit the World's Fair. Yanni quickly agreed, thrilled. A trip to Europe was just what he needed to lift his spirits.

Yanni's parents took him to the airport to see him off, waving from the observation deck as he walked across the tarmac to board the plane. Chatting happily, Yanni took the window seat and Jack took the aisle, fastening their seat belts and leaning back for takeoff. Eventually, the plane started hurtling down the runway, its thundering engines thrusting it forward. As the plane was about to lift off the ground, there was a loud pop. And then another.

The whining sound of the engines changed and the plane slowed down. Jack and Yanni looked at each other, puzzled. Soon after, the plane swerved off the runway onto the grass. The port wing hit the ground and the plane came to an abrupt stop. White smoke enveloped the fuselage and all the lights in the cabin were turned off. No one screamed or spoke. Even in these tense moments, Yanni remained calm, looking at his watch and wondering how long it would take before the fire engines showed up. His war experiences in Erytha were much worse, he thought. A scant five minutes later, the crew opened the doors and the passengers were quickly ushered out through the emergency chutes.

At the observation deck, Yanni's parents had watched the aborted takeoff, the plane veering off the runway, and the shuddering halt, with smoke billowing from the damaged port wing.

Silvia's knees buckled and she nearly fainted. "We

have no children anymore!" she cried out. "We just lost our last one!" She collapsed in heartrending sobs as Andreas tried in vain to comfort her. She didn't stop sobbing until she looked up, incredulous, to see Yanni standing there, reassuring her that he was fine.

The passengers were told to go home until a replacement plane could be found. Jack asked Yanni if he still wanted to take the trip, on a different airline. Yanni thought about it for a minute, his nerves jangling, then decided to go. He was still in a bit of shock after the near disaster, and he was still on edge after Georgia's death. At least, he rationalized, if another crash was meant to be, then so be it. At least he would be reunited with his sister, his cousin Maria, and his beloved grandparents.

Fortunately, the rescheduled flight was perfectly smooth and seamless, and the Savoy Hotel in London was the epitome of Old World chic. Yanni was far too busy with meetings and business luncheons, carefree dinners and sightseeing, to worry about planes crashing.

Brussels was even more fun. One night, Yanni and Jack went to "the Needle," a tall, thin tower with a glass-enclosed restaurant at the top. From their magical vantage point above, they could see all of the fairgrounds below, and the city stretching out to the horizon. Yanni feasted his eyes on the view, thinking poignantly of his sister, who would never have a chance to see such a spectacular sight, and of his own future. It seemed to stretch out below him, with endless possibilities, shining as brightly as the lights of the city that flickered on in the deepening twilight.

PART IV

A FACE
IN THE CROWD

A sweet hour....
Sensuous scents are in the air,
the spirit waits for nothing any more.
—From "Athens" by Kostas Karyotakis

The old man got up and stretched. He was almost in tears. Reminiscing was just too painful. Yet as the memories continued to flood his senses, he wanted to continue reliving his past.

For a moment he was distracted by the beauty of his surroundings, and he walked to the edge of the terrace. Fat pots of colorful bougainvillea and jasmine flanked each end, and he ran his fingers over the profusion of blossoms. From a neighboring house, the scent of strong Turkish tobacco wafted over on a gentle breeze.

It made him think of another cigarette, one that led to a terrible tragedy. There had been an explosion on a tanker in the process of discharging crude oil to a refinery. Tragically, a crewmember died after being burnt alive. Yanni took the deposition of the deck officer, also from Erytha. He testified that he saw the man who ended up dying, come out of his cabin and light the cigarette that triggered the explosion. Every man on a tanker knew never to smoke when a ship was discharging, as the fumes are highly volatile. Yanni was grateful for the information, however, because it meant a claim could be made against the ship's underwriters for crew negligence. Otherwise the owners would be hard-pressed to explain what caused the explosion. If the underwriters weren't convinced the explosion was caused by an insured peril, they could deny the claim, causing the owner to lose millions of insurance dollars. Based on the deck officer's testimony, the claim was eventually approved. The owners were compensated for the full insured value of the ship, and Yanni's law firm earned a handsome fee.

Years later, Yanni ran into the deck officer during his summer vacation in Erytha.

"Mr. Yanni," he said, "there is something I need to tell you. Something that has been weighing on my conscience for years."

Yanni looked at him, bewildered.

"It never happened," the man went on. "Not like I told you about the ship explosion. There was no lit cigarette. I had to invent that story so I wouldn't be blamed for it. That crewmember was totally innocent. He died a horrible death, and what's worse, he got blamed for it. The explosion was my fault." He sighed deeply. "I am very sorry, but I felt like I had no choice at the time. Because I was in charge of discharging and had made a mistake in controlling the transfers. I would have been fired and my career ruined and my life threatened. I had to think of my family. I hope you can forgive me."

Yanni was so shocked at this unexpected confession that all he could do was nod and walk away.

Sometimes, he told himself later, *you never know what people are capable of. You just really never know.*

The old man sat back down on his chaise. The happy chatter of the children next door filled his ears as he closed his eyes, and remembered more.

CHAPTER 11

Courtship and Conflict

I can't believe I'm thirty," Yanni said to Matteos as they sat in a sunny midtown coffee shop for lunch.

"I can't believe it, either," Matteos said with a smile. "Because that means I'm over thirty."

"And you're the most successful dentist in New York," Yanni replied.

Matteos laughed. "Not quite. But if I'm the most successful dentist, then you're the most successful lawyer and marine insurance expert."

"Hardly." Yanni grinned at his friend. "But thanks for the thought."

"Well, now that you're getting to be *old*, it's about time you settled down and found yourself a wife," Matteos said with a coy smile.

Yanni put down his coffee cup. "You sound just like my mother!" he teased.

"Oh, dear. That's the last thing I want to do to you."

Matteos' voice suddenly got serious. "No, really, I just want you to find someone who'll make you as happy as my Olga makes me."

"Me, too," Yanni admitted, shaking his head. "But where is she?"

He didn't want to tell Matteos just how hard it really was for him. Late at night when he couldn't sleep, he often wondered if there was something wrong with him. If his stern upbringing in Erytha, the years of his erstwhile love for Isabelle, and his intense, difficult relationship with the mother who he still felt had abandoned him, made it impossible for him to break down his emotional boundaries. Whenever his parents broached the subject, his mother punctuated the conversation with deep sighs about the loss of her daughter and her lack of grandchildren. This only made Yanni shrug with seeming indifference. Occasionally, he dated the eligible daughters of family friends, if only to stave off the loneliness and put a temporary halt to Silvia's nagging. But nothing had ever come of it.

What did it really mean, Yanni sometimes asked himself, *to truly fall in love?* He suspected what a thunderbolt that must be, because he'd been struck by one long ago when Isabelle had come home from school, flashing him a welcoming, bashful smile. But that one having lost its firepower by now, he didn't want another such jolt, with all its messy complications. He wanted stability. He wanted a loving companion, someone lovely and decent and kind, with whom he could share his life, based on their respect for each other and the same values and ambitions.

"Well, today's your lucky day, my friend," Matteos went on. "I know just the girl for you."

"You do? Who is she?" Yanni asked, his interest piqued.

"Her name is Irene," Matteos replied. "Her father works at an import-export company, and he has just brought his family here from Greece. My parents know the family well, and they said Irene is an incredible catch." He winked. "So, what do you think?"

"Is she pretty?"

Matteos laughed so loudly that the other diners turned to look at him. "Is that all you care about?" he eventually asked. "No wonder you're still a bachelor."

Yanni smiled, his spirits lifting. They agreed Matteos would arrange a meeting.

Silvia was thrilled when Yanni told her about it later that day. After a flurry of phone calls, the two families met one Sunday in church, introduced by a beaming Matteos. After church, Irene's mother invited them to their house in the suburbs for coffee and pastries. Irene was indeed pretty, but painfully hidden by shyness and quiet reserve. It was clear she had barely begun to adjust to life in America, and Yanni felt a sharp jab of disappointment, wishing she were a little bit more outgoing and comfortable living in New York. In fact, glancing at her old-fashioned dress and her face, that didn't warrant even a swipe of lipstick, he didn't find her particularly attractive.

Matteos would not allow Yanni's initial lack of interest put an end to his matchmaking. A few days later, he invited Nicholas to join them for lunch. He knew that Yanni was always happy to see Nicholas, who so graciously hosted their weekly Bible meetings at his sumptuous Fifth Avenue apartment. Yanni had tremendous respect for his opinions and lifestyle.

Soon, the conversation turned to Irene. "I don't really know her myself, but her father has had a lot of dealings with our company," Nicholas said. "He is a fine person, so that counts for something, right?

"And Irene was raised, as you were, in a traditional Greek family style, with strict morals and respectful obedience to her elders," Matteos added. "When she was still living in Athens, she went to a school run by Catholic nuns. And she is nobody's fool."

Both of Yanni's friends were persuasive. Silvia's eyes lit up, for the first time since her daughter's death, when Yanni recounted their conversation. She was in awe of Nicholas, too, for his beautiful apartment, lovely wife, and important connections.

"He has your best interests at heart," she told Yanni, convinced that Irene was just the kind of wife her son needed. "You know that. He is such a good friend. He knows what kind of person you are and the kind of wife who will be good for you. Give this girl a chance. You know how overwhelming it is to come to a new country. Once she becomes adjusted here and develops socially, she will be an outstanding wife and mother."

Her eyes widened into near panic, fearing that she was overbearing, but Yanni knew what she meant, and took no offense.

"Maybe you have a point," he said a day later, conceding that, this time at least, his mother could be right. He recalled that awful summer when he had arrived in New York. The feelings of disappointment and disillusionment before spiraling into depression and despair. Perhaps Irene had been so quiet and withdrawn because she feared saying the wrong thing. Perhaps, with a little bit of time, she would show her true nature, that of a beautiful, sophisticated young lady, able to meet Yanni on his own terms, as an equal.

And Yanni wanted to give his mother something nice to think about. He was very concerned about Silvia's condition, as she was still in deep mourning, fragile and depressed, often in near hysterics after her regular, even obsessive, visits to Georgia's grave. Yanni and Andreas desperately wanted to help her get better, to feel a little happier and hopeful for the future. "But I'm just not attracted to her," he confessed. "Plus, she is only eighteen. She is too young for me."

Silvia sat down and folded her arms. "So? She will grow up. You can help her. She was brought up the right way, not like these spoiled girls of New York. And she comes from a good family, a hard-working family," Silvia added. "And she's pretty. There's nothing wrong with her appearance, except not paying enough attention to herself and not using any makeup." She smiled, briefly.

"Back in the old country, young virgins do not use makeup!"

Yanni laughed. His mother's frank comments sounded a bit embarrassing, but deep down he knew they were true.

Shortly after that, they were invited to a casual dance at their church. Silvia spent days getting herself ready in a frenzy of excitement, even going to the local beauty parlor for a haircut and styling that morning. When they arrived, Irene and her mother, Joy, were sitting on folding chairs set up at the end of the large hall, merrily chatting with Matteos' mother. Yanni looked at Irene. She seemed very different. She furtively peered at him from under her long lashes, before shyly turning away. She was wearing a fitted, sleek dress that enhanced her figure, and her long hair had been trimmed to a stylish bob. Her lips were a subtle pink. She looked sexy and demure at the same time. Yanni's interest was definitely piqued. As he chatted with her, he missed the knowing looks among all the mothers in the large room. They certainly understood what Greek men found attractive!

Yanni and Irene soon started dating, following the unwritten rules of proper conduct that they'd grown up with in Erytha. A prospective suitor would arrive at his date's house together with his parents, and make conversation for a while. The young lady would then come into the room to meet the guests, politely chitchat for a few more minutes, and then demurely leave with her suitor.

Yanni liked Irene's parents, and enjoyed talking to them before driving Irene into Manhattan for dinner on Saturday evenings. A few hours later, he'd bring her back to her house, stay a short time, and then drive home with his parents.

At first, Irene was reserved, polite, and submissive, seemingly happy to defer to Yanni's decisions about where to go, appreciative merely of the chance to spend time with him in whatever restaurant he chose. His favorite was the Viennese Lantern, a cozy continental café on the Upper East Side, where a small band softly played romantic music. She seemed to agree with and echo his views about the world, about the way people lived, worked, and had fun. After a few more dates, though, Yanni's impression of this coy, demure girl slowly began to change. She was becoming more animated and willing to share her own ideas. Her personality began to shine.

One night, several weeks later, Yanni told his mother that he had changed his mind. "You were right after all, Mom," he said. "I like Irene a lot. I love her. I've decided this is the girl I want to marry. Next time we go to their house, for my next date with her, please tell her mother, Joy, about our proposal."

Silvia nodded, a peculiar look on her face. She called Irene's house and arranged a meeting, knowing that Joy would be happy and relieved at such a good match. As she hung up, the same peculiar look still creased her features. Yanni was troubled; she should have been ecstatic, as she had been nagging him to find a suitable bride, to give her the grandchildren she longed for. Yanni realized his mother was torn by ambivalence. Her mourning over Georgia was as unrelenting as ever. No woman could ever take Georgia's place in her heart, she was telling herself. But she also loved her son and did not want him to stay single forever.

Yanni watched the cloud of emotions pass over Silvia's features even as she was unaware of them, sitting in a chair in the kitchen, staring at the table. *It's not only the conflicts between my own future happiness and the pain from Georgia's loss,* he told himself. *It's the frustrations and the dismay about all the hardships and disappointments of her life.* She had never had a similar kind of courtship, and she never would. And her mourning over Georgia was the kind of pity she'd never been allowed to have, either.

Later that week, Matteos invited Yanni for lunch, intending, as ever, to be singing the praises of Irene and her family. Not this time. Yanni had already made up his mind. He was excited about his decision, and wanted Matteos to hear it first.

Matteos was thrilled and relieved at the news, assuring Yanni that he was making a wise decision, and that Irene would make an excellent wife and a caring mother. "Her father," he said, "will, I'm sure, be giving you a handsome dowry to get you started. We've known the family for a long time, and that's the kind of man he is. He would consider it insulting and embarrassing giving away his daughter, without making a handsome gift of money to the future couple." He leaned back and smiled. "Mothers-in-law in our village have a reputation of being particularly attentive and affectionate to their sons-in-law," he went on. "They just love them, and look after them as if they're their own sons. They cater to all their whims. At least mine does." He winked, and Yanni laughed.

Everything worked out that Saturday night as Yanni had hoped. His mother was in high spirits, which made him happy. As usual, his parents stayed at Irene's house, visiting only with Joy, since Irene's father was out of town on business. Yanni took Irene to the Viennese Lantern. As usual, they talked about anything and everything. This time, however, he found himself getting more and more excited. She was blissfully unaware that her life was about to change, and Yanni gave no hint of his momentous decision. According to custom, this was left for his parents to announce.

When they arrived back at the house, Irene was surprised when Joy opened the door, beaming. "Kiss the hand of your father and mother," she said, pointing to Yanni's parents. Irene knew what that meant, but she was too stunned to say anything. She obediently kissed her future in-laws' hands, and they embraced her tenderly, murmuring congratulations as Joy wiped tears from her eyes.

A formal engagement took place at Irene's home a few weeks before Christmas. Family friends and their local priest joined the party and Irene showed off the diamond ring Yanni had given her. Gifts were exchanged, delicious food was served, and everyone was in a jovial mood. The party was marred only by the absence of Irene's father, who was at a foreign port, still busy with work that needed his attention.

A long engagement followed, but as Yanni and Irene eagerly made plans for the wedding and their future, Silvia's state of mind again took a turn for the worse. She saw Dr. Elias frequently but nothing seemed to help. She was desperately conflicted. She constantly contradicted herself, veering between a deep desire to see Yanni settled, and an equally deep desire to keep some form of control over him. She had to know that she was still the most important woman in his life. How many times had Yanni heard her say to his father, "Our son should be married by now. He's thirty years old." Andreas would nod and agree. He, too, was unhappy that his son was still a bachelor. But he kept quiet whenever Silvia raged about her desperate unhappiness over her daughter's death.

A few weeks later, during a visit to Irene's house, Silvia's warring emotions reached a crescendo. "When Yanni marries Irene," she blurted out in the middle of an otherwise innocuous conversation, "my pain will go away!"

Irene and Joy's eyes widened at her inappropriate comment, but they were kind enough not to say anything.

Life became increasingly difficult for the happy couple. Silvia's initial enthusiasm about the engagement turned from ambivalence, to fault finding, to resentment. She would not allow any girl to take her daughter's place. Deep down, her guilty feelings drowned any sense of approval about Yanni's fiancée, and she veered from indifference to angry criticism with unrestrained, rude capriciousness.

Irene tried her best. She was a loving and dutiful future daughter-in-law, who knew she had to make daily phone calls and requests to visit Silvia to help with the housework. No matter how politely she asked, Silvia avoided or declined the requests.

"I just want to be left alone," she shouted at her son and husband, her previous joy at Yanni's engagement gone. "Why doesn't anyone understand how bad I feel?"

The weekly visits to Irene's home were pure hell for both, Irene and Silvia. Irene realized she had to ignore Silvia's moodiness and try not to take it personally. Silvia knew she had to keep up appearances. During these visits, she forced herself to be polite but distant, despite Joy's warmth and hospitality.

Yanni called Irene frequently, looking forward to their chats and to their weekly Saturday night dates. He longed to get away from the stultifying environment at home and his mother's unrelenting moodiness. The couple thoroughly enjoyed these dates, taking long drives or visiting sites in the city, talking sweet nothings and taking only limited liberties with each other. Irene was not like the other women Yanni had dated, and his strict upbringing would not permit going too far with his future wife.

They had their first kiss only on the third date after their formal engagement. They had enjoyed another romantic dinner, when Yanni pulled over a few blocks from Irene's home to say good night. They embraced, his face approached hers slowly, then he bent and kissed her sweetly on the mouth. He felt her entire body shudder, trembling like leaves of the Erythan trees fluttering in a warm summer breeze. It was obvious no man had ever kissed this girl before. Yanni found it adorable, knowing that Irene was thrilling for the first time to the sensuous fantasies of lovemaking.

Silvia's condition, meanwhile, was becoming worse with every passing day. No matter how hard Yanni and Andreas tried to cheer her up and distract with news about their days at work or with news from friends and relatives, they were met with stony silence or flashes of anger. How could they be so uncaring to speak about such trivialities when her daughter was lying in the cold, hard ground? How could they be so callous as to suggest she should look toward the future, when her daughter's death had robbed her of any interest in life? How could they not be mourning as she was?

Yanni had endless conversations with his father about what to do. He talked to Dr. Elias. He wrote to his aunts and uncles in Greece for advice. They all encouraged him to convince Silvia to get away, to travel back for a long holiday and spend as much time as she needed with her brothers and sisters in her homeland.

Late in the spring that year, Silvia relented and announced that she was ready to spend the summer in Erytha. Yanni arranged for a comfortable cabin on the Greek Line's sumptuous ocean liner *Olympia*, sailing between New York and Piraeus. When Silvia left, he heaved a great sigh of relief, hoping that the long-overdue visit would improve her state of mind.

Soon, letters began to arrive, with Silvia admonishing her son and husband to take the best possible care of Georgia's grave. To keep the candle lit and the flowers fresh and everything as clean and tidy as they could. Letters also arrived from Aunt Athena, detailing how Silvia's surroundings may have changed, but not her emotional state. She was just impossible, Aunt Athena wrote baldly. She found fault with everything and everyone. She found it impossible to relax. She was making her entire family in Greece miserable with her moodiness and anger.

Yanni and Andreas felt bad, but they were also relieved with the quiet calm in the house. They fell into an easy routine, both working hard and enjoying visits from Irene, who often came by to tidy up their apartment. After work, they'd relax, and chatter happily about their experiences during the day and Yanni's plans for the future. As ever on Saturday nights, Yanni took Irene out to dinner while his father dined with her parents. Yanni often took everyone for long drives on lazy Sunday afternoons, visiting some of the North Shore's deserted beaches.

⊰ ⊱

One early afternoon, Yanni received a phone call at the office from Diamandis, his future father-in-law, that would unexpectedly change his career. "I don't know if you would be interested," Diamandis said, his voice calm and impassive, "but Mike Stamos, a wealthy ship owner, and a distant relative from our village, approached me. He made an interesting proposition for you. It seems that the manager in his New York office is retiring, and he would like you to take his place."

Yanni listened carefully. He had great respect for Diamandis' judgment and business sense. "Your salary would be double of what you're making now," he went on, "and you'd be given a seven percent ownership in their newly built bulk carrier as a signing bonus."

"That's quite an offer," Yanni said. "What do you think I should do?"

"That, I can't tell you, my son," he replied. "I am not saying to accept or to reject the offer. Meet with him and see what you think."

Yanni thanked him and hung up. He wasn't sure what to do. He was comfortable and happy where he worked, ensconced in a nice office with the title of house counsel, and manager of insurance and claims. He had an assistant and a secretary and got along famously with everyone in the office. The owner of the company, TJ, an urbane, articulate Athenian, liked him a lot, which meant the world to Yanni. Once, in a moment of soul searching, TJ had looked at Yanni with a smile and said, "If I had a daughter, you would have been my son-in-law." That was high praise indeed. TJ knew what a valuable, and scrupulously trustworthy, employee Yanni was.

He had no reason to leave such a comfortable position, yet this unsolicited offer was enticing—a challenging change of career direction, the opportunity to learn everything about ship operations and to become the manager of a shipping office. He could earn a lot more money and also have a chance to own a small part in a ship. Yanni discussed it at length with his father and with his future in-laws, going over all the pros and cons. He agonized about his decision, but finally decided that as painful as it was to tell his employers, he was going to accept the offer without even having met with his future employer.

Soon enough, the meeting took place. Yanni was pleased when he described the terms of his new employment and his future boss readily agreed. Yanni had been expecting tough negotiations, and was surprised by Stamos' accommodating nature. At their next meeting, Yianni presented a detailed employment agreement he had drafted himself. He watched in amazement when Stamos read it quickly, made some innocuous comments, then signed it on the spot.

As expected, giving notice to the office was painful.

Yanni first spoke to Andrew, the efficient and all-business president of the company, a courteous man of honor and a true gentleman, dedicated to the company and its best interests. Andrew was disappointed, but made it clear that he realized Yanni had agonized over the decision and felt this change was in his best interests. Not so with TJ. His face flushed an annoyed red, though he tried unsuccessfully to feign indifference.

"You're making a big mistake," he said, shooing Yanni out of his office with a flippant wave.

⚎

Yanni pushed that memory away when he arrived for his first day at his new job, where he was given a nice private office. The former manager, Theodore, was not there, but he came to work a few days later and immediately took charge, totally ignoring Yanni. Clearly, he had not retired, and even more clearly, he told Yanni in a huff, there was work to be done attending to the American bulk carrier's daily chores. Also to communicate with the family's London office, run by Stamos' brothers, and tofollow up with their ships calling into American ports. Theodore had no intention of retiring; Stamos was the one who wanted him out, not his brothers in London. Conflicting signals between the brothers left Yanni caught in the middle.

This condition in the office became tense and awkward. Yanni always enjoyed going to work, but as time went on, he began to dread it. Gone in a flash was his good mood. Every day as he walked to the subway, where the hot, humid weather and the stultifying air made everyone cranky, he asked himself why he had switched jobs. When he walked into the large office building and took the elevator up to the tenth floor, his anxiety increased. He wondered what fresh complaints would be waiting for him from a smug and smirking Theodore.

Irene continued to make plans for the wedding, which was scheduled to be held at the Holy Trinity Cathedral in Manhattan, with a reception to follow at the swanky St. Tropez Hotel. Yanni found himself sounding vague and a bit short every time she called. The more she described how the invitations were printed, who was going to be in the wedding party, or how they had arranged for the reservations at the hotel, the more Yanni found himself beset by a subtle, indefinable distance. They continued to speak once or twice on the phone every day, and go out to dinner as usual on Saturday nights, but Yanni, plagued by depression and second thoughts about changing jobs, found no comfort in their conversations.

Irene knew him well enough by then, and she picked up on his growing unease. They began to argue. She was also struggling, adjusting to life in a strange country and fearing the prospect of a marriage with someone she hadn't spent all that much time with. When she tried to voice some of her worries, Yanni pulled away even more.

Not so with his father. Every night as they sat at dinner, Yanni poured his heart out to Andreas, who was patient and reassuring. "Every new beginning is hard," he would calmly tell his son. "You have a new job and, soon enough, a marriage and a new life. Things will work themselves out."

"I hope you're right, Pop," Yanni would say. "I hope you're right."

CHAPTER 12

A New Beginning

When Silvia arrived back home in early September, it was as if she had never left. Her mood was as sour and her complaints as endless, as they'd been before she boarded the ship for Greece. She tossed and turned all night, certain that Irene's sole purpose in life was to take the place of her sweet Georgia. She often snubbed her friends and future in-laws and was so difficult when in their presence that they didn't want to be around her either. Worse, she seemed happy only when her loved ones disagreed and argued. It seemed her sole form of pleasure came from the misery of others.

She particularly relished the problems that arose when Yanni decided to negotiate the purchase of the two-family house where he would live with Irene. A contractor with a fine reputation was building several two-story homes in Timberside, not far from his parents. The future owners could occupy one of the apartments and rent the other. Yanni thought this was a perfect building for them, as it would give the newlyweds an income from the rental, enough to pay for the mortgage. His parents agreed. Not so his future in-laws. They felt their only daughter should live in a private home, as she always had, in Greece and in New York.

"So what if they're giving you most of the money for the down payment," Silvia said, gloating, when she heard about the displeasure of the in-laws. "It just shows how much they know, that they can't see a good deal for their future son-in-law, even if it hits them in the face."

Yanni ignored her, and drew up a spreadsheet to show his future father-in-law. He hoped that seeing the figures and the benefits to the new couple, would change his mind, and put an end to any disagreements. They calmly discussed the pros and cons, and Diamandis, an experienced businessman of quiet, measured judgment, agreed this building was the right one to buy.

Silvia was as morose about Diamandis' change of heart as Yanni was exultant. Nothing made her happy, and the tension at home grew even more.

"Did you see her wedding gown?" Silvia asked Yanni one day, knowing that he hadn't. "It's so ordinary. I can't believe they didn't consult me about it. They have some nerve."

Yanni kept quiet, although her words pained him. He feared that whatever he might say Silvia would eagerly pounce on.

"I can't believe they decided all by themselves where

the wedding reception will take place," she went on, relentless. "Do they think we've never been to a luxury hotel in New York?"

Yanni again bit his lip. While Silvia had been away in Greece she had been asked numerous times if she agreed with their choices. She had never replied.

"I don't care how swanky it is," she added. "If I'm going to the reception, there will be no music. If I hear music, I'm going to leave." She set her lips in a frown, her chest heaving with indignation.

Irene's parents were very unhappy when a crestfallen Yanni reported his mother's demand. They'd never once been to a Greek wedding without music and dancing. Yanni hadn't either. He wanted all his friends and loved ones to celebrate his happiness in the way they knew best—with a wonderful Greek band playing the tunes they'd grown up with and knew so well. The music of home.

"Can't we maybe have a string quartet, playing a little soft music to entertain our guests?" Joy asked Yanni tentatively.

Silvia was enraged when Yanni put the question to her. "I can't believe your in-laws," she shouted. "I said it before. If I hear music, I'm going to leave. Shaming my own son at his wedding. Don't think I won't!"

Yanni looked at his father for help, but all Andreas could do was shrug. He was bearing the brunt of his wife's rage when Yanni was out of the house. Silvia's mind was made up. Nagging Yanni for years to get married, to find a nice Greek bride was a mistake, she thought. Worse, in her mind Irene was the wrong choice.

The gloomy atmosphere at home, at a time when there should have been nothing but happy anticipation and excitement for such a blessed event, made Yanni edgy and impatient. He had no escape from the misery. At home his mother was perpetually teetering on the brink of a nervous breakdown. At the office, with a boss who could never make up his mind, and Theodore, who delighted in making Yanni miserable, life was increasingly unbearable.

As final wedding preparations were taking place, an ugly argument over the phone almost derailed the young couple's plans. Yanni's frustrations left him angry and stubborn, and he unfairly accused Irene of being a bad apple and hung up. A few minutes passed. The phone rang again. A somber Irene tried to placate Yanni—apologizing even though they both knew she wasn't in the wrong—but Yanni was still so mad that he hung up on her.

The next morning at work, Diamandis called and invited Yanni out to lunch. They met at a diner near Yanni's office, and Diamandis sat calmly, unfolding his napkin, before dropping a bombshell. "Last night, Irene and her mother decided to call off the wedding," he said, his voice even. "I asked them again this morning. They both said they hadn't changed their minds."

Yanni stared at him for a moment in disbelief, his heart thumping and his head swimming so suddenly, he thought for a minute that he might faint. Call off their wedding? *Terrible.* He loved Irene. He wanted to marry her.

"I am so sorry," Yanni said quickly. "I don't want to call off the wedding. I don't know what else to say. It's just been very difficult lately, with—"

Diamandis waved his hand and Yanni stopped talking. "Say no more, my son," he said.

Yanni nodded, but he could scarcely think. He was horribly upset. He picked at his lunch and said goodbye to Diamandis before slowly walking back to the office. His thoughts were jumbled. He barely paid attention to the sour frown on Theodore's face and got little done that afternoon. He thought about his life and if he truly was ready for marriage. And, if so, was Irene the woman he wanted to share his life with? Was he acting towards her in a loving manner? Was he allowing his frustration with his mother and his job to take advantage of his fiancée's loving and trusting nature? Was he acting like the man he truly wanted to be?

I do love her, Yanni realized with a jolt. I love her deeply and truly. Irene might have been quiet and innocent and demure, but she possessed a strong will and knew what was right. She was the ideal match for him.

I must apologize. I must go to her and ask for her forgiveness, he told himself. Thoughts of self-deprecation flooded his mind. His behavior had been inexcusable. He had no right to be so harsh with the one woman who understood him better than anyone else. Who was always unfailingly kind and polite to his mother, even as Silvia treated her with obvious disdain. Who loved him the way he was, faults and all.

Yanni left the office early and took the subway to Irene's house. Her mother answered the door and smiled warmly when she saw the contrite, desperate look on his face. "She's upstairs," Joy told him, and Yanni bounded up the stairs where Irene was curled up in a large chair in her parents' bedroom. He flung his hat on the bed and knelt down at her side. "Forgive me, my love," he said. "I've been a horrible idiot, and I am so sorry."

Irene's eyes filled with tears.

"I had no right to talk to you that way," Yanni went on, the words of apology tumbling out. "No right at all. It's not your fault my mother is the way she is. I am so embarrassed about the way she has been treating you. I can't believe you put up with her. Or me."

Irene smiled, giving Yanni hope. "Please forgive me," he repeated. "I love you so much. I want to marry you. I want to share my life with you."

She pulled him close for the sweetest of kisses. "I love you so much, too," she said softly. Yanni's heart swelled with happiness. "Just forget it ever happened. I know the strain you've been under," she added.

Yanni kissed her again. "I don't deserve you," he said, full of remorse.

"It's all going to be fine," she replied. "You'll see."

Yanni was determined to make it fine, counting

the days till their wedding. He ignored his mother's moodiness and the incompetent bullies at work. He had more important plans to think about. Plans that actually made him feel good.

⊰⊱

The wedding day arrived, and the service in the cavernous cathedral was heartfelt and loving. Yanni's heart filled with joy at the sight of Irene in her beautiful gown, her cheeks flushed with happiness and her eyes shining with love. Two priests, one a close friend of Yanni's, performed the engagement service, blessing the gold wedding bands before pressing them to the bride and groom's foreheads. The Dean of the cathedral, assisted by the priest of Yanni's local parish, officiated over the wedding ceremony. The Dean placed the traditional crowns on the heads of the beaming couple, who held lit candles. Everything seemed to pass by in a flash. Yanni and Irene heard the blessings and became husband and wife.

The reception at the swanky Central Park hotel was jubilant, loud, and joyous—even though there was no music. Yanni was not going to let his mother's problems ruin his special day. He was floating on a cloud of enchantment, greeting the guests and speaking to them animatedly. Irene, too, was exuberant, surrounded by her friends and family, everyone rejoicing.

"We don't need music to have a real celebration,"

Yanni whispered to her at one point, and she hugged him tight.

After the reception, Yanni and Irene changed and bade good-bye to their parents. They were going to spend their first night as a married couple in the bridal suite at the Waldorf Astoria. Three marvelous weeks in the Virgin Islands, Jamaica, and Miami Beach, were planned. Just the two of them. Far from the chilly autumn air and the clammy coldness of the office and the endless moodiness of Yanni's mother. Nothing mattered except to be together.

Diamandis insisted on walking the happy couple out of the hotel. When they got into a taxi, he leaned over the window. "I wish you the best," he said, his voice cracking. "I wish the world will be kind to you, that there will be no clouds in your future, that you both may live very long, deep into old age."

Irene's eyes filled with happy tears at the sight of her adored father wiping his eyes. "Thank you, Papa," she said. "I love you."

"And I love you," Yanni told her once the taxi sped away. He carried his bride through the door into their suite that heavenly first night, and their life together began on the most perfect of notes.

The honeymoon was just as delightful as their wedding, with hot, lazy days by the pool, and lingering dinners, watching the sun slowly set into the Caribbean and hearing the chatter of the birds, together with hotel guests. They pretended that the telephone didn't work and called no one. There was no one they wanted to talk to, except each other. Every so often, an idle thought about his unhappiness at work crept into Yanni's mind, but he pushed it away. Nothing was going to mar the splendor of this honeymoon.

At the end of their second week, Irene called her parents to check in on them, and they were thrilled to hear from her. When Yanni called his parents, though, Silvia was dismissive and abrupt. Until she said something that surprised him.

"I've reserved a room for you at the Hotel Edison, in midtown," she announced. "Your house will not be ready when you get back. It'll take a couple more months."

Yanni was so astonished that she'd done this without talking to him first, but he meekly agreed.

When they returned to New York and rented a room at the hotel, they quickly realized it was a mistake. There was nothing for Irene to do all day. The room was bland and impersonal. None of her friends and family lived anywhere nearby. And the expense would be considerable the longer they stayed. They were relieved and grateful when Irene's parents called one evening, inviting the new couple to stay with them, where they'd have their own room and bath, and the privacy they coveted.

It was just what the newlyweds needed, especially as the winter that year turned out to be unusually cold and snowy. It was bliss for Yanni to come home after a miserable day at work and see the shining eyes and bright smile of his wife; to receive a warm welcome from his in-laws, who couldn't do enough for him. It was a much-needed change from the angst and misery that still enveloped his parents' home. Yanni often visited after work, mostly to see his father, who bore the brunt of Silvia's mood swings.

If only work were as gratifying as life at home. Stamos had proven to be the exact opposite of Yanni's previous boss. Often, what Yanni was asked to do made no sense. He would gently point out the problems, but Stamos would insist that he was the boss, and he knew best. Yanni would then do as he was told, but when things went wrong, as he expected, he bore the brunt of the blame.

To make things even more stressful for Yanni and Irene, Diamandis lost his job when his company ran into financial difficulties, giving the employees little warning. Fortunately, the manager at the office soon started his own import-export business and hired Diamandis in an even better position.

⚐⚑

A call from the contractor in early February confirmed that the house in Timberside was ready. Yanni and Irene were thrilled. After an uneventful closing on the title, they moved into the modest two-bedroom apartment on the second floor. They owned the whole building! Privacy and calm at last. Tenants quickly rented the first-floor apartment, and their rent helped pay for the building's mortgage and other expenses, just as Yanni had planned.

"I can't believe I ever thought this was a bad idea," Diamandis said as he and Joy came over for a visit, admiring the shiny new kitchen and floors, and seeing the curtains fluttering in the other rooms. It was gratifying to have a son-in-law who not only loved their daughter, but who had such a good head for business.

"If you only knew how much I used to hate math!" Yanni told them with a laugh.

Irene took over the management of the household. She quickly learned to be a good cook, and she scoured different stores for furniture and accessories that made their lovely furnished apartment a home. Yanni always looked forward to the minute when he walked in the door after work, and was greeted with a kiss and tantalizing aromas from the Greek specialties she'd concocted for dinner.

On Sunday mornings, they went to the local church, often with Yanni's parents. After church, they would drive to their in-laws' house for lunch. Predictably, Silvia objected every time, fearful that her son would become closer to them. Time and again, she found reasons, imaginary and petty, to argue with Yanni, just so she could vent her frustrations.

"You never really forgave me for leaving you behind in Erytha," she kept telling him. "If you only knew how I felt when the ship was pulling away from the dock. My heart was torn apart. I cried for the whole trip."

Now that Yanni was blissfully married, living in another house, Silvia simply could not wrap her head around the idea that he still cared and loved her. She demanded constant visits and attention, but was cold and often cruel when he came by. Yanni felt terrible for his sad and vulnerable mother, knowing how hard it was for her to understand his loving commitment to Irene, even as her nagging and insults wore him down. She criticized his in-laws, always calling them ignorant, or provincial, or some other insulting words. She criticized Irene, finding fault with how she dressed, how she cleaned the house, how she poured the wine, how she had burnt the lamb the last time she cooked for them. The comments about his beloved wife wounded Yanni, even though he knew his mother would say anything just to cause controversy and pain. No matter how much Yanni denied it, Silvia kept telling him there was no space in his heart for his mother anymore.

⚶⚶

In the early spring, Irene told Yanni she was pregnant. He was ecstatic, yet he knew he had to make some hard decisions. Establishing a thriving career in a shipping office with an erratic boss and an unpleasant colleague was never going to happen. There was no point in staying at a job where his contributions weren't appreciated, and where he was unfairly treated. Bad enough that he had to deal with a mother who was unstable and conflicted—even worse to deal with colleagues like his. Yanni was going to be a father soon, and he didn't want to be a miserable, nervous wreck anymore; not with these new responsibilities looming. He made up his mind to leave. Time, Yanni decided, to use the degree he'd worked so hard over—for four, long, arduous years. It was time to join a law firm and start practicing admiralty law.

He knew just who to call—a good friend from his previous employer's office, who had contacts with law firms. His friend introduced him to Ted, a partner in a small, three-member firm, with an office on the ninth floor of a modest Wall Street building. Yanni met Ted for an interview, and was thrilled to be called in a few days later and told he would be taken on as "of counsel." It meant there would be no salary, only one-third of any fees he brought in. He'd be working out of a tiny room off Ted's office, where he'd be able to set up his desk and telephone.

Yanni accepted on the spot. He knew it meant renouncing his lucrative employment contract. He knew it was a huge risk, going out on his own, with no clients, no guaranteed income and a pregnant wife. He knew he'd be building his business from scratch. But that didn't matter—he needed to preserve his sanity and regain his peace of mind. He couldn't wait to get started.

Stamos was not happy when Yanni broke the news, giving his boss two weeks notice. He reminded Yanni angrily that they had a contract.

"What contract?" Yanni replied. "You've never lived up to the contract. My salary is less than what is specified in the contract. You never gave me the seven percent share in your ship as the contract provided. Theodore did not retire, and has no plans of retiring." He looked at Stamos, who had a chagrined expression. "I was hired under false pretenses, because you didn't like Theodore and hoped to force him out by hiring me. If anything, I could sue you for breach of contract."

Stamos shrugged and silently walked away. The last thing he wanted was a lawyer going after him for breaking his word. Besides, deep down he liked Yanni and admired how hard he applied himself.

"Tell you what," Stamos said the next day, "let's forget about the contract. Why don't you handle our casualty claims, on a fee basis?" He held out his hand and Yanni shook it. That was an unexpected and much-appreciated gift.

Yanni left the office at the end of the second week with a smile and a lilt in his step. A sense of relief flooded over him. He was going to start a new career, this time as a practicing lawyer; doing what he'd always wanted to do, on his own, the way he wanted to do it. It didn't matter that all he had were some meager savings, a pregnant wife, and the daily stress of worrying about his mother. He had courage, that much was certain. He had faith in his abilities and his integrity. He believed in himself. He had earned the right to do it his way. Most of all, he had the desire and drive to make it work. He was going to succeed, he knew it.

And he was going to be a father.

Life could not be sweeter.

Epilogue

Let me stand here. And let me look for a moment
At the wide open space
The cloudless sky's morning sea
Bright brown and yellow shore; all so
Beautiful, great, and glistening.

Let me stand here. And let me believe that I see them
(Frankly, I saw them for a moment when I first stood up)
And not here in my fantasies, my memories, the idols of
blissful pleasure.

—From "Morning Sea" by Konstantinos Kavafis

The old man stopped reminiscing. He opened his eyes, staring up into the brilliant blue of the sky, the soft breeze caressing his cheeks like a lover's kiss.

It was a good life, he thought. *Often a hard life and a painful life, but still a good one.* Snippets of more memories flowed by, one melting into another.

His school days, the horrors of the German nightmare, his Athens days, the stolen kisses with Isabelle....

The ship bringing him to New York, his mother's tears of thankfulness, his dark depression and painful days, his college years, his busy days at work and long evenings at law school, his endless hours trying to make something of himself....

The volunteer work he did for his church, and his advice as legal advisor to the New York Society of Erytha, trying to help the new arrivals. He never tired of helping those immigrants whose anxieties about their new lives in America resonated so strongly with him. He would never forget that first year in New York, and the struggles he confronted—and conquered....

The fundraising he oversaw for the Greek day school he helped establish at his local church so his children could go to a private institution. The proud smile on his father-in-law's face as he cut the ribbon at the opening ceremony. What satisfaction that brought, seeing this school become a reality, the school where his children received their primary education....

The advisory board he chaired at a Greek studies program in a Queens center, and, with Irene, the professorship they established at his college alma mater in Philadelphia. His induction as an Archon at the New York Greek Orthodox Cathedral....

The endless hours in the office, the mountains of paperwork, the travels to exotic locations investigating ships' fires, collisions, groundings, explosions, sinkings—

some with tragic consequences—and the satisfaction of a job well done; the hours spent doing his best for those he cared about most....

All those memories, those struggles, successes, failures, happiness, disappointments, laughter, tears. All that pain yet all that hope....

How did I ever have the energy? Yanni wondered, as he knew that the strength of his body and mind were slowly and inexorably receding. The clock ticking its endless circle. Time pressing on.

Most of all, memories flooding his mind about the love he found and the love he gave. The kind, gentle love of his grandparents. The stern, faithful love of his aunt and uncle. The steady, unwavering love of his father. The complicated, tortured, hapless love of his mother. The pure, sweet, genuine love of his Irene. His partner, his soulmate....

And his children, his legacy, his earthly foreverness. The old man thought of his three blessings so gratefully as his eyes watched the dimming sunlight fleck the azure waters....

How cold it was when he drove Irene to the hospital, wincing in pain, and how snowy the night his eldest was born. "It's a girl!" the doctor announced a few hours later. "She's healthy and perfect. Your wife is doing beautifully. Congratulations."

A girl? A fleeting sense of disappointment at not having a firstborn son was quickly overshadowed by euphoria; then an overwhelming sense of sober responsibility.

How he walked down the hall to the nursery, together with his overjoyed mother-in-law, who had arrived to keep him company, to see the rows of bassinets in neat rows behind a large window. There, through the protective glass covered with the fingerprints of happy relatives, seeing his newborn daughter, swaddled and sleeping peacefully. Tears coming to his eyes as he watched her, so tiny, so helpless. With her mother's lovely rosebud lips and Silvia's heart-shaped jaw, just perfectly, utterly beautiful.

The old man recalled those momentous days following the birth of his little girl. First checking in on his beloved Irene and the condition of their priceless gift from God. Then trying to reach his mother to give her the happy news and ask her what they should name the baby. Not finding her anywhere and eventually calling his father, who suggested they name her Silvia. After her grandmother. His and Irene's dismay that his father did not suggest they name the baby after Yanni's dead sister.

And then when they arrived home from the hospital, the admonition by the tenant's kindly Italian wife. "From now on," she said to the new father, "you must be careful whenever you cross the street...."

It was snowing for the birth of his second child, too, the old man recalled. This time, his father and in-laws joined him for the anxious wait until the doctor walked in. "Congratulations," he said, smiling, "it's a boy."

He remembered how hard a time he had believing

the doctor at first. "It's okay, doctor, you can tell me the truth," he had said.

"It's a *boy*," the doctor had repeated with a laugh.

He was in a daze so overwhelming that he could barely eke out a thank-you to the doctor when his mother-in-law wished, ecstatically, "May our little Andreas have a long life."

Then Yanni's father, overwhelmed, asked for a cigarette from a beaming Diamandis, even though he had stopped smoking years before.

When the doctor blandly informed them that the newborn had some fluid in his lungs and needed to stay in an incubator, his euphoria disappeared in a flash. Remembering that, not too long ago, President Kennedy's son Patrick, who had also been born with fluid in his lungs, was placed in an incubator and had tragically died after only two days, struggling for every breath.

The old man then remembered how he sank into a chair, despairing and praying hard to God to please, *please*, keep his baby safe. And how for many years afterward, when his son had recovered and grew up into a fine young man, he looked at him and always felt he was the greatest, most precious gift God had ever given him on this earth. And how this experience had left a permanent scar in his heart, as he was unable to let go of his anxiety that his son be protected and kept safe from unknown, invisible risks looming, unbidden, in furtive dark corners....

And, when his third child was born. His little Joy, named after her grandmother. How thrilled everyone in the family was. How her siblings took her into their fold and looked after her as protective little angels. How sweet and carefree and beautiful she was to everyone, and especially to her father. She would always be his sweet baby....

The old man remembered the annual summer vacations he took with his family, watching his children splash in the ocean or fight over who got the last scoop of ice cream. Long gone were the days when a short drive in a hot car to a Long Island beach was seen as the height of luxury for the family. Yet the old man looked back on those simple jaunts, from his happy days as a newlywed, with the same humble pleasure he took in remembering the sites of the world that entranced his loved ones when they were older....

Thrilling to the completion of the first home he had built to his specifications, after endless months of delays and crises. The joy when they finally moved in, and first came home from the office, with his children shouting out, "Papa! Papa!" in greeting and running into his arms. Irene welcoming him with a kiss and a glass of delicious Greek wine, flooding him with peace and happiness....

⊣⊨

The memories toppled one upon the other, the years speeding by. One bright autumn morning, when the air was just beginning to turn crisp and cool, the family driving little Silvia to the lovely campus of the small Pennsylvania college she'd be attending. Her brother helping carry her clothes and books to the dorm, with Irene nervously rattling off last-minute instructions about what to eat and how to do the laundry. After their last good-byes, when they drove away, the sharp pain as Yanni watched his daughter recede, waving as she stood alone in the growing distance. How could his gorgeous little baby girl, his adored firstborn, be old enough for college? How it was just yesterday that he was driving carefully in the wintry air to the hospital the night she was born? And then, before Yanni seemed to blink, watching his Silvia graduate from college and get a job in a public relations office.

Then seeing Andreas off to a small college in Connecticut. On another sun-flecked autumn day, the family driving him to the sprawling campus, where he showed no anxiety about his new adventure. As they bid good-bye and walked sadly to the car, Andreas was already heading towards the dorm without looking back. And Irene's brother Michael, who was along for the ride, commenting, "That boy is going to go far in life."….

When, years later, Andreas became a lawyer and ended up working at Yanni's firm, the furtive gratification swelling in Yanni's heart that his son had followed in his father's footsteps—and yet, the old man recollected, that *his* own father had been content to work in restaurants and have a simple, uncomplicated life. But Yanni had always wanted more—and had gotten it. Later, his son was on the same path....

The old man sighed deeply and looked out at the sea, his memories vanishing. The phone was ringing, he realized, and he went into the house to answer it.

"Hello, my love," Irene's voice came across, clear and loud. "Is it all right to bring my cousin Eugenia and her husband for dinner tonight?"

"Of course," Yanni replied. "When will you be back?"

"I won't be long," she said. "I have one more stop to make, and then I'll pick up our guests and drive home. See you soon."

Yanni went back out to the veranda. Erytha's majestic twilight was about to set in. From the west, the last rays of a setting sun were reflected off the tiny island situated halfway between Erytha and the Turkish coast. The first light flickered from the island's lighthouse, a warning beacon in the distance, calm and steady, like time itself. His children had once been so little, the old man thought, and now they were all grown up, happily married, giving him beloved grandchildren.

He smiled, remembering the time years before, when Andreas and his lovely wife Tasia, had come home for Mother's Day.

"We have an unbelievable gift for you," Andreas told his parents as he handed a flat package to his mother.

"What on earth could this be?" Irene said as she tore it open and saw a framed chart, covered in short and longer vertical lines in neat rows.

"It's chromosomes," Tasia said, her eyes twinkling. "Of a baby boy."

Irene sat down, stunned.

"Our baby is going to be a boy," Andreas said, practically bursting with pride. "Your first grandchild is a boy. Are you happy?"

For a moment Yanni was speechless. Irene threw her arms around Tasia and blissfully chattered away.

"What are you going to name the baby?" Irene asked. Yanni tried not to flinch. In just those past few moments, so much had changed. An amazing miracle would soon arrive as a tiny little newborn. He suddenly realized that he wanted so badly for this baby to come into this world healthy and thriving, to ensure the family's immortality.

"Why, Yanni, of course," Andreas said, beaming.

As Irene clapped her hands in pure joy, Yanni excused himself and went upstairs to the bathroom. He didn't want anyone to see the silent tears that were spilling out of his eyes.

You are going to be born again; yes, you, Yanni, he told himself as he splashed cold water on his face and stared into the mirror, gazing at his immortality. *A new baby. A new Yanni! My family will live on....*

A deep feeling of gratitude overwhelmed him. *I will be born again,* he kept saying.

Yet the clock kept ticking. Why was it that time

seemed to move so slowly when he was a child, and everything seemed to move so quickly now that he was old?

How can I be so old, when I was young just a few seconds ago?

Yanni sighed, and a sad memory filled his heart. The death of his father-in-law, who passed from a painful cancer when Yanni was away working on a case in South Africa. The death of his mother-in-law, also from cancer.

When Joy still had some strength, Yanni took the entire family out west, to thrill at the Grand Canyon, Sun Valley, and Mount Rushmore. His mother and Joy had joined them. It was a memorable trip of pure Americana. Joy proclaimed it was the best vacation of her life. It was just a few months before she died. Even Silvia seemed to enjoy the trip. Yanni and Irene were secretly thrilled that their mothers were finally getting along so well, and that Silvia had positively bloomed on the trip.

"There is just no understanding my mother," Yanni would say ruefully, and even through her sadness, Irene had to laugh....

The death of his father. It took only a year for Andreas, who'd always exuded vibrant health and energy well into his eighties, to succumb after being diagnosed with lung cancer. His struggle at the end was so painful that it was a tragic blessing when he was finally at peace.

Yanni had arranged the funeral with the same family who had so poignantly helped them when Georgia had died so young. His sadness alternated with bitterness and disappointment. *If only my father had never smoked,* Yanni told himself in despair. *If only cancer hadn't chosen him.* But it was too late for ifs only.

And he had his mother to worry about. She was an aging widow, with few friends. Andreas had always been the buffer between Yanni and her complaints. And now he was gone….

⧗

Ah, Silvia. In the last decade of her life, she had overcome the chronic contradictions of her moodiness and the bitterness in her heart. She was grateful and helpless, warm and loving, an entirely different woman. Now, in and out of hospitals, at ninety-eight, she was nearing the end. She was weak and weary of her long and often unhappy and painful life.

"I want to die at home," the old man recalled her saying one day. "I don't want to go back to the hospital, Yanni."

He had nodded as he took her hand, so frail and thin. "Don't worry, Mom," he had told her. "I'll take care of everything. You know that. I'll get the best people to look after you and you'll be very comfortable."

"You're my good boy," she would say as she summoned the energy to kiss his hand. "You've always been the best son to me. I feel so terrible that I missed the joys of bringing you up. Bringing up such a sweet, loving little boy. Such a wonderful little boy, you were."

If the situation weren't so painful, Yanni might have laughed at her poignant gratitude. All her rages and conflicts, her paranoid complaining, her endless fault-finding, her ambivalence about Yanni's love, all of that was long gone. She missed no opportunity to say how thankful she was for the love and care Yanni had given her.

She had finally become who she was meant to be, the loving mother he had wished for. The mother who loved him unconditionally.

"Isn't God listening?" she'd asked him months before. "Why is He taking so long? I think He forgot me."

"Don't say that, Mom," Yanni had replied. "God would never forget you. He's just not in a hurry. He wants you to stay here, with us."

"You're right," she said. "Life is sweet."

She would perk up when her grandchildren came to visit, but then would relapse in pain and exhaustion.

Oh, about the sweetness of life, Yanni said to himself. He recalled his mother's comment years ago, during a quiet mother and son conversation in the comfort of her living room. "Listen, Yanni," she said. "One day we are going to die. There is no reason dying 100 times a day worrying about it."

Yanni knew when she was ready. She kept asking him and Irene to pray to God to take her. "I want to see my children again," she'd say, over and over. "I want to see my Andreas. I want to see my parents. I want to see them all."

The end was peaceful and quiet, just as she had prayed for it to be. Yanni had stopped by for a short visit on his way to the office that morning, and her two aides were giving her a sponge bath in the bedroom. She nodded when he touched her from the back, but was too worn out to say anything. The call came a short time later, when Yanni was on the train heading into the city.

The funeral was somber and painful. Father Peters, Yanni's beloved priest, was compassionate and soothing, and touched Yanni's heart when he read a kindly message from the Archbishop. Yanni, although he'd been steeling himself for the inevitable, was deeply sad and despondent that his mother had finally passed on. He kept his composure both at the wake the night before and in church during the funeral service. But as soon as he sat back in the limousine after leaving the church, he broke down into uncontrollable sobbing. Irene tried in vain to comfort him, but to no avail.

❧❧

Yanni's second life—the one that had started when he was eighteen and had crossed the Atlantic to be with his parents and sister—flashed across his mind. So many images, so many memories of the tumult, the sufferings, the unhappy confrontations, the accusations, the abandonment, the heartache, the expectations, and the disappointments all rushed in, and left him overwhelmed and distraught. That life was now over.

When did I get to be so old? The old man asked himself. *How can I be old, now, when I was so young just a few seconds ago?*

A few stars had come out in the twilight, winking at him from eons past. The neighbor's grandchildren had gone inside for their supper. Everything was still and silent.

Time, the old man knew, was his biggest enemy and biggest friend also. Time ruling every passing day, bringing him closer to that ultimate ending, knowing, as all humans must, that the moment we are born, we are condemned to death. Yet time is what shapes our days, keeps us moving forward, keeps us alive, even as our bodies age, slow, inexorably—and finally become still forever.

Like Georgia. Yanni's sweet little sister. Out of nowhere, snapshots of Georgia flew into his consciousness. Georgia with eyes shining as she gazed up at her big brother for the very first time at the New York docks. Georgia ripping the gaily colored wrappings of the Christmas presents under the tree. Georgia sitting bored and frustrated in her parents' restaurant in Pennsylvania. Georgia lying thin and wan on her deathbed, lamenting her fate with such stoic resignation that Yanni's heart broke at the sight of her. Georgia in her coffin, her body finally at peace, her spirit in heaven, her family bereft.

She will forever be twenty, the old man realized. She

never had to worry about getting as old as he was now—but she never had the chance to live the life she wanted to live, either. And it was one of the great regrets of Yanni's life that he never got to know his sister better—that he was robbed of the opportunity to see her grow up and fall in love and have her own children and her own lifetime of happiness like the one he shared with Irene.

Was Georgia's time that much different from my own, knowing that her illness made it that much shorter on this planet? the old man asked himself with a sigh. Or was time something God had created at some undefined point in the infinite universe, taunting us forevermore with the mysteries of creation? When did time begin, if ever? Will we ever know? Or if we were told, would we be capable of grasping the enormity of the answer, if indeed there was one? Or is time a complete circle, without a beginning or an end, bringing Yanni back to the island where he was born and raised, now, in the twilight of his life?

Time has stopped for so many people I have loved, the old man thought. First, his beloved grandfather, then his young cousin Maria. All those islanders who perished in the war, starved and killed by the cruel invaders. His parents. His in-laws. His aunts and uncles and cousins. His cousin Isabelle, the gorgeous, glamorous, sexually charged Elizabeth Taylor of the family, who had five marriages and who had looked up to him till the end. His friends and classmates and playmates. His cousin

Costas, who had come to New York for heart surgery, and stayed to recuperate.

One afternoon, a few weeks after the operation, Costas was sitting on the porch of Yanni's country home. The one he'd had built to his exacting specifications, overlooking the endlessly swirling currents of Long Island Sound. The waters that reminded him of the island he loved so much.

"There is nothing like the sea," Yanni said to Costas, reminiscing about their days in Erytha. The years disappeared, and it was as if they were boys again, sharing the same tiny bedroom with its narrow, uncomfortable beds. "Especially for island boys like us."

"How did we get to be so old?" Costas jokingly asked. He had regained much of his strength, and was no longer pale and thin.

"I don't know," Yanni replied. "Our children are now so much older than we were then, when we were growing up. Those were the days, weren't they?"

"Well, some of the time," Costas said. "They certainly weren't the days I want to remember during the war."

Yanni nodded. Those terrible years of fear and deprivation seemed to be no more than a passing dream.

But Costas was gone now. Even Dimitris, his beloved friend, was lame and sick.

And it will be my time someday, the old man had to admit. Everything he made; everything he acquired through hard work and relentless effort; the money he earned and the debts he paid. All things dear and valuable; all are left behind, abandoned. His own funeral, with his loved ones holding back tears, people milling around, whispering quietly, then all leaving to face their own sorrows. His own burial, when he would be placed into that small, solitary, immovable spot of earth for all eternity. What then? Is that when he would fall into an infinite void of nothingness?

Perhaps faith is the invisible wall that protects us from despair, the old man told himself. *My faith is strong, unyielding. It shields me and comforts me. My faith will be with me when my time comes.*

⧗⧖

He sat up on the chaise, watching, as more stars sparkled into view. One last memory came to him, of that heartbreaking day when his mother had been buried. Hours after they returned from the cemetery, when all the visitors had finally gone home, Yanni sat outside with a glass of wine and stared up at the stars.

The very same stars, he realized, *that he was gazing at now, in the serenity of the Erythan twilight.*

That night, years before, he had known his mother was at peace, but the sadness was overwhelming. And then Irene came outside and handed him the phone.

"Grandpa, Grandpa, are you okay?" said the adorable little voice of his granddaughter. "I love you so much."

Yanni's eyes filled with tears and he choked them back.

"Oh, how sweet of you to ask, my darling," he recalled saying. "I really am okay. And I love you, too."

Yes, it was a long, bumpy ride, Yanni told himself as he stared at his blank diary. *A lonely ride filled with pain, broken dreams, and endless turmoil, but also love.*

Love for his family. Love for his Island. Love for the sea that nourished and sustained him and made him whole.

The doorbell rang, shaking Yianni out of his musings. It was his wife, Irene, with the guests.

"Hello, dear. I'm sorry I took so long," she said. "I hope you are ready, but it's time to go to dinner."

Acknowledgments

Ever since I was a teenager, growing up in a remote Aegean island, I enjoyed writing essays, short stories, and an occasional poem. I had ambitions of being a professional writer. So while the trajectory of life took me in other directions, my yearning to write never left me.

This novel which, to a large extent, is based on my life story, is the culmination of those inner urgings, the incessant desire to communicate my emotions with the outside world, in print. Achieving this goal would not have been possible without the help of some wonderful ladies. Each of them, in her own way, played a crucial role of transforming this life story's ambition into reality.

The novelist, Karen Moline. Her months' long, extensive editing, suggestions, redrafting of the manuscript, and collaboration over several lunches, have been invaluable. Her work with me established a distinctive and lasting imprint upon the book's character, reflecting her professionalism and unique writing talents, for which I will always be thankful.

My loyal, quietly efficient, longtime secretary, Debi Farina, whose skills, work ethic, and attention to detail over the years have made her my indispensable assistant. Debi, in her own precise, careful way, helped with the editing, printing and copying of the manuscript.

My daughter, Erini, the "intellectual" in the family with a Ph.D. in English Education who, strangely enough, was not asked to help in the writing, as I did not want her to read the manuscript until it was ready for publication. However, as a published author in her own right, she guided me through the intricate straits of publishing and, in effect, became my business manager. I suppose this has been her way of returning some of the heavy doses of admonitions she had to endure as she was growing up in our household, the youngest of three siblings.

But above all, my wife Maro; my soulmate, my fellow traveler on life's long road; the woman who endured me for more than half a century; sustained me when the sky was dark; tolerated my strange, sometimes bizarre ways; shared and helped me to achieve my ambitions; always stood by me and gave meaning to the word family.

To those lovely ladies, I express my lasting gratitude for being there, for helping me carry this story from the fragile, imperceptible crevices of my heart to the hands of the reader.

Christopher Stratakis

CHRISTOPHER STRATAKIS was born and raised in Greece. After moving to America, he graduated from Drexel University in 1951 and New York University School of Law in 1955. Shortly after joining the law firm of Poles, Tublin & Patestides in 1960, he became a partner, specializing in admiralty and corporate law. He has written and published several articles, lectured on professional and historical subjects, served as Legal Advisor to several non-profits *(pro bono)*, and was an arbitrator in maritime disputes. He is the author of *Mnimes* "Memories" (2010), a book of essays, short stories, and poems which he wrote as a teenager. In 2015, he co-edited *Chians on Parallel Roads*, a book published by Panchiaki "Korais" Society of New York. In recognition of his extensive community involvement, he has been the recipient of several awards from religious, governmental, and educational institutions.

Mr. Stratakis lives with his wife in New York City. He is the proud father of three and grandfather of three. This is his first novel.